# the FIX

## AS ABOVE BOOK THREE

To all the shadows we sat alone with.
May they show us how bright the light really is.

"To live is to suffer, to survive is to find some meaning in the suffering."

-Friedrich Nietzsche

# Playlist

# Band Members

<u>**Character List:**</u>
Not all of these characters will make an
appearance in this book, but will be around.

As Above band members
Rex Thompson— vocals, guitar, songwriting
Finland Montgomery— guitar, backup vocals, songwriting
Tobias "Toby" Jeffers— bass, rhythm guitar
Mac Thompson— drums, nickname designator
Leo Keenan— band manager, cat herder

Sentry Security
Ian— Head of Security, Rex's detail
Lugh— Second in command, Toby's detail
*Peach*— Fin's detail
Jordan Kauffman— Mac's detail
Jonathon— The floater

and more …

# A Note from the Author

## Xx

This is normally the place that I suggest there's some content in this book that may be difficult for some readers. It's where I'd say that there's a list of content warnings at the back of the book (and there are, click here), but this story needs a little more introduction than that.

Because while this is the third book in the series of interconnect standalones and can be read on its own, it's my heaviest one yet.

It took me six months to write. Endless hours of research.

Laughter and the first tears I've ever shed while writing.

It wasn't even supposed to be the third book in the series, but here we are.

One heartbreakingly beautiful story of an alcoholic and his recovery later.

This work is strictly fictitious, but does include very real topics that might be uncomfortable. It is also strongly character driven, including making some rather large mistakes along the way. While I have done my best to handle the events encompassed with care, it does *not* reflect the entirety of the journey to recovery, and should not be used as any kind of reference to real life.

If addiction (namely alcoholism) is a concern of yours, please proceed with caution.

The full list of content warnings can be found after the acknowledgements.

Please keep in mind that this is a romance with spice meant for audiences of eighteen and older. There are 232 *fucks,* several filthy nicknames, one dirty talking bassist, and plenty of dick.

Enjoy the ride.

Part I

"It is an art to live with pain."
—Eddie Vedder

# Chapter One

## TOBY

"I DON'T UNDERSTAND WHY we still do this shit."

Perched on a stool, buried under packages and envelopes covering the counter, I toss another folded page to the growing pile at my feet. The discard box is already full, but I keep letting letter after letter flitter down.

"Um, because we *should*."

"Shut up, Mac."

My eyes scan the page in my hands, this one typed out in scrolling font, and scoff. "It's asking Rex *not* to marry Aria. *Too fuckin' late.*" Another addition to the pile at my feet. "Have we ever found anything decent in the last five years?"

"We've been doing this for eleven," Mac corrects.

"Exactly," I mutter and push the pile aside to make room for my forearms against the surface, though it only causes shit to fall off the opposite side. "Oops."

"Seriously?" I lean up to see Mac, my band's drummer and nickname extraordinaire, has migrated to the floor just beneath the bar on the other side of my station, covered in another layer. He snags a handful and tosses it back up at my face, only for more to fall off of the counter. "Motherdicker."

"That's what you get, Mackie." Snickering, I plant my ass back in the stool and snag my highball glass to take a drink.

And maybe push more shit aside so that it falls on his head.

"Pretty sure rock bands are *not* supposed to get this much mail."

"Oh, so you think the panties thrown on stage is plenty?" I pause mid-drink, glancing over the pile into the living space where Fin Montgomery lounges on a couch with his own pile of shit to wade through. *The bastard.*

"I actually like those," I say and take a sip, except nothing meets my lips when I tip the glass back.

"Dirty fucker," someone mutters from another couch. Probably Rex, our band's lead singer, songwriter, and twin to the drummer. I flick another envelope at Mac, hoping it sticks in his ever-present bandana headband.

*Today, it's white.*

*And for some reason, so are his nails.*

*It'd match perfectly.*

"What?" I chuckle and pour a fresh taste from the bottle at my elbow. "Like you bastards didn't enjoy the shit, too. Y'know, before your balls sagged so much, you needed assistance holding them up."

"Some of us like having our balls handled," Mac mutters wistfully on a scoff.

"Oh, I like my balls handled. *Fondled.*" I cup my hand and wiggle my fingers. "Tongued. Just not by the same set every night."

Shaking my head when I get a round of grumbles, I take a swig and lean back, no longer interested in the handwritten letters proclaiming love and sacrifices for people they've never met. *We've* never met.

*Of course they love us. We're* As Above.

My drink settles heavy in my gut; the tension in the air thickening, thanks to my bandmates and brothers ignoring that this used to be fun. Getting bras thrown at us was funny and sexy. Getting laid in a different city every night was our life. And letting the world drool over us was our way.

*Not anymore.*

The bachelors left in our group are dwindling fast, and I'm beginning to think As Above's days of chaos have officially come to a screeching halt. Even Mac has been weirdly *off*. Distant and permanently tired looking.

Show nights have stopped including after-parties with booze and girls and blow.

Tours are paused for the foreseeable future.

Even writing new music and practices have been capped.

*All thanks to the permanent pussy these bastards picked up.*

Grumbling, I push up from the stool with a spinning head and wrap a fist around the bottle I've been nursing.

I'd rather be drunk off my ass than sit here any longer with a bunch of old bastards that have given up on this rock star life we were all so desperate for as kids. Dreaming and planning about, *together,* since fucking grade school.

*We couldn't fuckin' wait to get our hands on it. Now look at 'em.*

"Bunch'a nannies. All of you." I gesture around the room at the big tatted bastards I call brothers that fit right in when they should be standing *out* against the frilly decorations and whitewashed walls.

*Just like my granny's place. She blended in so much with that shit I almost got myself in trouble a lot.*

Like that time I tried to sneak two chicks in after a garage show, only to be stopped by the old cockblock of a woman jumping out of the dark.

"You mean Nancy's," Mac corrects with a scowl I meet through a haze.

"I said what I said." Flicking a hand in dismissal and realizing it's my bottle holding hand, I forgo the glass and pull straight from the neck.

The whiskey *used* to burn when I drank it straight like this. But at some point, the hair on my chest thickened, and now I don't even bother with a mix or a chase.

"Dude, it's snowing outside," Rex calls when I make it through the mountains of fan mail clinging to all the surfaces in this room and the kitchen.

"It's cool," I say on a shrug and whip open the door, then hold my bottle up as the chilled wind rushes in. "I know how to stay warm."

I don't wait for any more protests. Or for someone to call Leo and *report* me like some kind of misfit kid that needs a sitter.

*I don't need a damn sitter.*

Instead, I step out into the winter with only the leather vest over my tee and damn near lose my untied boot in a pile of built-up snow blocking the stairs. It's abnormally icy and snowy for this time of year, the shit soaking into my boot as I walk the slick sidewalk.

They think they're so much better now that they have steady broads. Better now that they have *someone waiting for them* at home.

I can't count the number of times I've heard that shit, and it still pisses me off every time they bring it up. Because they all do, except for Leo.

And Mac.

Like it wouldn't take the right groupie on the road to change all that, but whatever.

*Means more for me.*

# Chapter Two

## Anna

"Have you seen Toby?"

Juggling a crazy amount of crap in my arms, I manage to tuck my phone between my ear and shoulder before it tumbles into the snow. *Or worse, I lose my travel mug.* "No, why? What did he do now?"

I hate that my first assumption is Tobias Jeffers has done something incredibly screwed up, but that's the persona he's given *himself*.

"He—*Uh.*" My caller huffs, and I feel it down to my exhausted bones, doing my best to walk the snowy parking lot without losing my balance in these heels. They aren't stripper tall, but they're tall enough to make slick weather difficult.

*But they're also one of my favorite pairs.*

"Let me guess," I say as my car beeps with the unlock. "He's disappeared again."

I settle my files that didn't fit into the leather binder in the passenger seat, my heavy purse following close behind. The load is probably heavy enough that the seat belt sensor is going to go off again, but I'd rather have it all within my reach. Even if I'm driving.

"Uh … Kind of. But that's not all."

I adjust the travel mug in my grip so I can hold the phone with my now freed hand and stretch out my neck.

*Calls involving the bassist no longer get me amped up.*

"So spit it out, Leo." I round the car and open my own door to drop into the driver's seat.

"Just … Can you get here? It's hard as fuck to explain."

*That's not good.*

Sighing at the situation *and* my boss, I engage the engine, the Bluetooth taking over the moment the car is on. "I'll be there in twenty minutes."

"Okay, we're at—"

"Really?" I scoff at Leo's nerve, click my seat belt in place, and put the car in gear to pull away from my spot. "Did you forget who maintains your calendar?"

"Right." There's a subtle chuckle that flitters over the line, but then it's gone.

*Boy, this is bad.*

"See you in nineteen."

I press the button on the steering wheel to disengage the call, my mind already running over all the possibilities of what the entitled rock star could have gotten up to, but there're too many options. I settle on listening to the soft rock song coming from the stereo instead.

The music eases more of my nerves than I care to admit. I feel like I am both walking into the hornet's nest, and preparing to calm Leo's over-exaggerations once I arrive.

He tends to freak out first these days, his mind too focused on all the things he could lose as an indie band manager making deals for his *own* label for the first time ever.

It's been almost two years. He hasn't crashed and burned yet.

But since I'm the only connection from the label world he kept, we've both had to wear every dang hat imaginable. Had to make uncomfortable sacrifices to keep up with the As Above reputation.

Like my salary and my move to a studio apartment that doubles as my office instead of the constant five-star hotel stays.

*Or my ability to slip away for personal reasons.*

Honestly … I hate it.

I mean, not the *job* itself. It allows me more access and freedom to the things I need. It's just …

It's a thankless job even before the compromises. The perks I got helped deal with the overworking conditions for a long while until eventually that wasn't quite enough.

*Nothing feels like quite enough these days.*

But going with Leo got me out of a terrible contract with a sleazeball, and for that, I'm willing to put up with the crap.

*For now.*

Including the unruly rock star that prefers to test the patience of everyone around him regularly.

With the car parked and a mad dash through the freezing temperatures, I secure the essentials just in time for the door to open and my pace to not slow.

*Keys.*

*Phone.*

*Hot cocoa.*

*Pocket sanitizer?*

All secured.

"Thanks for coming," Leo says, closing me in the house with the rest of his band—As Above. While I used to be intimidated by the massive muscle and rebellious ink covering each member, I've grown to ignore it.

*Mostly.*

"I was heading out to get some work done anyway." I shake my head against Leo's offer to stow my coat and instead tighten the furry material around my body. "So why am I here?"

"Well." Leo leads me through the foyer to the back of the house where I know an addition was added and Fin agreed to share the space with Leo for *band meetings*. "Ian found something in the mail and I wanted you to see this shit before it got any worse."

"Oh, boy." Coming around the back of the original portion of the converted condominium built in the late 1800s, Leo leads me into the modernized version of the house where a massive formal dining table takes up the room.

It might be modernized—as in recently built—but this place looks like it's straight out of an old Victorian home. It matches Fin's significant other perfectly.

*Gothic and dark.*

The table is not the only thing that takes up space in the room, calling all attention to it like a volcano warning of eruption.

"What's this?" I gesture to the mountain of mail left on the wooden surface.

All of As Above converges, including the band's resident security members from Sentry Protection.

Everyone speaks at once, all drawing together in a way that deflects around in my head until I hold up my hand for silence. "One at a time."

Clearly, whatever this pile of mail contains has everyone on edge.

*It's my job to get ahead of whatever it is.*

"Sentry sorts the mail. Checks it—"

"I know this," I add, cutting off my boss's explanation.

"And a few included what seemed like innocent declarations," Leo explains.

"That's not abnormal. As Above's fanbase is insanely attached. They practically grew up with the band."

"Uh-huh."

"So this one in particular has been going on for a while." Ian, Sentry's head of security for their contract with As Above and Rex Thompson's main protection detail, steps up to me with a stack of envelopes in his hand. I stretch my neck all the way back to maintain eye contact. "We originally dismissed most of it. We see so many names that it's hard to keep track. Anything remotely threatening gets archived, and anything the guys may want to see gets sent over for them to look at when they can."

"Fan mail. This is all about just some fan mail?"

His lips flatten into a thin line as he tilts his head in confirmation. "It's *what* came through the mail."

Ian presses a particularly bulky envelope into my offered hand. "This is just the most recent development. I found everything I could."

I nod and step aside to place my travel mug of hot cocoa on the table. Then I peek into the already open parcel and pull out the contents. Unfolding the page, I can't help the squeak of surprise that escapes my lips when I'm met with a pregnancy test taped to the page.

A *positive* test.

*I'm going to need that sanitizer now.*

There are only two sentences on the page accompanying the capped stick. "*Toby, it's yours. Call me.*"

I'm already spinning headlines in my head, debating which ones the media would eat up first, as I replace the worst attempt at gaining fame I've seen back into the envelope, ignoring the included phone number.

I hand the note over to Leo and fish the travel-sized bottle of sanitizer from my pocket, only mildly concerned about the bacteria I might be transferring to my coat as I reach inside. Squeezing some gel into my palm, I rub my hands to dissipate the remaining moisture. Meeting Leo's glacial gaze, I frown.

Because he's offering up another envelope similar to the last.

This one bulges in a different way, appearing to hold *two more* pregnancy tests.

"That's not all, Anna."

That tone. That's the one that makes me purse my lips and sigh at my boss.

"There's another tape."

"Okay," I draw out.

"And a fucking DNA test that looks awfully … *official.*"

# Chapter Three

## Anna

After hours of reviewing, deliberating, researching, and gallons of sanitizer, I finally throw my notes at the band's manager and try my best to smooth the stray hair sticking out of my slicked back ponytail. Or what once was. My clothes are rumpled beyond recognition, my shoes lost somewhere under the table that became my work station until I could no longer hold my eyes open.

I passed out for only a moment after refusing to accept a bed in a strange house with a weird sense of smell that only comes from adding brand-new materials to an old house.

*Musky and fresh.*

*It's weird.*

"What's this?" Leo stirs on the uncomfortable looking loveseat some-one dragged in when we refused to leave, the creases around his eyes digging deep.

"The plan," I reply, hands on hips.

"Uh-huh," he mutters, scanning the page the book is open to. "And we keep Toby out of the loop?"

"Yes. Lest he mentions something to the wrong person and blow it all up."

The bassist who caused this whole mess is still noticeably absent, while the rest of us take care of *his* problems. Security mentioned he made his way home and has been passed out—not alone—since about six this morning. God knows what he was doing before that.

My nerves are on the verge of snapping when Leo continues to stare at the page and says nothing. "Well?"

His gaze flicks to me, then back to the page with a scowl. "Well."

Huffing, I snatch the notebook from him and spin back to my workstation, dropping my butt back into my chair. "Maybe if he wasn't such an ass, we could ask his feedback—"

"Did you just say *ass*?" I ignore the drummer's mocking tone as he enters the space with a half grin on his handsome face and coffee cups filling his grip. "How original."

"Then what would you propose, Mac?"

He edges closer, sets a steaming cup of what I hope is hot chocolate next to my pile of pages, and shrugs. "She would have signed an NDA, right? So any shit she shared, or shares, publicly makes her in defiance of that."

Leo gasps in jest, his hand going to the undone top buttons of his wrinkled dress shirt. "As if we didn't think of that."

Mac flips his manager the middle finger and sips from the second cup in his grip. "She never signed one?"

"We would know," I answer on a sigh. "If we could *find it*." The last words are growled off of my lips, my scowling brow turned to Leo.

"His file is literally thicker than the dictionary," Leo adds, rolling his eyes.

"The generic verbiage in the NDA somehow *doesn't* mention pregnancy," I inform Mac.

His brow furrows, his cup paused in front of his lips. "Seriously?"

"Yep."

"How is that?" Mac's question is to his manager, but my boss shakes his head. "I mean, I know mine had to be different, but for real?"

The hearty sigh that escapes Leo is almost loud enough to echo in the formal dining space. His brow pinches in defeat, his shoulders less proud than normal when he leans up and braces his forearms on his knees. "Apparently not."

I scoff, my professionalism long gone, and lean back over my open laptop. The screen displays different windows of tabloid sites that love to paint As Above in a negative light. They would jump through hoops at the chance to have some kind of *scandal* like this. I can already imagine the headlines.

**Tobias Jeffers impregnates fan.**

**Toby, As Above's backup guitarist, loves to love it and leave it.**

Mac's clearing throat brings me back to the conversation. "How did legal miss that?"

"I have no idea. That's Leo's department."

Mac snorts and turns to his manager and friend and offers him the cup he's been sipping from. "Bet you paid extra for it, too, didn't ya, owl toes."

Leo chuckles, but it's tired. Quiet. *Defeated.* "You have no idea," he mutters, accepting the cup from Mac, only to smack his lips. "You fucking *drank it*?"

"I left you a sip." Mac arches a brow, his eyes light with humor he tries to hold back but fails. "Seriously, though." He sighs and flops into the seat beside Leo. "What *can* be done?"

Seeing them squeezed onto the small loveseat, covered in tattoos and dressed complete opposite, is almost as humorous as Mac's banter. Leo's shrug is as disheartening as his exhausted gaze when he swings it on me as if silently asking for me to become a witch and do magic.

*I'm good. But not* that *good.*

"Well, since you nixed my plan, I'd say the only thing left is to see where the cards fall. You or I"—I gesture between Leo and myself—"can try reaching out to her and hear her demands."

Leo growls and throws back the last sip of what I presume is cold coffee based on the wince that returns. "I hate that idea."

I wing a daring brow at the manager, hoping he shoots down another idea of mind when he's yet to present one of his own that won't end up with As Above labeled as some kind of crappy *baby-daddy* drama band. We already fought those vultures off when the media found out about Aria taking the twins to the park, alone, on a day that Rex was busy in the studio.

*At least that was easy to overshadow.*

Post a few of the millions of pictures where Rex is obsessed with his children.

Wait.

Then plan an interview with a popular radio disc jockey where said lead singer gets asked questions only a present dad would know.

Which is supposed to be conducted today, including an even more exclusive VIP meet and greet with fans, to keep the narrative flowing.

"I don't hear a better one, boss."

"Ugh, I hate when you're right," Leo grunts as he pushes to stand but not without landing a backhand on Mac's chest first.

The drummer only snickers, hooks a finger in Leo's suspender strap, then lets it snap back against him with a loud *crack*. "Fuck!"

"You're awake now."

Leo spins and growls, his fist closed and drawn back to toss a punch when Mac darts off the loveseat and across the room.

"That was for Anna. She was totally right."

"I am right," I state and tap at the keys on my laptop. "I'll schedule the meeting, but you're going. We'll hear her out, see *how* she accomplished a DNA test already. Need to demand one for ourselves to confirm and handle things from there. First step is to keep it *quiet*."

The manager nods, one hand massaging the ache from his snapped suspender.

"And keep it away from Jeffers?" I confirm with a quirked brow. "Are you sure?"

"Should be easy enough. Otherwise, he might open his mouth at the wrong time."

*Said every overly confident entrepreneur ever.*

# Chapter Four



"**D**UDE, YOU GOTTA DO something with that beard."

I slap away Mac's hands and grunt when he reaches across the bucket seat we share, aiming for my face again. "I'll bite 'em, twinkle nuts."

"Oh, you noticed?" Mac's cheesy grin lights up his face as he leans back and arches his hips into the air. "I'll tell J—"

"*Seat belt.*" The single growl from the passenger seat of our SUV has Mac slamming back into the seat and laughing.

"Seriously, Tyro," Mac calls up to his bodyguard. "Tell Tob his beard is garbage attached to his face."

"Fuck you." I run a hand down the facial hair being harassed and flip a middle finger to Mac. "They're not going to see our *faces*. It's a damn radio interview."

"Annnnd," Mac draws, his eyebrow quirked high enough to disappear behind his bandana, "a fucking meet and greet after. Duh. Where have you been?"

"Not listening, clearly." The quip comes from the driver this time, the seat filled with none other than Sentry's second-in-command and the absolute pain in my ass—Lugh.

*He's no fun.*

"I was listening," I rebut, but then lose track of what we were talking about. "What's this meet and greet shit?"

Mac bursts out in a laugh that has him slapping his knee. "Holy *fuck*, Tob."

It takes more than a few minutes for Mac's hysterics to die off enough for our bodyguards to resume their run down of the events before we park and walk in.

*Talking with Nitro from Reaper Radio—live on air.*

*Answer stupid questions.*

*Get thrown into a room with a few people who paid a lot of money to see us.*

*Sign shit.*

*Go home.*

Easy.

We pull up to a back entrance where another SUV is already parked next to a Prius and  my top lip curls instinctively.

We're ushered inside the brick building, with our bodyguards behind us. Mac leads the way down the long hall that looks familiar, but I can't place it.

"You've got twenty minutes," a female voice fills the space the moment Mac opens the door and leads us into a green room. "Read the questions, your answers are already prepped. Just say what's on the cards and leave it at that. Oh, good—you two made it in one piece."

I roll my eyes at the snarky comment from the woman I still have yet to see through the group when Mac passes me a card baton-style that has only two answers written neatly in handwriting I definitely recognize.

*Shit.*

"No one will see you during this interview, so if you get stumped, pass it to a bandmate or deflect." Mac finally steps aside enough for me to stand shoulder to shoulder with him as he does the same with his twin brother on the other side.

In front of us, directing and ordering, could rival that of a drill instructor on his worst day.

*If they wore tight skirts and fire-red hair in buns so tight their brains had to hurt.*

"Where's Le?"

The question gains me a raised, perfectly sculpted brow—so perfect, I think the woman threatened it to stay in place—and a purse of her pale lips.

There's almost no color to her face. Or her, in general, with the plain wardrobe and the lack of makeup that makes any of her good qualities stand out.

*Bland.*

*And annoying.*

"He had to step *out*," Anna nearly hisses, her face barely hiding the eye roll as if it's somehow my fault that the manager had manager shit to do and left her in charge of us. "But if you're done interrupting me, we can get this over with."

"Oh, burn," Rex snickers but snaps his lips shut when As Above's PR rep turns her steely green gaze on him.

"Rex, you are responsible for answering the questions. Make sure you only say what you're comfortable with and nothing more."

My bandmate nods and accepts the final card from her pinched fingers.

Even her nails are a similar shade to the woman's tan skirt.

Where most of the women in this industry would be covered in ink, Anna is not. They'd wear massive amounts of paint on their faces in various colors, especially black, but not her.

In fact, I don't think this woman owns a single black item.

And most would be down to fuck any one of us. They'd throw themselves at us like the last PR rep Leo fired or way too many of the groupies that follow us.

*Not goodie-two-shoes Anna.*

"Any questions?" she calls to the room, making eye contact with each member of As Above.

"Nah," Fin responds.

"Not our first rodeo," Mac quips, the last word coming out as *ro-day-o*.

"All good," Rex answers and reaches around his by-blood-brother to slap my shoulder. "Right, Tob?"

I nod to my lead singer and follow the rest of my band out into a viewing area where we get to watch the DJ of this radio show headbanging to a song he's playing for the listeners in prep for our interview.

"All right, *all* right, metalheads. For those of you listening at home, you've got Nitro with Reaper Radio and we have a very special guest for you tonight." The man claps his heavily tatted hands, and winks through the glass at us. "As Above is in the house, ready to answer some burning questions and talk music for us. They're on after this! So stick around."

Rock music fills the space as Nitro hits a few buttons, then tips his headphones off and waves us in. The audio tech smiles as we pass, closing the door behind us.

"Hey hey, guys." Nitro stands and reaches out to shake hands with a grin. "So glad you guys could make it out."

"Thanks for having us." Rex is the first to shake and take a seat, headphones situated on his head.

"It's been, what, three years?" Nitro asks the group as we each return his offered hand in greeting. "Too long, I know that. How's the families?"

Finland snickers, and Rex smiles proudly. "Well, that's what we're here to talk about."

"Perfect." Nitro slips back into his seat, headphones on. "We got about thirty seconds before we're live."

I sit and lean into the table, my headgear securely in place, letting the end of the song calm my sweating palms.

I'm not nervous. I just hate talking in front of people, especially when I can't see them.

Helps that it's a song I like from Hardy called JACK.

*Where is the Jack?*

"Welcome back," Nitro emphasizes into the giant mic that covers most of his face. "In case you missed it, we are *here* with As Above!" The man makes his own crowd noise in a quieted yell, then turns to us. "So this hangout sesh is a little different where we are not accepting callers, but I have a set of questions that you all asked online. I am just the voice for you. The voice of the *people*."

The interview goes along just like every other damn interview As Above has ever done. Nitro asks all the same questions, all the same comments prying in search of new songs or albums. Rex handles most of the answers with a grin I don't understand, Fin filling in the gaps when it seems like Rex is answering too much. Even Mac quips stupid nicknames and snickers. I, on the other hand, zone out.

*Is there any whiskey back here?*

The only difference this time is Nitro asking about Rex's twin kids and searching for if Fin and Cedar are planning any spawns any time soon.

*Can we get this over with already?*

"Now, Toby." His voice pulls me back to the land of the living and has me gripping the card cupped in my hand, preparing to answer the stupid questions. "I've heard some things ..."

My brothers and bandmates go deadly silent as Nitro's gaze lands on me, and I *feel* the atmosphere change.

*Something's off.*

The hair on the back of my neck stands and my mustache tingles enough that I reach up and scrub a finger across it. "What's that?"

Nitro's grin ratchets up and my stomach gives a wicked twist. "This was a last-minute addition, and I know that rumors are rumors, but I wanna know. The people wanna know."

I spare a glance at my band who's all pinched brows and confused. *This is not how this is supposed to go.* "Know what, man?"

"The grapevine claims you've also started settling down, yeah?" Sweat builds on my back even though I've had this question before. They always want me to be like Rex. Settle down. Find a woman and make little rocker spawn like he did.

*So why does this feel different?*

"Oh, nah, man." I glance at my cue card for help when I feel Nitro's gaze burning a hole in my head. "Not me."

"Serious?" Nitro pushes with a grin. One that seems like I'm full of shit and he's just waiting for the *gotcha* moment. "No one expecting?"

I can't help but glance at my brothers, wearing a clear *what the hell* expression, only to find each of them staring back at me intently. Their gazes are too focused, too scrutinizing.

"Nah." I force a smile. "Might wanna ask Rex, though. He won't stay off his girl."

*Deflect with humor. Should work.*

"Man," Nitro says on a shake of his head and raps his knuckles on the table with a chuckle. "I thought I had a good source."

"*Interview is over.*" I frown as Anna's declaration fills my ears and spin to find the woman standing opposite the window, hands to her hips and face tightened with fury.

Nitro speaks into the mic as if the end of this *hangout sesh* was planned for right now. "All right, folks. That's all we got for tonight. Drop your comments and questions on the socials and let's get these guys back in here!"

Music fills the room when I pop off the headphones, but it's not a reprieve for long.

Because the door slams open, and Anna rushes in.

"What was that, Nitro?" Anna corners the disc jockey with a dangerous pointer finger. "What the h—"

The two are closed in together, and even though we can't hear what's being said, it's clear that Anna is giving the radio DJ a piece of her mind, judging by his raised hands and the flush to her face.

*Huh. There is color to her.*

"What the shit is going on?" I ask the room even though I don't take my eyes off Anna as she spins from Nitro, her shoulders raising and lowering with a deep breath. She smooths her hair and her skirt, squares her shoulders, and reaches for the door.

The smile that meets us is manufactured. Forced. *Bland.*

And completely cut off from any further questions.

"Ready to meet some fans?"

# Chapter Five

## TOBY

**M**Y FACE HURTS FROM forced smiles, and my fingers cramp from all the writing. Though playing guitar has strengthened my hands, nothing compares to writing the same thing over and over and over again.

*When does the real party start?*

It's only when I see Anna flushing for the second time tonight, amid a crowd of fans, that I toss my Sharpie onto the table. "Who do you think she's talking to?"

"What do you care?" Mac asks and tips his chair back on two legs beside me. Our PR rep switches the phone to her other hand as she paces nearby, away from patrons but not too far from us.

"Because shit's been weird as hell and it's creeping me out."

Mac snorts and accepts another Pride flag for his signature, the fan bypassing me, even when I make a move to offer my pen.

"It's because of your beard. No one wants to tell you how ugly it is."

The comment catches me off guard and has a laugh bubbling up. "Where's the fucking whiskey? I'm over this already."

Mac elbows me in the ribs as a fan scowls at me, another signature bypassed. "Could you at least *pretend*?"

It's the first time tonight that he looks serious, his chair now on all four legs and his brow furrowed.

"Pretend what?"

"That you give a fuck. *Duh.* You're throwing all kinds of weird vibes," Mac says, muttering something else under his breath that I miss. Then, in an instant, he's back to his usual self, the joking drummer.

*Literally.*

He snatches my marker and starts piddling a beat on the table's edge with the plastic.

A few cheers sound around us, accompanied by flashes of cameras, spurring him on. He begins to tap his foot as if it's his kick pedal, his other hand joining in with his own marker, creating a series of annoying *clinks.*

*How his bodyguard deals with him on a regular—*

"Excuse me, Toby?" The female voice has my attention snapping away from the bastard beside me and landing on a soft smile and an As Above tee.

*Now that's what I'm talking about.*

"Hey," I greet, grinning for real, and she blushes. "You got something for me to sign?" I tilt my head to the papers in her grip, and she gets an even deeper shade of red in the face.

*Hmm, wonder what else is flushed?*

I like 'em shy. Hell, I like 'em confident, too.

*Equal opportunist and all.*

And this chick just landed on my radar for a potential bed mate for the night.

*Let's see how easy she can corrupt. That's my absolute favorite.*

"Y-yeah," she stammers and steps closer.

"Please collect your things and move along!" Anna calls from somewhere behind the chick in front of me, making her jump and my brow dip.

"Don't worry, hun." I hold a hand out in offering. "I'll make it quick."

The woman leans in, close enough that her thighs touch the tabletop, and her grimace grows into a forced grin. "That's what you said last time I saw you."

*What?*

Confusion contorts my features, making me drop my hand when she slaps papers over top of the few posters strewn before me. It's some kind of typed-up, official-looking paperwork with a signature line at the bottom and a complete contrast to the band posters beneath.

"Sign this," she hisses through gritted teeth. "Or I go public."

I feel like I'm the mouse caught by the tail.

"The fuck is this?"

"You know exactly what this is," she whispers and taps a chipped black nail on the papers.

*Is she trembling?*

My gaze flips to Mac, my brow furrowed, the hair on the back of my neck standing on end. "Okay, c'mon. Where are the cameras?"

I force a chuckle that goes unreciprocated. Because Mac looks just as dumbfounded as me.

*This has to be a shitty joke.*

*Right?*

"No cameras if you sign," the chick responds, her eyes darkening, her tight smile thinning.

"There a problem here?" I spare a glance at the papers when Lugh's voice cuts in and double-take. I'm up out of my seat like it's on fire, sweat prickling my brow as I fist the sheets the chick laid out for me. Only a few of the printed words register in my head.

Words like *child* bounce around inside my skull and threaten to pop out.

*Child.*

"There's definitely a fuckin' problem," I growl to the bodyguard who appears at my side and accepts the shitstorm in my hands. Without another word, Lugh rounds the table and grabs the chick by her elbow. Her face drops when the bodyguard turns her away from me and she begins to struggle.

"Hey! Let go of me—"

"Hell no," Lugh responds, and even though he moves them another step away from me, my stomach drops.

*No way it's real.*

Is it real?

"Get off me," the woman nearly screams, gaining just enough attention from those around her, promising a scene if Lugh doesn't get her the fuck out of here. "Let go, or I'll sue—"

"We gotta go." I feel eyes on me. Hands. Cameras. The whispered comments filling the room as it goes silent aside from the grating feminine voice beside me, urging my feet to move. "Jeffers, go. Now."

*It can't be real.*

Fake pregnancies and pretend babies have happened with As Above. It's one of the easiest ways to get attention in our world. But none of them have ever had *paperwork.*

*Real life, honest-to-the courts* paperwork.

My head spins. My feet shuffle. My hearing tunnels as I wrack my memory and try to place her face.

*Did I ever sleep with her?*

*Why can I not remember her?*

"Toby."

*It's not real.*

"Tob, c'mon."

Not even Mac can muster up a weird name. I hear his voice calling after me, feel his presence, and yet …

"This can't be real." The words tumble from my numb lips, my fingers tingling at the tips as I look around me and feel only eyes. They're on me, only me, filled with different levels of *judgment* and sympathy.

It is real.

*I'm just like them.*

Just. Like. Them.

I'm gonna be tied down and washed up. Wrung out and pinned to the spot, waiting and wishing and filling with regret with each day that passes.

With each day, I'll lose my freedom.

My breathing becomes labored, my heart racing in my chest, my bandmates staring intently, waiting for the explosion that is my life. Waiting for the inevitable collapse of all that is me.

It's all over.

My dream ... *our* dream.

It's over.

# Chapter Six

## Anna

"**G**ET HIM OUT OF here!"

Barking and yelling orders is not generally my style, but when Tobias Jeffers starts hyperventilating, I fear destruction is next.

*It's his thing.*

Feel stuck, caged, or just plain too freaking high to know that the dragon isn't real?

*Smash everything.*

Many a hotel room, green room, and venue have seen his noxious ways, resulting in one too many fines for Leo's label. It's chaos I'm not looking forward to, should it erupt.

*Especially here.*

It takes a second forced yell from me to get the stunned guys moving.

Security members fling arms around Toby and practically carry the man to the back of the studio. Once we're outside, it's a flurry of bodies piling into different vehicles.

I pause in the freezing cold, knowing my car is still here and that I shouldn't leave it, but I'm more concerned about Dr. Banner going Hulk as he's shoved into the back seat of a blacked-out vehicle.

"Crap," I mutter, my breath forming a cloud in the cold air. Ignoring the sensible voice in my head suggesting to drive my own car, I make my way toward Toby's vehicle and slide into the back seat next to him, just as the door slams closed.

I'm forced to shove Toby's leg over since he's taking up the entire back seat and plant my butt against the chilled leather, my phone already to my ear and ringing before security can pull us out of the lot.

"She wasn't fucking here," Leo answers, sounding somewhat out of breath. "I can't find her."

"Because she's here." I shove at Toby again, my freezing hand landing on his warm thigh and digging in to get him moving over far enough for me to snap my seat belt.

"*There?*"

"At the studio," I answer and raise my shoulder to hold the phone to my ear and free up my hands. "She had papers, Leo."

"Fuck," he snaps, and I reach for the purse I'm lucky I was able to grab with all the distractions.

I search my bag and silently groan when I remember that Lugh never handed the papers over to me. He kept them in his hand when he took off with the woman.

*He stayed behind.*

"We had to leave the studio," I say into the phone and secure my purse at my feet. "She was causing a scene."

Leo's heavy sigh echoes over the line, accompanied by the slam of a car door on his end. "So, he knows now?"

"I ..." I risk a glance to my left where the man in question sits awkwardly across the remaining seat cushions not taken up by my butt. He hasn't moved. Hasn't spoken. "I'm fairly certain he's dissociating."

In fact, I'm fairly certain I hear a continuous low growl coming from his side of the car and we're running out of time before he decides to do something stupid. Something like jumping out of a moving vehicle.

"Sounds about right," Leo huffs. "Fuck, any brilliant ideas?"

It's my turn to sigh into the phone. "I have no idea, Leo. But I do know that we don't have much time."

He lets out a long string of curses, vocalizing the storm brewing beside me because we both know what comes next with Tobias Jeffers.

*Binders. Destruction. Disappearing.*

*And little me left to clean up the dang mess the bassist leaves behind.*

Not to mention whatever was caught on camera tonight slipping to the media and growing like wildfire with rumors and partial truths Leo and I will have to fight the backlash of.

"Let me talk to him."

"Not gonna happen."

"Anna, let me try."

I hear the desperation in the band manger's voice. I hear how much he both cares for the man he considers a brother *and* how badly he doesn't want this to go sideways for himself. The band, the label.

*For Toby.*

It's something I've yet to understand about this strange group of men. They *care* to a fault, in a way that's almost sheltering. They downplay the things Toby does. Put up with his antics and insanity without much fight.

*Enable his addiction.*

If it were up to me?

Tobias Jeffers would be gone.

*Guess it's a good thing it's not up to me.*

Except right now, I have more control over the situation than the manager does. I'm here and he isn't.

And while the man on the line might be my boss, I know better than to chance what's happening. No one knowingly tempts the Hulk.

"No."

He huffs.

"Ann—"

"No, Leo. He's not okay, but he's not throwing things." His stress-filled sigh nearly cuts me off, but I continue, "He needs to stay like this until we get wherever we're going. I'm not going to be in a moving vehicle with him while he rages. You've seen him, how he gets. This is not the place for that."

"You're such a dick."

It takes me a moment of blinking my mind into focus to realize the words came from beside me and not from the phone.

"I can fucking *hear you.*" The words are growled, and when I look in Toby's direction, I'm met with such ferocity in his chocolate-colored eyes that I'm taken aback. He's not just mad at me or my words. He's downright feral.

I'm already leaning against the car door, but the handle digs in further.

"Well," I state and quirk a brow in his direction, despite my body's natural reaction to retract. "I'm the one who's gotten you out of trouble."

A literal growl reverberates from him, something I'd equate to a cornered wolf, and I grip the phone just a little harder.

"Fuck you, Anna," Toby spits.

"And you, as well, Jeffers."

Toby looks away, breaking the stare down and taking with him most of the intensity he's emitting into the small space. I will the little hairs on the back of my neck to settle and my breath to slow.

"Anna." Leo's voice draws my attention away from the beast sharing my seat back to the immediate problem. "I don't wanna do this."

"I already don't like it if that's how you're starting it."

"We gotta get him away from here," Leo continues, saying words like *clearing the air* and *waiting it out,* but I already know what he's going to suggest.

*The cabin.*

It's a place in the middle of the mountains with minimal service, no neighbors for miles, and a tiny house that he had plans to fix up in his free time.

*He's had so much of that.*

When he first bought it, I thought he's crazy. The lot didn't even have a driveway; one had to drive through the brush to reach it. Or a housing structure I'd consider anything beyond a shack.

It's a place of nightmares for city girls like myself.

"No." I cut off his justifications with a tightness to my chest. "No way."

"I know it's not ideal, but we're out of options—"

"Bull. We can figure something out here."

"Anna, listen. We don't have another choice. You said it yourself, we need to act fast."

"Send Lugh. He's the one that's supposed to be keeping—" I flick my sight to Toby, who's staring out the window, and dampen my comments. "It's *his job.*"

"I need boots here. You can do what I need you to do from there."

"Le—"

"Pack a bag, Anna." His determination is unwavering. I sigh out my defeat, knowing deep down he's right. Keep Toby out of trouble by keeping him the hell away from *everything.* Especially other people. "You're going to a retreat."

"I swear, Leo …"

"You'll be fine. The internet was upgraded last week."

"I hate you."

"Oh, I know." He almost chuckles, and my cheeks heat at the prospect of becoming a *babysitter* until this all blows over. My stomach twists, and my brow prickles with sweat. "But it's the only way."

*Of course it is.*

"I still hate you."

# Chapter Seven

## TOBY

"HE'S STILL PASSED OUT—"

*I'm not.*

I haven't been for some time. I think I did for a moment, but the voices surrounding me don't give a shit about anyone sleeping in the vicinity.

*Rude bastards.*

"—c'mon, Leo. There's another way. Someone else. I can't even walk away from him to pack his bag."

"No, Anna. There isn't."

From my position—which happens to be face down on the couch, though I'm not sure whose furniture I'm crashed out on—I can hear every word uttered about me and my condition. My issues. My *problems.* My anger—which I keep *contained,* thank you very much—and, for some reason, my inability to be in the public.

All thanks to Ms. Straitlaced Prune and her perfectly plain skirt, with her slicked back hair in that same damn tight-ass bun she always has holding her damn forehead back.

*Does she ever let the shit down?*

The woman has no problem calling shit out and making even Leo pause on occasion.

But for some reason, he's more adamant. Steadfast. Unbudging.

*I think.*

I'd probably know more if my thoughts weren't fuzzy and my face wasn't numb.

*Not even sure why we're here and why they keep talking about going somewhere.*

Certain that if I squinted hard enough, I might be able to recall why Anna is railing the shit out of Leo, but I'd rather enjoy the buzz that started in the car with a blunt and continued through the bottle of amber I'm still holding onto.

*Where are the guys? It's drinking time.*

*We could make a game outta the number of times Rex says 'fuck'.*

I try to push myself up, but I don't get far because the couch spins beneath me, and I flop face-first into the cushion. Something *thuds* along the floor beside me, but I pay it no mind.

*Damn, that's good shit.*

"And how am I supposed to manage that?"

The words pierce my brain and make my tongue feel funny with a retort I don't even try holding back. "I got somethin' you can *manage.*" My words sound muffled and far away to my ringing ears.

"*Ew,*" Anna shoots back.

*Goal accomplished.*

Chuckling, I wedge an arm beneath my ribs and maneuver my upper body until the light penetrates my pupils and drives a nail into the sockets, killing off the levity almost instantly, along with some of my buzz. "Shit, why is it so fucking bright?"

"Leo, I can*not.* Will not. Find someone else."

I get my arm out from under me and throw it over my eyes. "Am I not pretty enough for you, Ms. Prune?"

"It's *prude.* Prude," Anna corrects, agitated, her hands flying out as she talks.

I know this because it's what Anna does when she's super mad, which I normally enjoy watching. I can also see portions of her flailing limbs from underneath my arm. "I said what I said."

*What's with people correcting me?*

*Bastards.*

Her growling response is all I get back but it still makes me chuckle until Leo chimes in, "Toby, this is serious."

"*Sooo serious*," I mock, because I honestly can't remember why it's so important. "So, so serious."

"Fuck, Toby, c'mon. Can you at least *try*?"

*Why does Leo sound like Mac now?*

"No!" Anna answers for me, loudly. Forcefully. "No, he freaking *can't*. That's the whole *problem—*"

I sit up from my position, sway for a hot second, and then drop my arm. The lights are still blindingly bright, but I'm sick of hearing about the shit.

Sick of hearing Anna's mouth droning on and on about me and my *problems.*

*I. Don't. Have. Any.*

"Leo," I say through the cotton in my mouth, "take me wherever the fuck you want."

"Okay." The man sighs and runs a hand down his tensed face that's covered in an abnormal-for-him amount of scruff. He's still wearing his normal white dress shirt and suspenders and he looks ridiculous to me, but I'd bet my faded Ozzy tee under my leather vest looks just as fucked up to him.

He's put together. Formal. Planned and scheduled.

*I'm not.*

"Just not with *her*."

"Oh, fucking hell," Leo mutters and throws his hands up. "You're both being ridiculous." He paces in a circle that makes me dizzy the longer I watch. "Beyond reasoning." The man's hands go to his hips, his fancy shoes stopping just in front of me. "You're going to the cabin, Toby. And she's going with you."

"No, thank you." Before I shake my head, Leo crouches in front of me, his features set like hard stone, his eyes bloodshot and emotionless.

"You will go. And she will go. Or you both are out of fucking jobs."

His words slap me in the face so hard, I fall back into the couch. "Fuck you, Le. Threats? Seriously?"

His chin lifts in a single nod of confirmation, his face no less harsh than it was before the words left his lips. "Seriously. You, Anna, cabin."

"Le," I growl and pitch forward to grab his fancy shirt in my fist.

My band manager's jaw clenches as he grips my wrist, pressing into the pressure point. My hold loosens and my buzz fades. "Or you're fucking done playing for As Above."

# Chapter Eight

## Anna

Escorted to the edge of town as if this is some sort of prison transport, the last Sentry SUV finally pulls away from our tail. Toby and I reach the base of the mountain, where the cabin is located deep in the forest, with only a few minor problems along the way. It's several winding roads later that we finally pull into the driveway.

It's still difficult to maneuver, mostly hidden by brush and barren foliage, but in a better state than the last time I was here. Which was during its purchase. The driveway curves and steeps, forcing me to slow the vehicle or risk missing the trail in the blanket of fresh snow.

I'm so focused on the road with a death grip on the wheel that it takes Toby grumbling from the passenger seat to capture my attention and a gasp escapes me.

"Holy crap," I mutter, as the car rolls to a stop in the front yard of a nearly restored log cabin.

Smoke plumes from the chimney, and a cozy glow radiates from the large front windows, the cabin framed by a blanket of snow like a scene straight out of a romantic comedy or the front of a small-town greeting card.

"Can you at least say *shit*?" Toby scoffs, his large frame bowed forward in the seat, his sight on the building in front of us. "This place is worth more than a *crap*."

Rolling my eyes, I park the car. "It's a massive step up from the last time I saw it. Hopefully, the inside is just as good."

"It is," Toby mutters, opening the door and filling the cabin with chilled air. A lit cigarette hangs between his lips before he completely exits. His leather jacket draped over his shoulders despite the freezing cold.

I, on the other hand, am quick to snag and burrow into a puffy coat I had stored in the back seat, with a fur lined hood. I pocket the keys, double check my sanitizer bottle, and grab my travel mug of hot cocoa before slamming the door and wading through Toby's footsteps in the snow.

The crisp white layer only disturbed by his tracks seem to be a few inches in depth, but the width of his strides have me nearly jumping to reach the next crater created by his foot.

*Better this than snow in the shoe.*

He's already at the door, punching a code into the lock and stomping his boots out on the mat that I'm fairly certain is covered in a floral pattern when I reach the porch.

*Not at all what I would expect from Leo.*

"Whoa, hey," I say as I grab his elbow. He pauses in the threshold, his lit cigarette now pinched between his fingers, and wings a brow in my direction. "No smoking inside."

Grumbling, he rolls his eyes. "Why the hell not?" He puts the stick to his lips and takes a deep drag, the smoke blowing from his nose. "We own it."

I scoff and shake my head. "*We* is not on the deed to the house, I can guarantee that." I snatch the cigarette from his fingers and flick it into the snow.

With one challenging look, including a raised brow and pursed lips, I push past the man and enter the house before I freeze to death arguing over cigarettes.

"So damn plain."

I choose to ignore his mumbled words as I set my mug on the counter because I'm not here to impress Toby Jeffers. In fact, the less he likes me, the better.

Instead, I focus on the expansive layout in front of me. The open concept kitchen leads to a living space that is encompassed by floor-to-ceiling windows, tall enough to stretch up past the second story and touch the apex of the roof.

A one-hundred-and-eighty degree unencumbered view of the forested mountains lay out in front of me like a painted portrait.

"This was definitely not here last time."

Somehow, I've edged closer without realizing it, until my nose is nearly pressed against the glass.

It's gorgeous. Breathtaking.

*But it's not for me.*

"It was there all along." Toby's deep timbre startles me with its closeness, and I turn to see him admiring the view, an amber-filled decanter lifted to his lips. "Just needed the elevation."

"Right." Broken from the spell of a beautiful view and reminded all over again why I'm here, I stalk across the tiled floor. My short heels tap with each step back to the kitchen that smells of fresh citrus cleaner. My luggage is already there by the door, alongside the duffel Toby packed.

*That's … odd.*

"Did you …?"

"So you wouldn't break your neck in those fucking heels and have Leo blame me for your murder? Yes." Toby speaks to the window, raising his glass to his lips.

"Thanks, I guess."

Brushing off the weird feeling his words stir in the air between us, I snag the wheeled case and turn down the short hallway to my right. I pass open bifold doors holding laundry equipment that looks like it might be original to the cabin I remember, and I sigh.

*Of course the man wouldn't care to remodel the laundry. No way my poor delicates can go in there.*

I continue down the short path to the only archway left to explore in this portion of the house.

"Where's …" I trail off the spoken thought about any other rooms in the house, entering the primary suite with a lift in my hopes. "Wow."

Another wall of windows just as tall as the living space opens the room up to the setting sunlight that bathes it in a pleasant glow.

But that's not what has me rushing forward.

This time, it's a massive four-poster bed that resembles a cloud in all its blindingly crisp white linens and intricate frame.

It beckons me. Calls to me.

I bypass running my hands over the wooden encasement to see if it's actually carved and allow myself to fall face-first into its softness.

"Oh, God," I mutter into the comforter, my words muffled by the fluff settling in around me like a cool embrace.

*It's so peaceful.*

Exhaustion, heavy and damning, weighs down on me and threatens to steal my consciousness with each moment that I lie here.

So I push myself up to sit and pull my case onto the mattress beside me.

It's a stake. A claim for the room lest my new roommate thinks this space is fair game. There's no way he's getting this luxury when he's the sole reason we're stuck in this damn cabin.

*Speaking of … Tobias Jeffers has been too quiet.*

I slip out of my heels and leave them neatly by the bed. My curiosity pulls me across the plush rug in the direction I had just come from, distracting me from my quest to save the bassist from himself. *Toby duty can wait.* Three doors stare at me, two set into the wooden wall at the front and another to my left.

*Which door?*

I settle on the one closest to the entryway I came through and push open the solid panel to reveal a bathroom equipped for a queen. There's a tub the size of a pool, a dual vanity setup, and a small closet with a shelf running around the room just below hip height.

*Impressive.*

I promise myself a more thorough exploration later and move back into the suite to open the next door. Inside, a closet as large as my entire apartment greets me, complete with an excessive number of fancy lights and built-in mirrors that likely double as storage. Shaking my head, I close the door and turn to the next. This one, a frosted glass door typical of those leading to back patios, hints at the outdoors.

Cold air rushes in when I pull the door open, and I gasp at the sudden chill when I step out onto the porch. Another picturesque view is trapped between the roof and the railing. I pull out my phone to capture the moment.

*Maybe this won't be so bad.*

Soft strumming draws me back to the freezing porch. The sounds mingle with the hum of a motor, drawing my gaze from the snow-capped peaks to a cloud of steam in the porch's far corner. As I approach, the smell of chlorine hits me, and the air grows noticeably warmer. *Of course, Leo installed a hot tub.*

The smile I felt pulling up drops when I notice Toby perched on the edge, his feet dangling in the water, his old acoustic in lap.

"Good to see you've made yourself at home, Jeffers." I roll my eyes as I turn back toward the open door.

"Still not pretty enough, huh, Ms. Prune?" Toby retorts, drawing an audible huff from me.

"If you're going to insult me, can it at least make sense?"

He snorts, fiddling over the strings. The melody sounds familiar but unidentifiable, as I step into the toasty cabin and shut the man outside.

*Maybe he'll freeze to death and solve all of my problems.*

But then, that would be a lot to explain to not just the local authorities, but my boss as well. Then the media.

"Crap," I mutter, rolling my eyes as I head to my suitcase in search of something warmer to wear.

# Chapter Nine

## TOBY

WHEN MY fingers ARE about to freeze despite the amount of alcohol heating my blood, I finally slide my ass into the tub and attempt to keep strumming on my guitar. The water makes it difficult, the song evading me, but I don't let that stop me. I gulp down the last of my drink and reach for the bottle on the steps next to me. As I pour another, I hear an incredulous, "Seriously?"

Blinking through the fog of whiskey and steam, I make out Anna standing opposite the hot tub, her hand wrapped around the neck of my floating guitar.

*Oops.*

Her little growl of irritation makes me smirk. She tips the guitar, draining the water from its body, then disappears as quickly as she appeared, guitar in tow.

"I wasn't done with that," I snap, arms stretched wide.

"I know. Just—" Her voice fades into the misty air, the dim lights overhead doing little to pierce the steam. "I've got the articles lined up. All we have to do is decide when."

"What the hell are you talking about?"

"I think it's the best bet if you want this tamed."

My brow furrows as I slide through the water to stand on the side closest to Anna's pacing figure.

"Gimme my guitar back."

"No."

The single word has that familiar tickle of irritation running up the back of my neck and tensing in the base of my skull. "Anna."

She moves to the bench along the cabin wall, her head tilted away from me like it'll help her ignore me. Irritated, I swing a leg over the tub's edge and hoist myself out, water dripping from my soaked clothes. I tower over her when she cranes her neck to finally look up, her phone plastered to the side of her head as water cascades from me and lands on her covered knees. "Jesus, Jeffers!"

"Gimme my guitar," I growl.

I could easily take it. Grab it and head back to the bubbling water calling my name. It's just sitting next to her, propped up against the back of the bench with a towel underneath to catch the water dripping down the glossed surface.

*But what would be the fun in that.*

"So you can ruin another one? No." Anna's scoff drives straight to my skull like nails on a chalkboard.

"And you're the instrument police now?" I return her scoff and lean in close enough that I can hear the voice of my band's manager speaking through the phone.

"Toby," Anna shrieks, her manicured hands flying up to thrust against my chest. It only serves to release more of the water trapped in the fabric when I refuse to step back, the phone tossed aside and forgotten. "You're getting me wet!"

A dark chuckle escapes me as I lean in and rest my grip on the back of the bench, one hand on each side of her. "Is that so?"

Her spine snaps straight at the inuendo, her hands pulling away from my chest as if I'm on fire. Even her breath barely lifts her chest.

Her fiery gaze collides with mine, her words vehement, her hands still stuck up in the air. "Back up."

I smirk, my tongue poking out to wet my lips as her breath flutters over my face.

And then her eyes flick to the movement so fast I question if I really saw it.

"Guitar." The single word comes out somewhere between a growl and a low groan of frustration.

"If it'll get you out of my face, take it. I don't care." The venom bites me through her words, her eyes narrowed as she stares me down.

The pure lava she's flinging my way with just a look is almost enough to heat my blood and keep me in place if only long enough to see what she'd do next. But I stand tall and snatch the guitar from its seat beside her. With a huff, I walk across the porch, swing my leg over the side of the tub and sink right back into the steaming water. Guitar and all. My back faces her, but I still hear the scoff that rings across the wooden surface between us.

"We're going to be here for a while, Jeffers. If you ruin that thing, I'm not getting you another one."

"Oh yeah?" I mutter and strum, this time keeping the strings of the instrument above the bubbling surface warming my skin. "Maybe I'll need something else to do with my hands." Tossing a grin over my shoulder, I catch Anna shuddering—whether from my comment or the cold is still up to interpretation.

Either way, I laugh.

"You're literally the worst person to be stuck on a mountain with," Anna growls, the sound of her phone unlocking sharp.

"Oh, just you wait, Ms. Prune." I play into the night, lit by twinkling lights above.

*Just. You. Wait.*

# Chapter Ten

## TOBY

BY THE TIME ANNA makes her retreat into the cabin, the ends of my hair are practically icicles and my fingers are too wrinkled to keep playing. The propane heater in the corner of this little setup is meant for keeping the space just on the good side of freezing during the winter days, but now that the night has thoroughly claimed the land, it's having a hard time battling the cold.

*And that's my cue.*

I inhale deeply, then haul out of the water, snagging my guitar and the bottle that I tuck under my arm and make a run for the door.

*Thunk.*

My shoulder slams into the glass, rattling the pane in the frame, but otherwise unmoved by the impact.

"What the fuck?"

A shiver racks over my limbs as I jiggle the handle a second time, but nothing happens.

"Motherfucker," I mutter and glance around the porch for a better solution, only to come up empty. "Anna!"

Nothing.

No movement, no shadows. Just a big heap of *nothing* on the other side of the pane.

"Goddammit." I cross to the main cabin entrance, my bare feet stinging with the threat of frostbite, and punch the code into the keypad.

*Beep. Beep. Beep.*

Flashing red warns me against what was perceived as the wrong code, the lock remaining firmly in place.

"Son of a motherfucker!" I slam my knuckles into the heavy wood and punch the code in again, this time coming back with a flash of green that has me barreling into the house with heaving breaths. *"Fuck."*

My body rattles violently, teeth chattering as I slam the door shut and slam my back against it. My head *thunks* against the wood as I close my eyes, feeling my muscles vibrating with chills that dislodge trails of water from my wet clothes.

"Hot cocoa?"

Anna's voice, dripping with snark, snaps my eyes open. She stands next to the island with a steaming mug held to her pale lips, eyebrow arched.

"Throw some Bailey's in it and I'm in." Another massive shiver takes over my limbs so intense that I prop the guitar against the counter, setting the bottle on top.

My shirt is the next to go, dropping at my feet in a wet *plop*.

I decide that the shorts really should stay for the moment while I wait for Anna, but when my gaze crashes to hers, she remains mostly unmoved. She sips her coca, her gaze fixed on me.

"Water's still hot in the kettle. Packets in the cabinet."

She brushes past me, that damn mug still held high to her mouth and it's then that I realize she's using the ceramic to hide a damn smirk.

I draw in a breath through flared nostrils.

*Two can play games.*

"Thanks," I snap out and hook my thumbs in the waistband of my shorts. They drop to the floor with a matching wet *flop* and join the puddle. The air bites at my damp skin, but that doesn't stop me from snagging a mug from the cabinet and filling the whole thing with the chocolate liquor from above the kitchen sink. I pop the mug in the microwave, the ceramic clanking against the glass turntable obnoxiously, and forty-five seconds later, I'm stalking across the open space to stand in front of the fireplace.

The heat is a welcome relief, thawing my muscles and bones.

*Feels pretty good on my cock, too.*

Glancing over my shoulder, I catch Anna perched on the couch with her face buried in her laptop and her hand absently raising her mug between her face and the table.

"Do you ever st—"

"Jeffers!"

*Gotcha.*

"What?" I snicker as Anna throws her hands up to cover her eyes. "Not enjoying the view?"

"God," she growls, lifting her entire laptop to block the sight of my bare ass on full display. A full blown laugh bursts past my lips when her pale face turns the same shade as her hair. "Where are your clothes?"

"Hm." I shrug and rotate, the flames now licking at my exposed ass cheeks. "They were wet." Sipping from my hot Bailey's, I run a hand through my hair to brush it back out of my face. "Didn't wanna catch cold. Or whatever that wives tale is."

The disgruntled noise that escapes the woman buried behind not just her laptop, but an added pillow as she sinks further onto her back in the couch, makes me chuckle.

"Go put *something* on," Anna snarls from behind her makeshift wall.

"Why?" My free hand goes to my hip as I sip from the mug. "Being naked is good for your health, I've heard."

"And you decide now's the time to test this theory?" she screeches, the top of her head barely visible over her protective wall, that same tight bun keeping her reddened forehead exposed.

"Now's a good a time as any, ain't it?"

"No!"

I snicker at her irritation and take a step closer to the center of the room when the flames lick at my ass a little too hot.

"Do. Not," Anna warns, her words dripping with so much venom, I'm surprised I'm still standing.

"Fine," I say, shrugging my nonchalance. "I'll go put something on."

I throw back the remaining sip of my drink and set the mug on the mantle below the TV. Taking my sweet-ass time, I stride across the living space to the kitchen and snag my duffel from behind the door.

With the strap secured at my shoulder, I start down the hallway off the kitchen but pause when I hear footsteps at my back. My lips quirk up when the sound quickens, Anna's feet carrying her closer to a realization I don't think she's prepared for.

"Whoa, wait," she calls, catching up to me and grabbing my elbow for the second time tonight. My cock bounces when I spin to face her, my laugh bubbling up at her hand hovering below her chin to block her view. "What are you doing?"

"Changing," I muse, my smirk untamable as I gesture with my shoulder to the room at my back. The same one I know Anna claimed. "Like you said."

"No."

"You say that a lot."

"No, I don't."

"Repeating the word won't change anything."

Her brows dip. "Change what, exactly?"

Mine shoot up in amusement. "You didn't scope out the entire cabin?"

"No," she snaps. "I've been working, all thanks to you."

I nod and purse my lips, then gesture back to the room. "Well, I'm gonna …"

"Jeffers, I claimed this room," Anna states, her shoulders squaring off like this is some kind of competition or argument she can win. "Go pick another one."

"Uh-huh." My tongue flicks over my grinning lips. "I saw you brought your shit back but not mine. It's cool, though."

"We are *not* rooming together." She grabs the strap of my duffle to keep me from stepping backward. What she doesn't realize, though, is that she's dropped her protective blinder and stepped closer to me, the heat of her rage radiating from her and crashing against my bare skin.

Her frustration makes me giddy, her proximity tingling me with excitement.

"Except—"

"No," she grinds out through gritted teeth, that reddish tinge stuck on her face.

"—you claimed the only room in the house."

# Chapter Eleven

## Anna

N<sup>o.</sup>

*No-frickin' way did I just hear him say that.*

"Seriously?"

"Yup."

Yanking the strap of the duffle until Toby relents, I take the bag and walk into the main living space of the cabin.

*I saw stairs. There's more than this here.*

Adamant and determined, I hike the bag on my shoulder and round the back of the couch to the narrow stairway.

I grumble despite the chuckles that follow me so close I swear I feel his breath on the backs of my legs. Dread settles into my stomach with each creaking stair I climb. My stomach churns when I breach the surface of the second floor, then drops completely as I reach the final step. It's a barren loft-like space that overlooks around the chimney spouting up from the fireplace below where Toby stood naked only a few minutes ago and hosts …

Nothing.

Only a few boxes litter the wooden floor; its surface not even finished and covered in a sheen of dust.

"No."

"There you go with that word again."

"Uggghhhh!"

Spinning, I shove the bag into his chest and push past him, rushing downstairs, and barrel across the cabin's belly, snatching up my laptop as I pass.

By my next breath, I'm barricaded behind the locked door of the only room livable in this house with my phone.

"You didn't tell me!" I yell into the phone before Leo even has a chance to finish his groggy greeting.

"It's four a.m. here," Leo sighs out. "What are you talking about?"

"That there's only one damn room in this whole place."

"Whoa," he mutters, the rustle of sheets echoing over the line. "Hey, now. Let's take a breath for a sec, Anna."

"No!" I bellow, much louder than I intend and totally out of character for me, because despite the banter and bickering with my boss, I do still try to remain tactful and professional. I do need this job, after all, if I'm ever going to find the answers I'm looking for. "No breaths, Leo. You didn't warn me there was only one freaking bedroom in this whole house."

"Ah," he sighs. "I hadn't got to fixing the lounge up yet. Is it dusty?"

I pace around the plush rug, my hand to my damp forehead. "Yes. No—" Impatient and frustrated, I walk straight to the bathroom to peel off my pantyhose, tossing them into the trash.

"So," Leo drawls into the phone, his deep voice betraying his confusion. "Was it dirty or no?"

"That's not the point." Setting the phone on the vanity, I engage the speaker. "It is, but it's also not livable."

"And?"

"And? And it means that there's only one freaking bed here! Hello? Are you still asleep?"

"Have Toby sleep on the couch. It's where he'll most likely end up any-fuckin'-way."

I flail my hands, even though the infuriating man can't see me. "How is he supposed to have any privacy? And where is he supposed to *shower*?" I huff and pace in a circle.

"You mean where can you get away from him." It's not a question, but a statement of concern I vocalized before I was forced in this hell to begin with.

"Yes," I hiss, my hands flying to my hair, my palms flat against the crown of my head. "He'll just be out there. Doing whatever guys do when they're alone."

I shudder at the possibilities.

"Anna," Leo soothes over the phone, his sleepy voice grating on my last nerve. "There's a bathroom that works upstairs. And the couch is good. I've slept on it myself before the bedroom was done."

"What about my morning routine, Leo? He'll be right there!" I scoff and swipe at my sweating brow. "He's already proven that he doesn't care about sporting his birthday suit around the whole dang place."

My breath races as I think of all the things I won't be able to do to keep myself sane with Toby Jeffers up my butt. No privacy. No peace.

Leo's chuckle does nothing to calm my nerves. "It's not for that long if the articles work. Okay? Just breathe."

"I can't do that."

"C'mon, work with me here. Breathe with me."

"I hate you," I snap, but force a lungful of oxygen anyway. "You're the worst boss on the planet."

"I doubt that." He snickers, then sobers. "I'll double check the shipments in the morning when I'm supposed to be awake." The exhaustion is evident in his words, his jab driving that point further. "I've got the shit to finish up the lounge coming; it's just not as easy shipping shit up a mountain in the snow."

I exhale a long breath.

"Shouldn't be but a few days if the snow holds off, okay? Just hang in there."

"Fine," I growl out, teeth clenched as I lean on the vanity over the phone.

"And maybe get some damn sleep, woman. You're atrocious when you're tired."

"This is all your fault, Leo." Growling when he laughs, I end the call before he can toss out any more unhelpful advice.

With my head hanging between my shoulders, I take a moment to try and tame my racing heart rate. It takes several minutes and a glance in the mirror to change my focus from the metaphorical cage wrapped around my head to the dirty feeling coating my skin.

I'm covered in dust I can't see and sweat that's dried and gritty.

Dark circles shine under my eyes through the concealer I applied almost twenty-four hours ago.

The tub calls to me, but the idea of sitting in the filth only adds to the dirty feeling already crawling across my skin.

Turning, I face the shower stall behind the bathroom door, its glass shining with my reflection. *Perfect.*

With a mad dash out into the bedroom for my toiletry bag, I return and crank the water in the shower to its hottest setting. While waiting for enough steam to fill the room, I strip out of my formal wear and lay the articles out in the tub.

Mentally, I add hand washing to the already long to-do list and step in.

*This is about to be the worst working* vacation *ever.*

# Chapter Twelve

## TOBY

Tʜᴇ ʟᴀꜱᴛ ᴛᴡᴏ ᴍᴏʀɴɪɴɢꜱ have gone exactly the same as this one.

Me, asleep, like a normal human. Only to be brought back from dreamland by the sound of the fucking blender before the sun has even finished getting out of bed.

Grunting, I flop over and wrap the blanket over my head to block out the noise. Yet somehow, it only seems to get louder.

*Or maybe that's just the hangover talking.*

I grumble, poke my head up above the back of the couch and stare daggers at the woman who thinks morning smoothies are the only way to start her day.

"Anna," I call, but it's no use. She's got earbuds plugged into her ears as she moves about the kitchen, mixing and chopping shit while the blender continues to pulverize whatever the hell she's already got in it.

*Goddammit.*

Whipping off the blanket with a huff, I curse the chill that settles into my bare skin and pad across the room to stand opposite the island separating me from Anna.

*At least I remembered to fall asleep in shorts this time.*

"What the *fuck* are you—"

"*OhmyGod*," Anna screams when she turns, her startled hands flinging the strawberries in the air between us. "Jeffers! Where are your clothes?"

"*Anna*," I mimic her high-pitched tone. "I've got the shorts on. Now, what the hell are you doing?"

She places a hand on her heaving chest. "Breakfast. Something you wouldn't know anything about."

"Oh, I've heard all about it the last three fucking mornings," I snap. "Some people like to actually sleep at some point."

Scoffing, she gathers the scattered fruit from the countertop and starts scraping the shit into the trashcan at her side. "Sleeping in is a luxury, Jeffers."

"What are you—" I snag some of the strawberries before she can throw them all off the side of the counter and into the dark abyss of the garbage. "So wasteful."

"I wouldn't need to toss them if you hadn't scared me half to death," she retorts.

Popping the handful in my mouth, I speak around the fruit. "Wouldn't have scared you if you knew how to make breakfast without using the goddamn blender before the sun's fully up."

She swipes her hands on a towel and pins me with a look.

"Seriously," I continue. "Who uses a blender for *breakfast.*"

"A blender is meant to be used for more than just margaritas. Jesus." She turns to the machine in question, it's low whir a steady sound she cuts off now that its contents are liquified.

"That's literally the only time I've used a blender."

Anna's gaze flings up to mine, a hand coming up to cover her dramatic gasp. "You know how to use a blender?"

"Har. Har," I deadpan and move around the island to the fridge. "There's all kinds of shit you don't know about me, Ms. Prune."

She sighs, doing her best to ignore me and pour her liquid breakfast into a cup.

Shaking my head, I retrieve milk and cereal and the biggest bowl I can find in the cabinet. The coffee pot is put on next and I lean against the counter with what used to be a butter bowl filled to the brim with floating Lucky Charms held beneath my chin.

They aren't my favorite, but it's what I'd opened last night before I realized there was a box of peanut butter puffs right next to it.

As I crunch the rainbow marshmallows between my teeth, my eyes follow Anna's silent form around the kitchen while she cleans up her mess.

She goes over each spot repeatedly, only stopping when she has touched every inch of the marble and returned every item she used—cleaned, dried, and straightened.

*As if she was never here.*

I'm left blinking after her when she finally disappears down the hall and slides the bedroom door closed.

*Holy fuck.*

Pushing off from the counter, I stand and stare down the hall as if the emptiness will explain what the hell I just saw.

It's not until the coffeepot beeps that I'm shaken from my stupor, heading to the machine, so many questions swirling around in my head.

*There's no way.*

When the first taste of brew finally hits my tongue, I shake away the inquisitions because the questions don't matter.

What *does* matter is how uptight the woman is about everything.

She's so stringent, straightlaced, and beyond stuck in the mud when it comes to anything even remotely fun.

We're in the mountains for Christ's sake and she's yet to even drink anything alcoholic, make a s'more in the fireplace, or get in the hot tub.

*Bet she doesn't even own a bathing suit.*

*And if she did, it would be beige. In a single piece that covers her from head to toe.*

But then an idea hits me at how I can make Ms. Prune let loose.
It all starts with a good old-fashioned wooded retreat experience.
Involving something alcoholic and some sticky marshmallows.

# Chapter Thirteen

*TOBY*

OPERATION: *REHYDRATE PRUNE.*

It's what I've deemed tonight's activities and any others that follow if this works to get Anna to loosen the fuck up.

She's still holed up in the bedroom like she has been all day, alone and not at all enjoying any bit of the cabin life.

I, on the other hand, have ventured out into the snow to retrieve the perfect sticks to use in the fire, gathered more firewood to keep this plan alight, and gotten myself two sheets to the wind.

Not three, because it gets ugly when I hit three sheets to the wind, but some of us know how to have fun.

*Even alone.*

I even took the time to record some guitar playing and sent it off to Leo for him to do his thing with the online shit that keeps our band at the forefront.

Now, I'm making my way down the hallway, cheeks burning with windburn and my favorite hoodie thrown on for warmth. It's half-zipped and doesn't match my gray joggers, but after freezing outside, comfort won. "Oh, Ms. Prune," I call, knocking on her door. "Time to come out of your cave."

"No!"

"C'mon," I shout at the door. "There's that word again!"

"Go away, Jeffers."

"I will knock until you come out."

Just to drive the point home, I tap my knuckles against the wood again.

"I'm *working.*"

"But it's nighttime," I retort. I have no clue what time it actually is. Hours and days just flow different when you're on rock star time. "Work's over now."

"Not when it comes to you," Anna growls from inside the room.

It's silent for a moment. No rustling, no shifting lights beneath the door.

So, I knock again.

"*Go away.*"

A slam against the panel separating the two of us has me jumping back a foot and a grin breaking out across my face.

*Time for a different tactic.*

"Aren't you hungry?" I ask, placing a hand against the smooth surface. "I'm hungry."

"If you ask me to make you food, you're getting locked out in the snow."

"Too late." I snicker. "You already tried that once."

Grumbling is all I get back.

"Knock, knock."

"Saying the words doesn't change the fact that I have plenty of crap to do in here, Jeffers."

Snorting, I replace my words with the action, except this time I don't stop pounding my palm against the surface. I do it so long I find a beat to it, keeping time in an eighth of a beat.

*Mac would be so proud.*

Lifting my arm, I'm halfway to adding a second hand to the mix when the door flies open and a flustered Anna snaps, "*What?*"

Smirking, I snag her wrist before she can slam the door in my face and pull. She fights my hold, but doesn't break free from me as I practically drag her into the living room, not stopping until we reach the fireplace.

Heat radiates from the stone, the flames on the smaller side, while the coals underneath burn red hot.

"Dinnertime," I mutter and drop down to the blanket-covered floor with crossed legs, careful not to disturb the trays already laid out.

"Um," Anna chokes out, her wrist twisting in my grip, "no, thank you."

"Not too good for weenie-roast, are you?"

I look up at the woman with a grin when she makes some kinda noise that's stuck between a scoff and a snort. "Uh."

Clicking my tongue against my teeth, I tug on her wrist and nod at the literal sticks leaning against the hearth. Sharpened and waiting. Just as I have done for the last twenty years of my life. "You know how this works, right?"

I'm teasing her. Pushing her. Waiting to see if she'll take the chance to live a little.

It's probably a dick move, but I'm nothing if not persistent. Possibly even an asshole.

*I accept this lot in life.*

She just stares expectantly at the fire with an arched brow and a robotic shake to her head.

"It's not gonna bite you."

Her pale throat moves with a swallow. "Why?"

The question catches me off guard, my grin slipping. "Why what?"

It's not lost on me, despite the buzz I feel fading away and a heaviness filing in, that her sight has yet to move away from the snapped off branches.

"Why are you doing this?"

"It's the cabin experience," I explain, my voice dropping as I watch the flames dance. "We used to come up here every winter. Roast hotdogs and make s'mores. It's what you do."

My stomach drops as my slipup settles into my ears before the question is even off her lips.

"We?"

*She doesn't know.*

"You know what? Never mind." I push up to my feet with a tightness in my throat and an itch to my palms. "I need a smoke."

*Or ten.*

I stride over to my jacket, fumbling for the cigarette pack tangled in the lining.

*Sinking.*

It feels like I'm sinking in a pit of quicksand fueled only by my emotions and getting deeper with each moment.

"Jeffers."

I growl, my jaw ticking as I yank. The pack finally comes free, but not without ripping the pocket. Emotions spiraling, I feel the heat from the fire on my chest, rising up my neck. I move to the door that slams at my back with a cigarette already hanging from my lips and the cold slapping me in the face.

*"Jeffers."*

# Chapter Fourteen

## Anna

I'M NOT CERTAIN HOW long I stand staring after Toby's hasty escape, but if my butt burning is any indication, it's been a while.

*And he's still not back inside yet.*

As a non-smoker, I'm not sure how long it's supposed to take to finish a cigarette, but I'm certain it's been more than long enough.

Deep down, I know that it was more than just me getting under his skin.

While there's a level of curiosity niggling at the back of my mind, it's not the lingering questions about Toby's interactions with the mountains that has me moving forward and picking up his jacket.

A sense of duty is what drives me to slide my arms into the men's outerwear, the scent of citrus and tobacco enveloping me as I wrap the sides closed around my middle and wander closer to the exit.

Frozen wind meets me when I step out, surprised to find the porch all but empty.

*He can't have gotten far.*

"Jeffers," I call out into the inky black wilderness that spreads beyond the reach of the single porchlight, my breath rushing out from me in a fog that blocks my view. As it clears, I move toward the cabin's edge, peering into the shadows where the hot tub lies hidden. The darkness swallows my efforts, offering back only silence.

*Did he really just go out into the snow?*

Reaching the railing, I lean forward, straining to see around the lattice that blocks my view of the porch's rear section. But it's futile; the darkness is impenetrable.

"Jeffers!"

I'm about to retreat inside for a flashlight when a flicker of red catches my eye—a cigarette cherry glowing in the dark. The familiar scent of burning tobacco hits me just as I regain my breath, my frustration flaring.

"Right here."

"Ugh!" I snarl, throwing my hands out at my sides. "You didn't hear me calling for you?"

"I did," Toby sighs, his tone a complete contrast to what happened inside. Jovial, almost.

Blinking at the shadowed figure leaning against the wall, covered by the shroud of darkness, I wait for him to say more, apologize even.

He stays quiet.

Which only makes me angrier.

"What is your problem?" I snap into the blackness, taking a step closer. "You come in here, acting like you own the place, then just snap when you're reminded that you're here?"

Silence.

"Do you even remember why we're here, Jeffers? In the freaking *mountains*?" I shake my head as more accusatory questions, statements, roll off my tongue without much effort. "It's because of you. Your mistakes. Your *crap* that you keep getting yourself into, for no good reason, only to go running away all over again. Well, guess what?"

Silence.

"You can't keep running away. Eventually, there won't be anyone left to clean up your mess!"

"You done?" His reply comes rough, clipped, as if he's barely holding back.

"You don't even care, do you?" I huff bitterly, shaking my head. "As long as you have your smokes and a bottle—"

"Why not?" he roars, his ragged breaths smacking me in the face, bathing me in the scent of whiskey.

He's close now. So close that I feel his anger radiating off him in waves.

The little voice in the back of my head tells me I've pushed too far, and that I should back away. Leave him be. That it's all so far out of my control and over my pay grade.

And yet … words whip from my tongue as if Toby deserves them all.

"Because people give a damn about you!" I yell, leaning up on my tiptoes and pointing a finger in his shadowed face.

Any semblance of professionalism has gone out the window, and in its place is … well … just me. *Aftermath Anna.* Here to figure this out on my own without any help from the infuriatingly striking man before me.

His once-brown irises take on a new shade of black as he stares at me.

"But do they?" The finality of his words are whispers over my lips, yet still slice through me as if he'd screamed them, making those familiar hairs stand on the back of my neck.

*Do they actually care about him?*

I know that they do. His rebound rate is the problem. His ability to hide the things from his own bandmates, men he calls brothers, appearing fine in front of them when he is so clearly not. I've seen things they haven't.

*I recognize it because I've seen it before.*

*They just don't get it.*

My resolve cracks, and in those crevices, my throat tightens and my calves relax me back down to flat feet.

"*Exactly*," he hisses, as if my retreat only confirms his suspicions. "That's why *you're* here and they aren't."

I swallow hard, the reality of his words sinking in.

*We aren't here because of his band.*

*We're here because of him.*

"You're right," I mutter into the frozen tundra, squaring my shoulders. "*I'm here.* So quit making my job difficult."

Toby grips my jaw faster than I can back away, his touch searing against the cold. I gasp as he pulls me closer, his face inches from mine, the scent of alcohol strong.

Our noses bump as he walks me backward, and I taste the whiskey on his breath.

My pulse races. My stomach clenches.

"You didn't have to come," he growls and crowds in, the heat of him pressing into me until I feel him everywhere.

"But I did," I fling right back, my hands biting into the railing keeping me from falling right into the mountain terrain at my back.

And yet … Toby pushes until I'm arching over the side of the porch and his hips are digging into mine, my feet barely connected to the wood beneath us.

"Why," he snarls, "do you give a fuck?"

"It's my job," I mutter, the words sounding way too small even to my own ears. Unconvincing.

Breathless.

*It* is *my job.*

*But it's so much more than that.*

It's too difficult to focus with him this close, the heat and surprising hardness of him battling it out against the cold on my back, my breath racing from me.

*It's what I'm supposed to do.*

"Bet this isn't."

Before I get a moment to consider a response, Tobias Jeffers slams his mouth against mine and steals all my thoughts through the tongue that slides past my lips and knocks into my teeth.

My body betrays me, and I gasp.

That's the only reasoning I can come up with when my jaw unclenches and my fingers unhook from the railing.

I want to raise my hands, push him away and put a stop to this, but his tongue touches mine and it takes everything in me not to moan. The taste of whiskey bursts against my tastebuds, and I grip the open zipper of his hoodie, the smattering of hair on his bare chest brushing my thumbs while his beard scrapes against my mouth.

*It's all so much and somehow not eno—*

"No." Popping back, I gasp, desperate for air and distance and the cold that seeps into the space created between my chest and Toby's. "No."

"There you go," Toby mutters, sounding nearly as breathless as I feel, "with that fucking word again."

My hands don't release his hoodie. "That … that did not happen."

He hums, then mutters softly, "It didn't not happen either." He dips to catch my gaze, his fingers digging into the backs of my knees, his forehead knocking against mine.

"It *can't* happen, Jeffers."

"Oh, but it already did." His mustache does nothing to hide the teasing grin pulling up the corners of his lips. "At least in my head, it did." He lifts me, my feet leaving the ground completely and my butt missing the railing.

I'm in midair before my scrambled brain cells can catch up, my arms reaching *up* instead of *down* as I fall.

"Jeffers!"

A scream prepped to burst from my throat gets lodged when my back collides and my arms flop to my sides, a dusting of white puffing out around me.

Blinking through the snow that flutters down over my face, I lay frozen in shock.

Shock … because nothing hurts. Nothing rolls. No aches.

And the mountain isn't eating me alive.

I sink further into the pile of fluffy, white snow, as I scrambled onto my knees. "Jeffers!"

A burst of laughter is the only answer I get as I trudge my way out of nature's pillow, the flakes clustered and clinging to every bit of me.

"Ready for that hot meal, Ms. Prune?"

# Chapter Fifteen



"**I** LITERALLY HATE YOU."

"Well, that's not very professional of you." I don't bother tamping down the snicker that rises.

"You're the worst."

*I regret none of my decisions.*

"How dramatic."

The sight of Anna covered in snow is one I will never forget, not that it's the only thing I want to see her covered in after a kiss like that one, but we're still ignoring that it happened.

It did, however, get her ass inside with a stick in her hand because it meant being close to the warm fire.

She cheated and found a metal skewer long enough to reach from a safe distance, but she's still next to me with some weird version of a hotdog currently burning in the flames.

"You know you're supposed to be able to eat that, right?"

"It's fine," she mutters and pulls the corners of the throw blanket closer around her chin.

"Not if it's fucking shoe leather, woman. Fuck."

She jabs the skewer further into the flames. "It's gotta be cooked all the way."

"They're literally pre-cooked dogs." I pick up the package and shake it between us. "You can eat them straight out of the plastic."

"Ew."

I shake my head, my tongue poking out to wet my grinning lips. "There's nothing wrong with them."

Anna just shakes her head, rotating her wrist to get another side of the hotdog into the heat.

"You won't die if you eat one." I shove the package in her direction and when she cringes and shakes her head, I pull back. "Fine. More for me, then."

"Go ahead."

Shrugging, I dig into the pack and pinch a hotdog between my fingers. Bringing the cold processed meat to my mouth, I take a huge bite.

"God," she groans. "You're the absolute worst."

"So you're saying …" I pause long enough that Anna drags her resentfully curious gaze to mine. "You don't want any of this?"

She rolls her eyes when I use the half-eaten hotdog to gesture around my mouth.

"Not even a little bit."

I know I've had enough liquor to completely forget why we ended up outside to begin with, but I swear the woman shudders. Like the thought of another kiss somehow disgusts her.

*Well then …*

*Challenge accepted.*

"I'd rather freeze to death," she mutters. "The only reason I'm out here now is because I'm starving and someone ate everything else in the fridge."

I shrug and snicker, undenying of her accusations. "Pretty sure food is a staple for survival."

"Lucky Charms and whiskey in your coffee is not survival."

Holding up my arm, I squint at the half-eaten hotdog through one eye. "Guess you don't count, either." It goes down the hatch, colder than the first bite.

Anna shudders audibly, but manages to slap her dinner on a bun, then nibbles around so long I end up roasting and finishing another dog.

"Tastes horrible, doesn't it?"

Grumbling, she tosses the remaining bits on the tray between us and sighs. "So bad."

I chuckle. "I fuckin' told you, Prune."

Growling, she pushes to her feet, the blanket falling around her seat. "I'm going to bed." She grabs the skewer and the tray and whisks them away to the kitchen.

I pretend not to watch her wash, rewash, and then replace each item in their designated space. She nods once she's done, only disappearing down the hallway when she double checks them all again.

I wrap my fingers around the neck of the guitar I left on the couch. My fingertips ache, the smaller cords cutting into my already calloused skin, but I don't let it stop me from playing.

The sound is not as rusty as it was in the hot tub, but I'm sure the water didn't help the instrument much.

I tweak the tuning pegs, and that helps create a better melody, but it's still not quite the tune I recall.

Growling, I scoot across the floor until my back hits the couch and the acoustic settles in my lap. I'm more engrossed in the flickering flames than the strings I play, but that doesn't stop my mind from wandering. Dreaming. *Wishing.*

It's almost as if I can hear the voices in my ears once the tune stops, my vision tunneling out so far that I don't see anything past the burning embers.

Emotions I've done everything in my power to ignore claw their way up my drying throat and release a sound that's on the verge of choked. The desperation burns behind my eyes until tears form, while anger and pain sear into my fingertips as they find the strings again. My skin splits, flaying open as I drag them across the cords, and yet I don't stop.

Time stands still as I bleed over the frets with raw digits, and when the instrument gives up on me by popping a string, I pick the bottle.

I don't stop until the bottom is dry and my vision is fuzzy and my head is swimming.

Then finally, it all goes black.

# Chapter Sixteen

## Anna

"What in the—" I exit my room the next morning, toeing my way down the clutter-filled hallway, with my palms slicking over.

What I'd expected to find this morning was a hungover but sleeping Toby passed out on the couch. Especially after hearing him play from my side of the door, so long that I fell asleep to the tune.

Instead … I'm met with complete and utter chaos as I enter the main portion of the house.

Dishes are discarded from their cabinets, silverware littering the counter, logs tossed across the floor. There're ribbons of paper towels hanging from the open cabinets and cereal spilled all over the coffee table beside an over-turned chair.

"Jeffers?" I whisper.

Several bottles—beer and liquor alike—dot the disorder like a trail of crumbs I follow, all the while doing my best not to touch or step on anything.

"Jeffers," I call out, stopping beside to the upside-down recliner.

*I heard the guitar but not this?*

"In ever gotto—" The words are mumbled, spoken so close together that I can barely make it out.

"What?" I crouch, careful not to let the wide legs of my dress slacks touch the floor, and peer beneath the armchair when a painful cry echoes out from the cushions.

That sound quickly becomes a grunt and the recliner goes flying.

Gasping, I fall back, pushing myself away in time for my ankles to narrowly be missed by the projectile that crashes against the stone hearth across the room.

In its place is a feral Tobias with not just bloodshot, but red-rimmed eyes, a layer of sweat coating his exposed skin, and pupils so blown that the already dark color is gone.

His chest heaves as he whirls around, his gaze not landing on anything before he's moving again.

"*Whereshe?*"

The scent of sweaty liquor permeates the room, and I skitter my way around the back of the couch, pulling my phone out as I duck behind the furniture.

Toby continues to mumble words I can't make out over the ringing phone.

My hands shake and my butt feels like it might be bruised but none of that holds a candle to the anxiety twisting in my stomach.

*I've only seen him this bad once.*

"C'mon," I whisper into the still ringing phone, my grip tight to the device when the line finally clicks. "Oh, thank God."

"Anna?" Leo answers, his end of the line bursting with noise. "Hang on, shit."

"Leo, Jesus Christ," I mutter. "He was fine last night—well, not entirely *fine*, but he wasn't this bad."

"What?"

"It's Toby," I whisper into the phone as the man in question tosses something and things go crashing to the floor. "He's losing his marbles and I don't know why."

"Did something happen?"

I shake my head and clammer to my knees, peeking over the couch cushions. "No—*yes*—no. I don't freaking know, Leo!"

"Explain." His clipped tone makes me scoff.

"Last night, he mentioned coming up here as kids. He freaked and ran outside. I have no idea if that's something or just Jeffers being freaking insane."

There's a long, drawn-out sigh. "Fuck."

"Um, *yeah*, that's what I'm saying. Because whatever it was that you guys used to do up here set him off. Now he's throwing crap and apparently drank all night."

"Not us," Leo corrects, and I drop back down, leaning into the couch.

"What's that mean?"

Mumbles reach my ears from both the man on the line and the man in the room.

"Leo, what's that mean?"

A string of cursing is what I receive and just when I'm about to open my mouth to start yelling into the phone for some kind of answer, Leo's words stop me dead.

"Get him a drink."

"No, Jesus." I scoff and shake my head. "That's the whole reason we're in this predicament."

"Anna, trust me." The somber tone makes me suck in a breath, my eyes going to the ceiling. "It's the only thing that'll calm him down. I've tried everything else."

"And what happens when he comes down from this?"

"He'll be fine. He just needs to chill out."

"I seriously think that's the worst answer." I'm shaking my head, my knees drawn up to my chest when some of Toby's words start to register through the chaos.

*Where is he?*

*I never got to show him.*

*Where is he. Where is he.*

With my heart in my throat, I push back up to my knees. "Leo, I'm leaving you on the line. If I scream, send the authorities."

"Wait, Anna—"

Setting the device on the cushion, I call, "Jeffers," calmly into the room as I raise my hands and step around the couch. "It's just me."

"Where did he go?" Toby wheels around the middle of the room, a bottle sloshing in one hand. "I gotta find him."

"Find who?" I ask and step closer as his unfocused eyes trail right over me like I'm not even here. "Tell me and we'll find him."

"We can't find him," Toby heaves out on bated breath. "He's not here."

Pulling in a deep, steadying lungful, I breathe out and step closer. So close that I could reach out and steal the bottle from his grip. "Then where is he? Tell me who we're looking for and I'll help you find him."

"You can't," he mutters, his blackened sight landing on me and piercing me with its intensity. "Can't."

"Sure we can," I say softly on a forced smile. "I'm sure he's around here somewhere."

"No," he snarls, his face hardening.

I wet my lips and shake my head. "Help me out, Jeffers. So I can help you. Please."

His throat bobs with a swallow, his stance unsteady as his eyes slowly meet mine, as if he's truly seeing me for the first time. The redness in his gaze grows, and it's like I watch the weight of the world settle onto his sagging shoulders. "Can't find him because he's *dead*."

I swear I feel the color drain from my face as my heart plummets into my stomach.

I know this has to be a hallucination that Toby is experiencing, but his conviction just feels so damn *real* that tears are tickling the backs of my own eyes.

"I know, Toby," I mutter even though I don't know and step up to the man with pain etched into his features. "And I'm so sorry." Instincts have me wrapping my arms around his bare torso, his familiar citrusy scent filtering through the alcohol sweating out of his pores. "I'm so sorry he's not here."

He's like a radiator when I press my cheek into his pec and run through all the information I've ever been told or read about Tobias Jeffers in the official files. Even some of the tabloids flash through my mind, and yet, I come up with nothing that would match his reaction.

Cinching my arms around his waist, I almost startle when his hands land on my shoulders and grip me, holding me close.

*Like he might float away if he doesn't.*

I want to ask questions, to understand better, but they get stuck behind the lump of emotion in my throat as I feel his tears dampen my hair.

"Our first show, As Above's—" Toby sucks back a sniff and runs his hands down my spine as if I'm the one in need of comfort, reassurance. "He was supposed to be there. I looked all night." His words are clearer now, but full of so much pain that my stomach twists. "Swear I still remember every face from the crowd that night." His bearded chin rests on the top of my head, and I blink back the tears that threaten when I feel his thick swallow against my temple. "I didn't know."

Biting my lip, I nod against him, silently encouraging him to keep going when I know my voice won't work.

"Did you know he's the one who taught me to play?" There's almost a hint of a chuckle edging the end of his question, like maybe the thought brings him some peace. Except it doesn't last. "He never got to see me play."

My hands shake against his back, my eyes clouded with tears as I force a swallow. I don't trust myself enough to speak the question, but that doesn't stop the whisper of words off my trembling and damp lips. "Who taught you to play, Toby?"

He shudders against me, his throat bobbing, his grip bruising. "My, um—" He sucks another tear-filled breath, his swallow sounding with an audible click. "My pops did. He taught me to play."

My jaw wobbles, the tears no longer held back as they flow over my cheeks and transfer to the skin of his chest.

"And he—" I can't bring myself to say the words, the pain too much to bear, but he takes them from me and makes it real.

"He never made it to our show that night." Voice thick, more moisture soaks into the top of my head. "Head-on collision with a drunk driver killed him." His chest pumps in short puffs, his shortened breath bursting over the top of my head. "And it's all my fault."

The dots finally connect. My body shakes with silent sobs, the connections all making sense as tears soak the chest I'm still leaning into.

*I can't believe I didn't see it sooner.*

"Toby," I state with as much strength as I can. "It's not your fault. None of it is your fault."

"He would have never been on that road that night if it weren't for me," he chokes.

I squeeze my arms around his waist, the heat of him making me sweat where we connect. "You weren't driving the car."

"I could've been, Anna." He shakes his head against mine, his voice cracking. "Since I was *fifteen*. Any given night, I could be."

I swallow against the realization he's spitting, my chest balled up in the worst possible ache. *He was so young.* "You're right," I say through gritted teeth and turn into him, my forehead resting against his pec. "So what are you going to do about it?"

"I ..." His jaw moves against my head like he's licking his lips and collecting his words. Except they still comes out broken when he speaks. "I don't know, Anna. *Fuck*, I don't know."

There are a million things he could do. But the one that he *should* do is abstain. Quit.

*Get sober.*

And the last thing this man needs is another reason to reach for a drink.

*I've got to make this baby accusation disappear.*

# Chapter Seventeen

## Anna

I T'S WELL PAST THE afternoon by the time I get off the phone.

Between giving Leo a piece of my mind, working through the plans, and calling a friend that has her degree in counseling, exhaustion settles in my bones.

I slump back on the bed, the door slightly ajar so I can hear if the bassist stirs, my phone gripped tightly in my hand as it blares warnings at me. A heavy sigh escapes me as I nibble on my lower lip, tapping the phone against my forehead.

*Winter weather warning: Snow mixed with ice inbound tonight. Six to twelve inches projected to fall in your area.*

The alert has my stomach twisting and my mind running a million miles an hour.

We need groceries that the local place refuses to deliver, the shipments for the loft furniture have been delayed another week, and there's a rock star in desperate need of a detox.

*There's not enough hot cocoa in this place for this amount of crap.*

And the bun on my head begins to feel so tight that it might pull the gray matter from behind my skull. Frustrated, I toe off my pinching shoes and unravel my hair, letting my red locks cascade over my shoulders as I scratch at my aching scalp, easing some tension but doing nothing for the upside down stomach I've battled all day.

*Jeffers.*

Tears threaten to build when I think about the younger version of him and his loss and I can't take the tightness that takes up space in my chest.

*He blames himself for his dad's death.*

I fumble through unbuttoning my blouse with shaking fingers and yank it from the tuck I spent twenty minutes perfecting in the early morning light. I'm in jeans that hug my hips and a tank I thank myself for packing less than a minute later, the air chilled to my exposed skin as I scramble for the socks and sneakers.

Making it to town is not going to be easy in the snow that's already fallen. But we're going to need supplies before the storm hits.

"Jeffers!" I call, hoping he's not deep in sleep, my mind still partly on his morning breakdown.

*Someone's gotta help him.*

The thought halts me. Wracks me right to my core.

*It's me, I'm the someone. Nobody else is here to help him.*

Nibbling on my bottom lip, I shake my head.

*It's my job. It's going to have to be me.*

"Jeffers!" I call again before cresting the end of the hallway and entering the living space. "You awake?"

*Will he even remember this morning?*

Part of me hopes that he doesn't remember spilling his secrets to me and things can go on as normal.

But a bigger part of me really does want him to remember falling into a peaceful slumber on my shoulder.

*Just so he can remember what peace feels like. That's all.*

"C'mon, we have to go into town," I say, standing by his feet, hands on my hips. "There's a storm coming."

*And I don't trust you to be alone.*

Not that taking a rock star to the grocery store is going to be any easier, but at least I know he'll be alive the whole time.

He groans and throws an arm over his eyes. "Let me sleep, woman. Fuck."

"Negative." I ignore the way his sleep-deep voice sounds and fist the fabric over his shin to pull the comfort away. "Get up or I'll break out the blender."

"I share my secrets and you threaten me with blenders?" He half snarls, half chuckles, and I ignore the way my body responds. "Savage, Prune."

Rolling my eyes, I ball the throw blanket. "So you do remember."

"I don't black out often. It's called *tolerance*."

"Right." Pursing my lips, I nod more to myself than the guarded bassist who's still hiding beneath his arm. "You wanna talk about it?"

"Nope."

"Then get up."

He chuckles, the sound muffled by a grunt as he rolls to his side and hikes a leg that strains the shorts across his surprisingly toned buttock.

I flush as I scan his inked skin, my eyes wandering over his half-exposed body. *Not what he needs, Anna.*

"I can feel you watching me."

Before I can retort, he's up, shoving his hand into his hair, pushing it back from his deep brown gaze that goes wide when it lands on me. "Prune?" Toby's jaw ticks, nostrils flare, his hand frozen in his hair.

"What?"

His sight is trained on the blanket in my hands, his lids sliding closed in slow blinks.

"Um." His blinking quickens, his throat moving with a swallow. "I'mma need a few minutes." I cock my head to the side. "And maybe for you to put that button-up shit back on." He grips the open hem of his shorts and tugs. "*Fuck.*"

I roll my eyes. "We really don't have time for your antics, Jeffers." Tossing the blanket to the loveseat, I spin away to search for something to help me combat the cold once we're outside. Dismissing my winter coat, I rotate back to Toby with hopes of borrowing a hoodie or three to complete my incognito look, only to gasp as his warmth caresses over my exposed skin before his actual touch feathers down my jaw.

"Tob—"

"Hush, Mama," he murmurs. "Let me look at you."

Just as promised, his lip pinches between his teeth as he leans back, his molten brown eyes trailing down my torso in a caress almost as intimate as the one still teasing my jawline. It's like I can feel his sight touch my bare shoulders, feather over the slight cleavage, then trail down the ribbed waist of the tank to the tight denim on my thighs.

"*Fuck*, those jeans are doing you just right." His trailing groan of approval makes me suck in a breath and I bat his hand away with widening eyes.

I'm no *prude* as Toby continues to accuse me of. I've had sex.

My southern parts have been touched before.

A pastime I have enjoyed.

But never has my body reacted to just a single look. A single sentence.

*A freaking groan.*

I spin away when I want to lean in, walking away from the infuriating man heating up my back with his gaze, and pluck his hoodie off the loveseat. He makes another provocative noise that sends a quiver right down into my pants. "*And* you're gonna steal my hoodie?"

*No, no, no, no.*

*Can't happen.*

*Won't happen.*

Shaking my head, I thread my limbs through the overly large sweatshirt. I'm bathed in the citrusy-scented fabric, a hint of fresh tobacco on its heels.

"You're making it worse, Prune," Toby growls. "So much worse."

"Oh, Jeffers," I chide. "You have no idea how bad it's going to get."

# Chapter Eighteen

## TOBY

**M**Y DICK IS HARD.

So hard that I had to tie it down with the waistband of my boxers, but even that is proving to only rub just the right spot and keep me solid through the entire barren cereal aisle.

Anna leads me around the store to avoid any high traffic areas, while I get to keep my sights glued to the peach of an ass she's been hiding.

I knew the woman had curves, but *damn…*

"*Jeffers,*" Anna whisper-snaps and eyes me around the frosted freezer door. *When did we end up in the freezer aisle?* "Stop watching my butt and help."

Snorting, I pull my beanie over my brows and step around the barely-filled cart. "Say *ass* and I will."

She rolls her eyes from the recesses of *my* hoodie's hood and tries to reach past the empty shelves. "You're the worst."

"Fine." I shrug and crowd her in. "Don't say it." Reaching up past her, I lean in until my hips meet her and her gasp of surprise fills my ears. "I like that sound better, anyway," I whisper on a dark chuckle and snag the last bag of frozen veggies to toss into the basket.

She skitters out of the freezer—*away* from me—before the plastic bag can even make contact with the crates inside the cart and practically dives into another section of mostly vacant freezer.

Smirking, I pull the cart and call on a snicker after the woman who darts along ahead of me, "Prune, wait for me."

"No!" she snaps and darts into another section, her fist white-knuckling around the handle.

"There's that word again ..." I trail off, my gaze traveling down the arch of her back to the ass that sticks out past the glazed pane between us.

*How have I missed this?*

"There's nothing *left*." She unknowingly struts along the aisle, her flustered hands sweeping at the static-infused hair that peeks out past her hood. I can't see them, but she's been doing it since we parked in the busy lot just outside this rinky-dink establishment—the only grocer within a hundred miles of our cabin.

It's been added to since I was here last—newish equipment put in and a wall knocked out for more floor space—but otherwise, it's the same old overly packed shithole with boxes still stashed along the aisleways, and paths worn into the dingy tile floors.

*Bet it's bothering the fuck out of her.*

"Prune." I reach out, my fingers pinching the fabric of her sleeve. "I know where the good shit is." Her wild eyes swing on me and it's the wideness of them that has me tugging her around. "C'mon."

"O-okay." She allows me to turn her around and walk to the back where the dry goods are kept.

The wall is lined with all the prepackaged goodness.

"I am so out of depth," Anna whispers, her unfocused sight trained on the boxes in front of her.

"Good thing garbage happens to be my expertise." When she finally spares me a glance, I shoot her a smirk that has her biting her lip, and even though I want to tell her to quit doing that shit, I know that's the last thing she needs. "Look, I know it's not kale salads or whatever the hell it is you make in the morning, but it's edible and doesn't require a fridge if we lose power."

"Guh, why do you have to remind me that's a possibility?"

Snorting, I move along the aisle and start filling the otherwise empty cart. "We can run through the freezers again and snag the last few healthy bags of crap that we can eat first."

Anna puffs out a resigned breath and reaches for a box of granola bars. "You sound like you've had to do this before."

I arch a brow in her direction and move down the aisle. "Course I have, Prune."

"Right." She tentatively places the granola bars in the cart and follows me. "Why don't you ever talk about it?"

Grunting, I dump more shit in the cart. "Just assumed most kids went camping or road-tripping at some point in their lives. Nothing fancy about it."

"That's not what I meant."

"I know," I sigh and shake my head. "There's just nothing to talk about."

"Except there's plenty to discuss," she presses, the green of her irises piercing me in a way I haven't noticed before.

Like she can see right through me.

"And you think," I start as I step into her, my boots hitting the toes of her sneakers, "now's the time? In the middle of a packed grocery store?"

Anna hums her begrudged agreement, but I don't miss the flick of her attention to the way my lips form the words. It's quick, but I see it.

The growl of appreciation is out of my throat before I can think better of it, the sound widening her eyes for a split second before she backs away from me once again, just in time to bump into a man reaching past her. "Excuse me," she rushes out as she spins to him. "I didn't see you there."

"No shit," he snarks back, reaching around her to snag something off the shelf.

It's only a split second, but he boxes Anna in against the racks, and my vision goes red.

"She said *excuse me*, motherfucker," I bark and grab her elbow, pulling her to me. "Back the fuck up."

"Keep your woman in check then, *bro*," he snaps, and I take a step toward him.

"Don't." Anna tries to tug me away from the douche with an inflated ego, but her efforts are futile because I'm yet another step closer.

"Oh, I guess your woman's got *you* in check." The guy actually laughs like this shit is funny to him. "Got that mixed up."

Boiling hot rage heats my blood when I push her behind me and step right up to the guy. "Leave her outta this."

He scoffs right in my face. "Then teach your bitch to watch where the fuck she's going."

My fist connects with his jaw before I even realize I've thrown the punch. Grabbing a flustered Anna and our cart, I head for the back employee-only exit. I leave three hundred-dollar bills under a box by the desk—more than enough to cover our groceries—as we make our escape.

"Jeffers, what are you doing? They have to scan the stuff."

My hand lands on her lower back to keep her moving. "I paid for it and then some. Don't worry about it."

"Wait, hold on," Anna hisses, her feet slowing despite my pushing. "We can't just—"

"Stop," I growl and spin her to face me. "It's this or finishing the fight with that guy." Narrowing her eyes, she sinks her teeth into her lip like a goddamned tease. "Let's go."

Snagging the cart with one hand and Anna's wrist in the other, I blend right into the horde of people that leave the store until our car comes into view.

It's a pain in the ass to toss individual packages into the trunk with a co-pilot that supplies more eye rolls than hands and enough grumbling to last the century.

"Seriously, just let me go back in and talk to them." Anna gestures to the storefront.

Throwing a glance over my shoulder through a haze of snowflakes, I catch sight of the guy that insulted Anna wandering around the store with a scowl that suggests he hasn't gotten over it. I can't explain what came over me in the first place, and I'm definitely not interested in finding it out a second time.

"No. Now, let's go before I finish the fight I started."

Huffing, Anna spins away and heads to the front of the car while I slam the trunk closed.

# Chapter Nineteen

## Anna

Tobias Jeffers is being way too casual.

About everything.

The self-restraint he exhibited in the store is enough to have me questioning whether or not I picked up a doppelganger somewhere along the way and just didn't notice until now.

During our car ride, *he* called the store owner and admitted to taking a cart full of products from their store and leaving money in the back.

It's almost as if being out here in the mountains is both a trigger for the bad memories, while also calming him. Changing him.

*I can't explain it.*

"You're creeping me out." Hands to my hips, I stare at the now shirtless bassist who chops an onion and then swipes into the sizzling pan.

*I didn't even know he could cook.*

"Rude," he mutters on a scoff, tossing a few cloves of garlic onto the board that his nimble fingers work over.

"And where is your shirt?"

A shrug is all I get before Toby's palm smacks the side of the knife against the wood, crushing the cloves beneath the blade he quickly chops, then adds to the sauteing onions. "You're lucky I'm wearing pants."

I snort. "Cooking while half-dressed is dangerous." And unsanitary, yet that doesn't seem to bother me.

He pauses, hands hung over the pan, and flicks his gaze to me. "Something you have some experience with, Prune?"

The flush takes over my face before I can stop it, which only serves to confirm whatever suspicion Toby has cooked up in his head.

He's wrong—I would never—but I also don't correct him, either.

"The things I didn't know about you …" he mutters, resuming his gait around the kitchen, adding various ingredients and spices to the pots heating on the stove. "Besides, I showered earlier."

I try to convince myself that the delicious smell is enough to keep my feet stuck to the tile but when my eyes refuse to leave the muscles of Toby's back, the tattoos standing proud against tanned skin that intrigue me rather than intimidate me, and the dusting of hair across his chest that leads to the southern part of his torso, I know I'm losing the battle. His fingers—so talented—as they work about the concoction, introducing a ground meat of some kind to the sizzling pan, then to the tomato-based sauce he's been nursing in a larger pot.

My eyes follow his frame as he swaggers around the kitchen like cooking is just something he does, while shirtless, with no one around but me to feed.

"Will you ever talk about it?" I ask, hoping that the calmness and the distraction of cooking will open him up enough to let some of the demons out.

*And I can keep my newfound ones in.*

"No."

*Not surprising.*

"Fine," I placate. "Wanna talk about the other thing?"

"Nope." He doesn't even look up from his tasks.

"Do you even remember her?" I push. I know it's probably the wrong way to do this, but I'm sick of dancing around the topics. Pretending that he doesn't know when he has to after what happened at Nitro's meet and greet. If we're going to fight the accusations, then I need the truth. From him. "Recognize her at all?"

This question pauses him. His brown eyes, a lighter shade than they were this morning, flick to me and narrow. "I thought no meant *no*."

I scoff. "C'mon, Jeffers." I shake my head. "Is there any chance it's *real*?"

"Real? I *always* wear a raincoat."

"That's not an answer."

"It's what you're getting," he growls and turns back to the stove. "It ain't mine."

I step closer. "Are you *positive*?"

*I need to be sure. For press purposes.*

The sound that comes from him is almost animalistic. Frustrated and defensive.

"Then why is there a DNA test?"

Toby scoffs, tossing the spoon onto the stove, red sauce splattering all over the cooktop. "Funny, Prune," he mutters as he snags a towel he wrings and turns away from me.

"I don't think any part of this is funny." Following him, we round the island and he stops to pull open the refrigerator.

"No shit," Toby says as he bends down and grabs something out.

"Can you be serious for two seconds, Jeffers?"

He whips around so fast, I don't even see what he slams against the counter he backs me into. "How about *you* be serious, Anna," he growls, his bare chest pressing into mine, his skin hot to the touch. "I know you're pretty fucking smart. Figure it the fuck out."

His eyes—dark and full of emotions I couldn't name—stare right through me. "What is there to figure out? It's a simple answer. Yes or no?"

"Let's see," he growls and bows his head, making sure those intense eyes are on mine. "What element do you have to have in order to do a DNA test before a baby is even fucking born?"

"DNA … I guess, saliva, blood, something like that."

"Bingo!" he calls out, his hands coming to rest on either side of the countertop that bites into my back, just above my butt, that would be the perfect height to— "And when have I provided any of those to anyone, Prune?" The smile that stretches his lips holds no humor as he closes in, so near that I feel the tickle of his facial hair when he speaks and the brush of his skin against my raised nipples through the thin tank. "Tell me. When."

"I, um …"

"Exactly." His eyes roll, the whites a severe contrast to the darkness in his irises. "How can this bitch have a positive DNA test when she hasn't compared the shit to *my* DNA?"

I release a puff of air in Toby's face. "But what about the tape?"

"Of?"

"I …" *I don't know.*

"Right," he spits, shaking his head. "You assumed, didn't you?"

"I …"

He rolls his tongue along his teeth, the flash of pink flesh doing enough to me that I can't form a thought, let alone a rebuttal.

"Did you even watch it, Anna?" he snarls and snags my wrist off of the counter. "Watch me sink this dick"—he punctuates it by placing my willing hand between his legs—"inside her pussy? Bareback and ready to make her cum?"

If it's possible, my entire body throbs when he bumps my palm against his groin and—

*Oh, God, he's hard.*

My heart is ready to pound right out of my chest, but he doesn't stop there.

Instead, he cups my hand, clamping my grip around him, and my fingers instinctively wrap along the hardness behind his athletic shorts.

"*Ung* … Mama," he nearly whimpers and leans in, his lips grazing my temple. "The only pussy I'm coming inside is the one I know is *mine*."

I can't stop the shudder that overtakes me, the heat that floods my lower stomach and beyond if I dare to admit it.

"But I'm not the bike that comes with training wheels." The grip cupping my hand squeezes, then disappears, leaving a frozen chill in his wake.

I pant against the countertop, while Toby returns to the stove. "Thirty minutes until dinner's ready." He glances over his shoulder, the heat in his gaze scorching me. "Why don't you go take care of *that*?"

His words send a shiver down my spine, and without hesitation, I clamor to the bedroom, needing to distance myself from him as fast as possible.

# Chapter Twenty

## TOBY

Fucking hell, I need a drink.

*Her hand wrapped around my cock?*

*Fuuuuuck.*

I've spent the last several minutes picturing what it would feel like to not have the barrier. Feel her hand on my bare cock. To see if her pussy is as tight as she is, and now I'm so fucking hard, there's nothing I can do to make this rager go down.

*But whiskey will.*

I'm halfway across the living room when I hear her door open and I can't stop my feet from freezing like I've been caught. Halting my escape to go take care of myself in the form of a sip.

*What if she's coming out for me?*

"It smells amazing," she calls down the hallway, the patter of her soles hitting the tile and bouncing around in my skull like a tease of what could be.

*Did she make herself come?*

I have half a mind to just fucking ask her but I feel like my torture will only continue either way.

No *means she's coming for me.*

Yes *means she already came for me.*

Grunting, I reach into my shorts and tuck my stiff dick beneath the elastic mere seconds before Anna enters the kitchen. In a cute little off-white frilly top that stops just beneath her tits and pants that mold to her ass, leaving a peek of porcelain smooth skin between the two pieces.

Her hair flows in waves around her shoulders, the red strands a bright contrast against her pale skin, and I can't help but picture the way my hand would look wrapped up in her locks.

*I've never seen her so relaxed.*

My dick pulses at the thought—well, at everything about her—begging for attention.

"Is it done?" Anna calls, her back to me with the teasing little patch of skin calling to me like a siren in the night, while she retrieves the serving spoon I abandoned.

"Yeah." Even I hear it in my voice, the gravel so thick that it almost comes out like a growl, when she glances over her shoulder in my direction, a slight pink tinting her pretty face.

*There it is.*

I groan when she shoots an innocent smile my way, then goes about stirring and fucking with shit in the kitchen.

It takes two full length deep breaths and a countdown from ten to get my feet to move me back across the living room and into the kitchen instead of up the stairs to the box of liquor stashed on the dusty floor. I lean against the island, my hands clutching the surface, the height a perfect cover for the boner that's refusing to settle.

But then Anna bends into the fridge, her perfect ass pushing up into the air, and it takes every bit of my control to white-knuckle the counter instead of vaulting over it.

*I need a fucking drink.*

Shaking the thought that keeps resurfacing in my head, I puff out a breath and run a hand through my hair.

After what happened last night, I've been doing my damnedest to ignore that niggle in the back of my mind, refusing that urge to pick up the bottle. It's been tormenting me all day, tempting me, calling me to take just one sip to ease the anxiety it's caused.

*I was on my way to do just that.*

The way her eyes looked up at me, all sad and puffy and full of fucking pity, is exactly why I've kept that night to myself for twelve goddamned years.

*I never want her, or anyone, to look at me like that again.*

Even the boys don't know the truth of the whole deal and even if they've figured it out, they don't talk about it because I don't talk about it.

*Talking about it hurts.*

"Jeffers." The snapping tone draws me back to another look I'm adding to the list of shit I don't want to see on Anna's face when it comes to me.

*Worry.*

"Yeah, Mama?" I meet her gaze, ignoring the little crinkle between her brows, and give her a nod of reassurance. "What'd you need?"

*At least my dick calmed down.*

"I asked you …" She pauses to lick her lips, the pink of her tongue drawing my eyes and tempting my dick all over again. "I asked how you liked your chili."

I take in the way her mouth entrances me to the proud cleavage dipping into the low neckline of her top. "In a bowl like a normal person."

She leans into the counter, the light illuminating the freckles that adorn her skin, light and barely there, yet enough to outline the tops of her tits all the way around to her exposed shoulders. It's an irritated stance, and somehow, it's sexy as fuck. I'm ready to get her on this countertop, beneath these lights, just to see what other colors I'd find on her body.

*And how rosy she'd let me get that ass from my palm.*

"Jeffers."

"Yeah?" Slowly, so very slowly, I trail my gaze down her, pausing at the peaked nipples behind the lace. "Need me to show you how to eat good?"

If I hadn't had my focus zeroed in on Anna, I would have missed the slight shudder.

"Actually …" Anna trails off, a flush rising on her cheeks. "I've been trying to eat healthy. I can't remember the last time I ate something like this."

*Hello, cold bath.*

"What?" I snap, my brows furrowing. "Like you haven't ever had chili?"

"No, I have." Anna flutters her hand between us dismissively, but that tinge of pink is still on her cheeks when she turns away and something about the color suggests it's not arousal. "It's just been a long time. How do you fix yours?"

"Load it the fuck up 'til it's goop."

"Attractive." She wrings her hands. *Just like at the store.*

I round the counter and snag her wrists, dipping to catch her sight. "I'm not going to judge."

I'm not sure what makes me say that, but it must be close to the right thing because she sighs and rolls her fucking eyes again. "You microwaved Bailey's. You have no room to judge."

"Exactly," I state. "So, what's the problem, Prune?"

Anna huffs. "I've been on this diet for forever and I—"

"Hold up," I interrupt. "Diet? For fucking what?" Lifting her wrist, I take in her curved stature, and for the life of me, can't find anything other than sexy standing in front of me.

She lets loose another irritated sigh. "What do you think, Jeffers?"

I narrow my eyes at her sarcastic tone. "Spell it out. Tell me why the hell you think you can't eat the chili."

"I never said I couldn't," she growls and wiggles her wrists in my grip.

"Then why act like it?" I hold tighter.

"Because!" she snaps, yanking free from me and spinning away.

Except, I chase. "Because why?"

Anna stalks in the direction of the bedroom, with me hot on her heels.

*I'll be damned if she thinks she can escape me this time.*

"Just let it go. Leave me alone." She throws up a hand as she walks, that ass of hers swaying with each step.

"No can do."

I hook an arm around her waist before she can cross the threshold to the bedroom and pull her back against my body. Her ass crashes into my groin, and I don't bother holding back the thick noise that escapes me.

"See," she hisses and forces her fingers between my forearm and her soft belly in an attempt to push me away. "I'm like a freaking *wrecking ball.*"

"*Whoa*, Mama." I cinch tighter around her midsection despite her resistance. "What the hell is that supposed to mean?"

"I'm—Just let me go!"

"Nope."

Anna growls, struggling more in my arms, and that's when I move. Lifting her up, her back hits my chest and her legs raise to kick at air. "Let me go, Jeffers!" she squeals, her nails biting into skin and her heels meeting my shins as I walk.

I ignore it all as I advance until the bed is in front of us and there's no room left to move.

Tossing her onto the mattress, I snag her ankle before she can skitter away.

She flops over, raises her free foot and kicks in my direction.

"I hate you!"

I catch the other ankle on her second kick and pull her body across the bed until my hips are snug between her thighs. "No, you don't."

She growls and arches her arm back, her fist flying forward to connect with my ribs. "Yes, I do."

Another fist lands on my torso, except this time, her face is more than just flushed from exertion. I tilt her chin up until her eyes meet mine and I see the heat that she's fighting in her piercing green irises.

The anger swirling in them.

The arousal.

"Stop fighting it."

# Chapter Twenty-One

## Anna

C LEARLY, I NEED SOMEONE with a doctorate in psychology to examine *my* behavior. Not just Toby's. Take a look at the marbles I think I have and tell me that I've lost them.

It's the only thing I can think of when Toby arches my neck back and stares at me like …

*I don't even know what.*

Like he wants to eat me alive, but also consider strapping me to the bed to feast on for days.

Instead of continuing to fight him off like I should … I am unbelievably turned on. More than I have been in my entire life. My arms fall helplessly at my sides as his dilated eyes dart between mine. I almost feel …

Deserving of the fight he put up to get me in here.

Not *overweight* or *fat*, like my sister called me when she had her drug-induced episodes, but …

Attractive.

Worthy.

*Sexy.*

"Mama," he says, his voice all gravel as his finger and thumb dig—not unkindly—into the soft spots of my cheeks and draws my gaze lower. Over his bare and tattooed chest, down the trail of hair in the center of his sternum that leads into the protruding waistband of his shorts. "The only wrecking ball here"—Toby cups the larger bulge in his shorts—"are these."

His words are vulgar, dirty, yet the urge that fills me feels criminal.

The desire to peel back his packaging and take him into my mouth feels … overstimulating.

*Overwhelming.*

But then the man calls me *Mama* and my stomach clenches.

*Who am I right now?*

"I see you." The hand around my mouth tugs me closer. So close I can practically taste the saltiness of his skin. "Stop fighting it and take it." He groans when my lungs heave, and a whimper escapes me. "Fucking take it, Anna."

*Have mercy on me …*

# Chapter Twenty-Two

## TOBY

I ASKED, DEMANDED ... and I fucking receive.

Because Anna's nails dig haphazardly into my groin, tearing the waistband of my shorts down until my dick springs free, and my balls are held up by the elastic.

One look.

For only one split second does her gaze flash to mine, before her lips spread and that pink tongue swipes across the head of my dick.

My escaping groan is instant when the feel of her tastebuds grazes over my sensitive flesh, and I force my eyes not to roll.

*I don't wanna look away.*

"That's it." My grip migrates from her jaw to the back of her head, the red strands of her hair threading through my fingers. "Fuck—"

She takes the tip into her mouth, licking and sucking. Tingles explode across my skin, rushing up the length of my dick and all the way down to my wiggling toes.

*It's perfect.*

*It's not enough.*

She sucks more of me when I press on the back of her head tentatively, mewls around me, and my head falls back. "Fuck, that's so good, Mama. Suck my dick like you hate me."

I grunt as I hit the back of her throat, her muscles constricting around me, the motion sending goosebumps straight to my balls and then all the way up my chest.

Anna's lips stretch around my cock and her tongue flicks at the underside of my head before taking me all the way back again until I feel the breath from her nose flutter across my abdomen. Goosebumps litter my skin when she moans around my shaft, the vibrations reverberating all the way up to my brain, and my abs clench. "Fuck. Open that throat. I'm gonna fucking cum down it."

Surprising the hell out of me, I grunt when Anna arches her neck, loosening up enough for me to thrust into her. Gripping her hair, I ride her face until my balls draw up tight and I shoot down her throat.

She gags and sputters, her muscles working against the intrusion, but she swallows me.

All of me.

Until I'm wrung dry.

"Fuck, Mama."

Lines of saliva drip from her chin when she pulls back and settles those intrusive green eyes on me. They're wide, disbelieving, but darkened.

"Get on your back," I growl.

Anna hesitates, swiping the back of her hand across her mouth. "Um ..."

I grip her chin again, my palm sliding in the mess left there. "I wanna know how juicy that cunt is. Now get on your fucking back."

Her breath shudders out of her, her lids fluttering closed, dark red lashes fanning out against her cheeks.

*More color.*

"Okay ..."

Anna falls back against the mattress, her arms going above her head.

Growling my approval, it's my turn to curl my fingers around the waistband of her pants and peel them away from her hips. Except, I do it slow, keeping our gazes locked as the material glides down her thighs and pools at her ankles, exposing her cream-colored panties.

More color rushes to her face, her chest rising in uneven pants as I dip and plant my lips against the pale skin above her hip. "I hope you're ready."

I don't give her a chance to respond, let alone think, before I'm ripping those pretty little panties down her knees and pressing her legs to her chest. Hands to the backs of her thighs, I lean in and take one long swipe from perineum to clit.

"Toby!" Anna cries out when my tongue touches the sensitive nerves, and her entrance pulses with need against my chin.

"Yeah?" I mutter against her flesh and pinch her clit between my teeth. She squeals at the pressure, the pain that I lick away, and buries her hands in my hair.

"*God*, keep doing that."

I grunt when she gasps, my dick perking back up the more she fights my hold on her legs.

Anna's near vibrating when I spread her wide open, a sheen of sweat building up on her porcelain skin when I tease her entrance with a finger.

My tongue flicks, and she gasps, as I thrust the digit inside her.

"*Toby*," Anna keens for me, and I look up just in time to catch her eyes rolling back into her head. The sight alone makes my dick jump and my finger curl, hitting her G-spot and making her back arch. "Yes!"

She whimpers when I lick, clenches when I thrust, and it only takes one more pass over her G-spot to have her pussy fluttering around my finger.

"That's it, dirty girl. *Fuck*."

I lap at her long enough for the aftershocks to slow, the pulsing to stop, and her body to relax in my grip.

"Oh my God."

*That's not the good oh my God.*

My gaze flicks to her face with a pang of worry, except she's covered it with both of the hands that were just buried in my hair.

"Shit," I mutter and release my grip on her. "Did I hurt you?"

"No," she mumbles, and I kneel on the mattress beside her. "I, um, crap—I can take more than that, I just ..." Her voice sounds thick—too thick.

"Just what?" I reach for her but pause, my hand hanging in the air above her.

I'm absolute shit at this. Terrible at comforting others—fuck, I can't even do it for myself—but I'm even more out of sorts when she *should* be soaring from the orgasm she just had. Not sound like she's crying behind her hands.

"Just what, Anna?" I push with an itch I can't explain in my palms.

"Just ..." She sighs behind her hiding spot. "Just leave me be, Jeffers."

"Anna..."

"Please leave me alone. I need a minute."

# Chapter Twenty-Three

## Anna

I'M FULLY PREPARED TO argue. To allow the projection of the anger I feel toward myself to bleed out of me and land all over Toby in the form of crappy words thrown at him.

I'm stewing.

Words hover on the tip of my tongue, ready to spill, when unexpectedly, the bed rises instead of sinking, and the warmth of his presence leaves my side.

*This was a huge mistake.*

One that's going to make things awkward and difficult until the point at which I have to tell my boss.

What I don't expect … is my heart to sink.

Fall deep and crack just a little bit.

This man is the definition of hot mess, and yet …

*I wanted him to stay.*

The tears fatten against my cheeks, rolling down and wetting my temples.

*But he's my client. My job.*

My throat tightens around the emotions, my body curling up to roll onto my side.

*Toby is the* last *person I should want.*

Except I'm hit with the coolness along my butt, a slickness between my thighs, and a whole new wave of tears flood my hands.

*This is screwed up.*

*I'm going to lose my job over this.*

"Hey, Mama."

I startle, even though the words are hushed, my squeak of surprise squeezing passed the lump in my throat.

"Jeffers," I growl out through my hands. "I told you to leave me alone."

"Uh-huh," he mumbles and the roughness of his calloused fingertips brush against my ankle. "I didn't listen."

I can't help the scoff. It's watery and yet blunt. "Clearly."

Subtly, I wipe at my face yet keep it covered.

"What are you doing?" I ask when he wraps those fingers around my ankle and lifts, my leg going willingly despite my brain screaming not to.

"Making sure I didn't hurt you." His free hand dances across the back of my thigh where he held me, his callouses teasing against my skin.

I don't want to want it.

I don't want my muscle to relax in his hands, or my skin to raise with goosebumps, and I definitely don't want the warmth in my chest at his return.

*I can't.*

I can't focus on the fact that I didn't want him to leave, and yet, here he is. Cradling me, tending to me.

So instead, I roll my eyes and jerk my leg from his grasp. "I said you didn't hurt me. I'm fine."

Toby huffs and snatches my leg back. "Then quit acting like I kicked your fucking puppy and let me clean you up."

My legs are parted and the tingles of terrycloth grate over my sensitive flesh. "Toby," I squeal. "That's too much!"

His deep chuckle warms my stomach when my back hits the headboard, and I cross my legs against the desire wanting to pool yet again.

"Can you hand over my pants?"

"Nope."

"Why?"

"I like you better when you're naked, Mama."

"Oh my God," I growl, covering my heating face. "You're ridiculous. What happened didn't happen, okay?" I grab the edge of the comforter and tug it free. Draping the white material over my thighs, I shove the corner under my opposite thigh. "It didn't happen."

"We're doing that again, huh?" The lopsided grin on his face screams he's going to do anything but forget this happened.

"Yes," I hiss and shove more of the material beneath my thigh. "I can't lose my job over some … some …"

"Head?"

My cheeks heat. "Yeah. That."

"Oh, c'mon." Toby waggles his brows. "Don't go getting red on me now."

I grit my teeth. "You're the absolute worst."

"I didn't hear any complaints a few minutes ago." The smirk behind his mustache is downright sinful. "Or do you need a reminder?"

I'm desperate for a distraction—and some freaking pants.

*How did we even end up in here?*

"And stop calling me that." I scowl, though, deep down, I like the nickname way too much.

But his head is tilted away from me, his hair a disheveled mess of attractive waves framing his face. He sniffs, his nostrils flaring with the inhale only a moment before his eyes go wide and he's hopping off the bed.

"Oh, shit."

He runs out of the room, leaving me confused and all alone.

Diving across the bed, I snag my pants from the floor and shove my legs through the material in time for him to call after me from the kitchen.

"Prune!"

I flatten the elastic around my waist and take my time joining the nuisance where he stands at the stove, serving spoon in hand.

*Oh, crap. We left the burner on …*

*God, how careless—*

"You're not allergic to anything, right?" I blink against the sudden interruption and automatically shake my head.

"No …"

"Good, here." A bowl is shoved into my chest, a layer of cheese already melting around the edges. "Oh, wait," Toby states, his hand still clasped around the dish I've also got my hands on. My fingertips touch his, the heat of both the man and the meal stirring more crap in my already swirling head. "Is there a texture thing?"

"A … texture …?"

"Yeah," Toby murmurs, his free hand coming to my chin and tipping my head back, his whiskey gold eyes meeting mine. There's a bit of a crinkle at the corner, a softness to his features, and I block them both from my mind. "I mean … is there shit you won't eat or touch because it feels weird."

I shake my head.

"Good." He steals the bowl from me and puts it on the island. "C'mere."

"Why?" I blurt and immediately shake my head at myself. *That's not what I meant.* "I mean—"

"Mama," Toby enunciates, "come."

*Why, oh why, is that so dang appealing.*

"I just meant why were you asking me that …" I mumble, joining him.

"Call me observant," he answers dismissively, already peeling back the wrapper on a sleeve of crackers with deft fingers.

*Fingers that were—*

"Did you wash your hands?"

Toby snorts. "Nope."

The chill that runs over me has my nose crinkling and my lip peeling back. "But you're touching our food."

He huffs, raises a hand to his nose and sniffs. "Smells like the perfect secret ingredient to me."

My hand goes to my rolling stomach, and I swear I feel the color drain from my face because it's all rushing south.

I have no idea how to act to that comment. It's both a turn-on and a trigger that makes me queasy.

*The germs …*

And yet …

"Anna, I'm kidding."

"What?" My vision fogs, and my breath rushes, as if I'm underwater.

"Anna, look at me." His voice, grating and somehow grounding, draws my eyes right to his chest. I want to look at him. I want to see his eyes, all bright, staring back at me.

But my brain feels like static and my ears feel far away.

"Anna," Toby snaps, commanding, and my eyes to crash against his.

*He looks worried.*

I don't even see his hands move, but now they're on my face and all I can see is him. His straight nose, his bearded chin, his thick hair.

He's everything that should drive me nuts in the wrong way. The exact opposite of everything that I am.

*Unkempt and wild.*

"I'm okay."

*I don't want him to worry.*

"I'm okay," I repeat the words, stronger this time.

*I'm supposed to be helping him. Not the other way around. This isn't about me.*

"Have you eaten at all today?"

"I'm …" I suck in a deep breath, the tunneling beating back slowly the longer I focus on Toby's furrowed brow and the space between them. "I'm good. I did. I just don't …"

"Like germs." He nods. "I got it."

That's not entirely the truth, but it's the easiest explanation when people question me about my … quirks. I hold myself to a level of unobtainable perfectionism that's coupled with an overachieving and obsessive compulsion to please. That, and the uncanny ability to concern myself with what others might think or say.

*Like someone finding out the fingers that were just inside me are now on the communal food packaging, even though no one else is in the cabin.*

*Or how my weight may be construed as something negative.*

*The way I dress. The things I say.*

I'm not compulsive enough to have a disorder, not afraid enough to have a phobia, nor am I ashamed of my body as it is. And yet, I know that if I don't flatten and fluff my top just right, then the world will only see my *larger-than-most* stomach. If I don't clean the utensils I used and return them to their original places, then something terrible might happen.

It's not logical, just as it's not linear, either. I'm aware of that.

*Which makes me difficult to diagnose.*

I chose not to follow through with the back and forth appointments, instead having thrown myself into my work and the reason I chose this profession.

"Two options," Toby murmurs, his sight trained on my lips as he speaks. "Eat the chili, or I eat you. Take your pick, Mama."

"But you just—"

"Mm," he growls and sinks his teeth into his bottom lip. "I could eat that pussy all night long, Mama. Try me."

My face burns with the embarrassment and arousal, and it's all I can do to just wrap my fingers around his wrists. "That won't be necessary."

"Then let's get you something to eat."

# Chapter Twenty-Four

## It's the Fist Heard 'Round the World!

Picture it—a simple grocery trip in the middle of blizzard ends in meeting a rock star. That would be a feat all on its own, right? But what if that same rock star—known for his aggressive and chaotic behavior—punched you in the face?

That's right, ladies and gents.

Toby Jeffers, bassist for As Above, was photographed assaulting a fan just this evening.

Come back in just a few for the full article on this crazed man and his wild exploits.

# Chapter Twenty-Five



I F I'D KNOW THAT a trip to the grocery would end up on the front page news of every tabloid known to the industry, I would have done it sooner.

Because not only is the asshole with the ugly mug that got too close to Anna on the front page but so is the swing I took at him.

*Serves him right. Little bitch.*

It has, however, put a damper in the evening because the woman I'd rather have my hands on is the one who's currently pacing around the living room with her phone braced between her head and shoulder as she taps away at a tablet.

*Guess you can't take me anywhere.*

I have no idea what she's doing, why it's taking so long, and I'm only listening to every other word she says into the phone.

Instead, I'm imagining those same lips around my dick, making me come again.

It's the only thing stopping me from reaching for the whiskey in the cabinet above the fridge. I wanna be sober for the feel. I wanna be clear for the touch. I wanna be here, on this planet, for the taste.

*If only my trembling hands would get the memo.*

"This would be less boring with some Jack. Or Coke. Possibly both, maybe one of each." I smooth my hands over the flat surface of the countertop I'm perched against, where I've been ignored for the last several hours.

Dinner went just fine, where I caught a few sneaking glances from Ms. Prune who was pretending not to enjoy the attention *and* the food, but that disappeared the moment her damn phone rang.

Since then, she's been strictly professional. Almost overly so with how much she's pretending I'm not here. Including the scowl she's throwing my way for the comment I shrug against.

*Fine.*

*Let's see how well that phone call fares against a few rounds of practice riffs.*

Anna's back is to me when I land my ass back in the stool, my six string in my grip, and a pick pinched between my teeth.

Plucking a few notes after replacing the string I'd popped, I rotate the tuning pegs until the sound is just right, the melody already playing in my head. I follow its lead, my raw fingers moving on their own, the song filling the space.

Calmness washes over me, smoothing against my skin and easing the tension in my muscles. A warmth fills my veins when I let my body go, my mind clear, my head bobbing along with the beat.

It's peaceful for a moment. Tranquil for a few more beats.

*Like the cabin always used to be.*

*Used to.*

Then the tension bleeds back into my chest as memories crash into me, my mind flashing, and my throat closes in on itself.

My strums become aggressive, the cords reverberating back an angry strain in a sound that's way too decent for what I'm doing to the instrument.

It only pisses me off even more.

I wrap my hands around the neck of the guitar, preparing to destroy the last worldly possession my pops left me against the marble counter, when my eyes fly open and a stunned Anna fills my vision.

"Jeffers …"

My ears ring with the sudden silence, and my heart pinches in my chest at the look staring back at me.

"Don't," I growl.

Her intense gaze is enough to bring me to my knees.

*I'm shaking.*

That warmth I was feeling becomes almost boiling beneath my skin and a bead of sweat rolls down my temple.

"We need to flush your system." The words are cold, distant, and everything that her eyes aren't. "Drink this."

*Did she have that in her hand the whole time?*

Gone is Anna's phone and tablet, replaced by a sports drink she thrusts in my direction. I'm shaking my head when my vision decides that it would prefer the vignette filter, the edges darkening until all I can see is her.

"Toby. You're gonna need this." The chilled bottle is pressed into my bare sternum until I accept it, the other clutching the last lifeline I have left of my dad. "Slow sips."

*When did I end up on the couch?*

My stomach rolls when I lift the sugary drink to my lips and catch a whiff. "There's no alcohol in this."

Anna scoffs, her deft fingers tipping the bottle close enough that my only options are to drink or wear it. I take a sip and almost spit it right back out.

"Hair of the dog works better," I grunt.

"That's exactly what has gotten you into this mess, Toby. Jesus." She mumbles something else I can't make out but then says, "How many times have you felt like this?"

I snort. "Every twelfth hour I don't have whiskey in my hand."

She lifts my trembling arm until the plastic hits my lips again. I swallow down the berry-flavored shit even when my stomach wants to reject it and tightens against the way the air has changed.

*Even sick, I can sense it. Just like I did that night.*

Except, Anna doesn't say anything like my bandmates did. She doesn't tell me it's just stage jitters or adrenaline. She doesn't dismiss it with a back pat and a '*go get 'em*'.

*She doesn't hand me a shot and tell me bottom's up.*

No, her reaction is far worse.

Because it feels too much like *sympathy*.

"Don't you have a phone to answer?" I snap.

She doesn't hesitate. "Not right now. Now drink again and stop being a grump."

Grumbling, I take another reluctant sip of the cool blue liquid that tastes weird without vodka in it.

"Good. Now tell me how bad this has gotten before."

"What?" Her question makes my brain hurt and it's already starting to pound in my skull.

"What else has happened when you ignored the shaking?"

*Is it that bad?*

"Um …" I raise a hand to swipe at my brow, but the bottle bumps my nose, and I nearly drop it. "I normally would have had a drink by now. And not this shit." I lift the bottle and tilt it, the liquid sloshing.

"Crap. Okay," Anna mutters and wraps a towel around my dripping wrist. "Think you could eat something?"

"We just ate, Prune." I roll my eyes, but that makes the room spin and my head pound. "Just need to sleep it off."

"Toby, this is not just a hangover."

I sigh, flop back against the cushion, and slide my eyes closed. "Pretty bad hangover. Hair of the dog works for that." My tongue dries and feels too big for my mouth, to which I raise the sports drink to my lips even though I know what's really coming.

My upper body pitches forward, the back of my throat burning despite the chilled drink, and my abdomen clenches.

A different kind of plastic is shoved under my chin and my body takes the opportunity to purge everything left in my stomach.

The sound and the smell surround me, pulling more heaves from my guts until there's not even bile left.

I cough as chills take over and spit into the bin in my lap.

"Think you're done for now?"

*Oh, Anna's here. She's such a prune. She's gonna hate this.*

"Super sexy, right, Prune?"

She hums half-heartedly before I feel her touch against my shoulder, circling around my upper back.

It's nice enough that I zero in on the motion, allowing it to settle my racing mind and my rapidly beating heart.

Until another wave of nausea takes over me, and I hunch over the small bathroom trashcan with more garbage coming out of my mouth.

Yet, her hands stay, and I hear whispered words coming from her lips. Lips I wish I could kiss, but I know that she'd freak the hell out if I did.

*Why do I want to kiss her so bad?*

Stunned and tensed, I'm not ready for the next wave that hits me like a freight train, ripping its way out of my gut and splashing into the already half-filled can.

"Fuuuuuck."

# Chapter Twenty-Six

## Anna

Tears prick the backs of my eyes.

*I wish I'd never found him like that.*

*I wish I didn't know.*

I flush the contents of the bathroom pail. I'm doing my best not to think about it as I wander over to the tub and clear out my dirty delicates before rinsing the container.

I know I don't have much time before he's ready to vomit again, but I can't stop my knees from hitting the tile and the tears to take over. My forehead hits the arms I have braced on the side of the tub and I just … let it flow.

The pain. The heartache. The exhaustion.

*The regret.*

It all bubbles up to the surface and drips off my jaw.

I chose the music industry *because* I know exactly how this is going to go. I've seen the alcoholics, the drug addicts, even the sex addicts.

I've seen the jonesing at its peak in people I knew.

And I've seen the withdrawals at their worst in people I loved.

*It's something I'd never wish on anyone.*

To carry this disease inside their minds with only those of us left around them to help carry the weight.

*It's so much weight.*

Which is why I pick my butt up and scrub the pail until it's clean and then wash my hands and my face in the sink.

*Those times before … she had staff and medics and hospitals.*

*Entire facilities that were supposed to help her.*

This time, Toby just has me.

When I return to the couch, he's asleep in a seated position, his head bent back against the cushion.

"Toby?" I whisper, half afraid that I'm imagining his chest moving with each intake of breath, but also certain that being passed out is what he needs most right now.

When he doesn't respond, I gently lay the pail in his lap, prepped for another round of vomit, should it come and find the remote for the TV over the fireplace. A soft brown noise fills the space, coupled with the sound of the crackling fire.

I hope it helps keep him calm along with my mind.

I stand there for a moment. Frozen with indecision in the middle of the living room.

*I can't leave him alone. What if he chokes to death?*

Sighing, I settle into the cushion and just look at him.

"What am I supposed to do with you?" My heart aches at the thoughts, so many of them running through my head. "Why did you have to tell me about your dad, Toby?" Of course he doesn't answer me, just steadily breathes through his open mouth with lips I've kissed and a beard that felt better than I could have imagined. "Why did you have to go and make me *like* you? I wanna know why you told *me*? Of all the people in your life, why me?"

His bare chest rises and falls evenly, the inked script along his left pec begging to be read.

*"The deepest darkness will always return to the light so long as my eyes are left open. It's with eyes open that I know love cannot be felt without pain. And it's that pain that acknowledges I have lived."*

Tears prick the backs of my eyes and I pinch my bottom lips between my teeth to keep them at bay as my eyes wander further down his torso to the clock—a pocket watch with wings in water color—painted directly in the middle of his flat sternum.

*7:52*

My stomach churns and the bite on my lip becomes painful.

Abstract mountains rest just above the waistband of his shorts, little peaks capped in snow across his right hip that remind me of the exact view I'd find if I looked out the windows over my shoulder.

The tears clinging to my lashes trail down my face.

"Every one of them are for him, aren't they?" I trace over his clammy skin as an ache like nothing else blooms behind my breast.

"Yeah, Mama. They are." His graveled voice startles me as he breathes out the words, drawing my attention to his red-rimmed eyes. He's staring at me with so much pain in those dark irises that the ache in my chest increases.

I don't bother stopping the choked sob that bubbles up, nor do I pull away from his grasp when it lands on my wandering fingers.

"C'mere." I don't fight him when he tugs me close enough that my head lands on his shoulder and my arm drapes over his ribs.

I'm stiff at first, the position awkward enough, considering the fact that my mind is screaming at me to back away from this whole situation, but then his arm wraps around my shoulders.

Tobias Jeffers holds me as if to console me, and I just let him.

He tightens his arm around me and pulls me as close as possible.

I let him rest his head on mine, his other hand against my shoulder, encircling me in his orange and tobacco scent.

"How?" His voice is grated and worn as it travels over my hair.

My brow furrows. "How what?"

His chest lifts with a deep inhale. "How do you smell like the ocean?"

"Oh." My cheeks heat, the skin tight with dried tears. "My shampoo is sea salt and kelp scented."

A deep chuckle rumbles his chest. "They literally bottled the ocean for you."

A faint smile tugs at my lips. "It's mass produced. Anyone can have the ocean in a bottle."

"I bet it doesn't smell like this, though." Toby takes another rough inhale, his nose pressed unashamedly to the strands near his face.

"Like what?"

Grunting, he falls silent.

It's not an uncomfortable silence, either.

In fact, it's warm and welcome and the most at peace I've felt in years, despite everything.

*I'm so screwed.*

# Chapter Twenty-Seven

## *Toby*

"**W**ANTING YOU IS THE only thing that makes fucking sense."

# Chapter Twenty-Eight

## Anna

"**W**HAT?"

Toby grunts and lifts, his arms sliding beneath my bent knees and around my shoulders. "Nothing, just go back to sleep."

I wrap my arms around his neck as he carries me. He could carry me out into the snow and I wouldn't give a damn about it simply because he's lifted me when no one else I've known since I was an adult has.

*This has to be a dream.*

The thought makes my insides feel all fluttery and gooey as he sets me on the mattress and settles in behind me. His arms are void of their previously clammy nature when he wraps them around me, his chest meeting my back, the bare spots around my bralette tingling.

*That's gotta be a good sign.*

"You feeling better?" I mumble, almost too distracted by the skin to skin contact.

"All thanks to you." I feel the gruffness of his words tease over my ear, and I shudder.

"Good . . ."

I'm not sure how long I lie there, focusing on his even breathing and staring off into the nighttime, before I realize his arms have stopped trembling and his presence just feels lighter.

As if there's a weight that's been lifted from him.

I'm not fooled into believing he's *cured*. There is no cure for addiction and trauma that has gone unchecked for so long. Or terrible habits that have taken over a life. There is no switch that means it's all over now.

But for the moment. This moment. There is peace in him.

*I'll take as many of those as I can get.*

"Mama," Toby murmurs against my neck, bathing me in his minty breath, the arm around my stomach tightening. "Tell me you're awake."

"Depends." I snicker and angle my head in his direction, but I can't see him through the darkness.

"This a good enough reason?"

Toby's lower half moves and something jabs me in the butt cheek.

"*Jeffers*," I squeal and tap his arm when he bumps me again. "That better not be what I think it is."

His husky growl is enough to shut me up. "Why not?" His erection presses into my butt and stays there. "Not like it wasn't already buried in your throat."

I suck in a breath at the reminder. "We shouldn't, Toby," I whisper.

"Mmm," he rasps. "You don't sound very convincing."

I'm not. Not at all convinced that this is a terrible idea when all I want to do is let him bury that thick length inside me, if only to ease the throbbing he's caused.

If only to ease the ache *he* created.

I cry out when he grinds against me, teasing me, testing me.

"Tell me to stop, Mama, and I will."

Toby leans up, and I fall back against the mattress in his absence. His body curls around me, his length still rutting against me, his hand grasping my hip.

"Anna, say something."

My lips pop open with a breathy gasp when his hand shifts to the inside of my thigh. I know that I should stop this. Yet, I can't.

I can't get myself to utter anything except, "Something."

He snorts. "That's not a *no*."

I'm flat on my back before I can blink, with my pants torn down my legs and a growl reverberating around the room when his hands meet my bare hips. "No panties? Were you waiting for me to find you bare, naughty girl?"

No amount of biting my lip can hold back the whimper because while I didn't intend to leave myself without undergarments, maybe subconsciously, I was hopeful.

*Was I?*

"Maybe …"

Toby hums at my admission and moves between my knees.

His skin is a stark contrast to the white blanket surrounding him, his hand unmistakably reaching for his already exposed length.

"Like what you see?"

He smirks at me and raises something to his mouth.

"Play with that juicy cunt, Mama. Get it ready for me."

I gasp when his vulgar words twinge my lower stomach and immediately I obey. The ache is almost unbearable as I dive between the folds.

*I'm incredibly wet.*

"That's it. Spread it all around."

I follow his husky instruction, all the while keeping my sight trained on his movements.

The wrapper in his hand tears against his teeth, and he arches his head to spit half of it out.

"Look at me," he demands, and I listen. "Eyes on me when you play with yourself." My lips part in a pant as I do, and he adds, "Now finger that wet cunt for me."

I gasp and slip a digit inside.

The hum of his approval makes me throb as he grips his shaft. "I wanna see two fingers knuckle deep. Work yourself open for me."

His graveled demands have a wave of wetness building between my legs.

"*Toby*," I whimper when my second finger slides inside, and I curl them to meet that special button that has my eyes rolling back.

"Don't come," he demands roughly on a pant. "Your next orgasm is mine, Anna, and it's going to be around my dick."

I moan. Unashamed and unchained. "Yes. Yes, I want that."

He hums, his knees shifting closer, his thighs hitting the back of mine. "You want to cum on my dick? Or you want your next O to be mine?"

"*Yes*," I gasp, my pumping fingers hitting the head of his covered shaft. "Both. All of it. Yes."

"So eager for me, aren't you?"

"So eager."

Toby has taken command of my body and I'm not willing to take the control back.

*It feels so freaking good to let go for once.*

The head of him rubs against the back of my hand. "Then tell me what you're eager for, dirty girl. Tell me what you want me to do to you."

"I-I-I …" I'm gasping, my entrance tightening around my fingers, a heat blooming low in my belly. "I want you to make me feel good, Toby." His hand wraps around my wrist, and at first, I fight his hold when he tugs my fingers free. "No."

"Tell me." He braces his arms on either side of me, and that's when I feel his erection bump against my wetness. My hips act on their own, lifting and chasing him when he pulls back with a *tsk*. "Say it and it's all yours."

My breath leaves me in pants and my body feels like it's on fire, the only cure is the man hovering just out of reach.

*He asked me for words.*

I swallow thickly when the statements evade me and lift my hips again, searching for him, answering him with my body.

Toby groans and leans close enough that his mustache brushes the shell of my ear. "So needy for my dick, aren't you?" I gasp, biting my lip to tame the sound. "Is this what you want?" His head slides through my folds and I nearly lose it. "Say that you're a needy little slut for my dick." His erection slips over me once again and my hips chase him.

*Can I orgasm from just words? Because I'm pretty sure that's about to happen.*

"*Oh God*," I cry when Toby's erection lands on the bundle of nerves between my legs and moves against me.

"Tell me you're my dirty little slut, Mama, and I'll fucking make you one."

It's automatic. As if I've been possessed and all I can think about is getting to that climax, consequences be damned.

"I'm your dirty little slut, Toby." The words are husky and moaned and sound nothing like me when they leave my lips.

But then he leans back on his haunches.

"Wait, don't go—"

"Hush," Toby hums and grabs my knees, lifting them to my chest. "I'm gonna fuck you. Don't you worry."

His knees edge closer until I feel his thighs against my butt, my core completely exposed.

"Take a breath for me." I'm halfway through forcing my chest to expand when I feel it. The head of his erection at my entrance.

My breath hitches.

And then his length inches inside me, breaching me, taking me.

Everything in me freezes, all of my focus on feeling every inch of Toby sliding inside me like he's staking a claim.

*Like he's ruining me.*

"*Fuuuuck*, Mama," Toby murmurs, his neck strained back. "Tell me you're my dirty fucking slut while I'm buried inside you." Groaning, he moves another inch inside of me. "Tell me you need the rest of my dick in you."

He's panting, his grip digging into my knees as he holds me still and the only thing I can do is take it. It's all I can think about, all I can feel.

*All I want.*

"Yes, *Toby*, give me all of it. I'm all yours. Your dirty little slut."

"Oh, you will be." He thrusts forward, leaning all of his weight on my shaking legs, and my eyes roll back once again. "You're gonna be fucking gone for this dick once I fit it all inside you. My perfect little slut. Made just for me to *fuck*."

"I want that. *Yes, please*." I'm rambling, disoriented, and flushed from head to toe, with the orgasm that's ready to take me at any moment.

"Look at the mouth on you."

He buries his remaining length inside me and there's no part of me that can stop the keening that rips from my throat. "*Please ...*"

"Please what, dirty girl?" He pants. "Say those dirty words I wanna hear so bad from your sexy little mouth."

I whimper when I feel his erection jerk inside me. "Please," I choke out. "Please take me."

"Oh, Mama," Toby makes a sound that's a half chuckle, half grunt, that I feel in my core. "I've already taken your cunt with my dick." He moves, his length sliding almost all the way out of me and making my eyes roll back, then slamming back inside me in one hard stroke that leaves me with a gaping mouth stuck in a silent scream. "I'm gonna ruin this cunt and you're going to take it, right? I know you want me to."

"Yes. Yes. Yes," I chant. "Ruin me. Use me. Make me orgasm. Toby, *please*."

Toby moans above me. "There's my dirty girl." *Finally*, his hips move. "Such a desperate slut for my dick, aren't you?"

"*Yes.*"

"Yes, what?" Toby asks breathlessly, his hips flexing, his length claiming all of me until there's nothing left but him.

"I'm a dirty slut for your dick."

He's in my mind. Coming out of my mouth. Taking up every piece of me that I'm opening to him.

"That's right. Made just for me."

And what I get in return is the ultimate pleasure in the form of his guttural groans, his rutting erection, his body slamming into mine.

The climax builds with each word, each thrust of him inside me, until I shatter into a million different pieces around him, his name screaming past my lips. "Toby!"

"That's it, come while you're stuffed full of my dick," he pants, keeping his erection buried inside me as his own orgasm comes roaring from him.

He takes each clench around him and meets it with a flex of his erection, each wave of pleasure coupled with his own.

Toby said he was going to ruin me.

*I'm already ruined.*

# Chapter Twenty-Nine

## TOBY

Now that I've had my taste of her, I can't stop.

I won't stop.

Last night was heaven, and for the first time in a lot of years, I remember every fucking second of Anna's dirty cunt sucking the life right out of me.

*I knew she was a freak under all that.*

She just needed the right man to bring it out of her.

The shakes have finally stopped, and while I'm still nauseous if I move too fast, my dick works and that means I'm as good as always.

"No, Leo." Anna scoffs into the phone and bitches to my band manager about how much snow has built up around the cabin, blocking the doors and blanketing over the driveway.

Pretty sure even the car is buried.

Which I have no intention of *unburying* because that just means I get to explore a little more with the Prune before life goes back to normal.

My grocery stunt has taken over the tabloids, restoring my shitty-bad-boy image with the media, which means as soon as the snow clears, we're safe to go home.

There's a twinge in my gut at the thought of leaving this place, this sanctuary of peace, but I'm also itching to get back into the studio. On stage. With my bandmates.

*After I'm done fucking Anna in every room available.*

"Anna," I call from my spot on the bed, willing the vixen to come to me. Hopefully without clothes and a wet pussy in need of touching. "Come help me with the sauna."

The pad of her feet echo down the hallway, her voice leading the way. "There's a sauna?"

She appears in the doorway, not naked as I wished, and with hands to her hips.

"Uh, yeah. What the fuck did you think was in the bathroom?"

Her brow pinches. "A closet?"

Snickering, I scoot to the edge of the bed, still buck-ass naked, and stand with a shaking stretch. "Come with me."

A flush takes over her face.

Snagging her hand, I make my way across the room, closing the bathroom door behind us.

"Jeffers—"

"Hush, Mama." I push open the sauna door and pull her inside.

"Why are you always freaking *naked*?" she squeals.

"You got a problem with it?" I ask over my shoulder and pull open the panel built into the wall that holds the controls for this room.

"What if I do?" Anna snarks.

"Do you?"

After setting the temp and timer, I start pulling the straps of her top down her shoulders.

"I'm so screwed." The words are mumbled, whispered, and don't compute.

"What?" I flick my gaze to her when she allows me to work the material over one elbow, then the other, and the top drops to her waist.

"Nothing," she grumbles.

Her tits are finally exposed and I see faint tan lines dipping between and along the sides of her.

"*Fuck*," I murmur, my fingers following each line that stops just beneath each tit. "You wear a bikini, Mama?"

Anna slaps my hands away, her face growing a deeper shade of red even though her hands go to her hips. "So?"

*So much color to her.*

I chuckle. "That's sexy as hell."

If it's possible, her flush trails all the way down to her exposed chest. "It's just a bathing suit. Which I have if you'd let me go change for this."

"Nuh-uh. Not now." I snag her wrist when she goes to push by me. Her body collides with me, those glorious tits smooshing into my chest. "I have other plans for you."

"What plans?" she asks, breathless.

"Dirty." I hook my thumbs into the waistband of her pants and watch as her eyes fill with want. "Filthy." I drag the material down her thighs and her chest rises with quick breaths. "Nasty." I drop to my knees, taking her pants all the way to her ankles she eagerly lifts. "No clothes required *plans*."

Anna shudders in front of me, the misters above us triggering with the rise of the temperature.

Rising to my full height, I toss the clothes out of the sauna and close us in it.

My skin grows damp and hot as I look at her, my gaze tracking from her toes—painted a bright teal that has me biting my lip—up to her creamy calves and thighs, dotted with a light smattering of freckles.

I want to kiss my way across each one. To memorize the colors of her.

Then her hips and belly. The woman has an ass I want to sink my teeth into, just like a fucking peach, that creates the base of her hourglass figure. Her waist pitches inward before flaring up her rib cage with full tits and peaked nipples I need in my mouth before we leave this room.

When my sight trails up her neck to her jaw, then those glossy pink fucking lips, my gaze collides with hers and she squirms.

Clenched thighs and all.

"You're so fucking sexy, Mama." I lick my lips and offer my hand. "Now come ride this dick."

She whimpers, fucking *whimpers*, and slides her palm against mine.

The heat of the room is what I attribute the burst of warmth behind my ribs to when she comes to me willingly, following me to where I have a towel laid out on the bench, a rubber or three hidden underneath the terrycloth.

I lower to the seat and spin her in one motion so that she's facing away from me and that ass of hers is directly in my face.

"Bend over," I rasp. Her spine curls into the perfect arch that pushes her ass up in the air. "*Perfect.* Widen your stance—*Good girl.*" I hold her steady with my hands to her hips. "Now I'm gonna eat this flawless cunt."

Anna groans at my words, before I have the chance to lean closer and run my tongue along her exposed slit, but when I do, she gets louder.

"That's it, dirty girl. Make it loud for me." My lips move against her flesh, sealing and sucking on her already swollen clit. She cries out, her raspy sounds bouncing off the walls and landing straight in my balls.

I hum into her and straighten my tongue, the tip circling around her entrance, then plunging inside her.

"*Oh God.*"

I hum and use my grip on her hips to pull her back against me until she's riding my face, impaling herself on my tongue.

"*Toby,*" Anna whines, and when her walls flutter, I know she's close.

So I pull back.

"Toby!" she growls like it's a curse but all it does is make me smile. Even more so when that juicy ass pushes back in search of me.

"Same rules as last night, Mama," I say with a grin. "Now come ride this dick."

Anna doesn't hesitate to turn and climb me, her knees placed on the bench on either side of my hips.

She wraps her fist around the root of my dick and strokes. Once. Twice. Three times before she lifts and slides the head of me through her soaking slit.

A groan escapes me at the feel of her wetness on my bare cock. *So warm and wet—*

Panic sets in, my brain catches up, and my stiffened grip on her hips halts her movement.

"*Ow*, Toby. What the—" I move her back, her ass settling on my thighs and my dick standing straight up between us.

"I wasn't ready." I make quick work of sheathing myself, my gaze colliding with hers.

"*Oh*." The flush on her has nothing to do with the heat of the room. "Oh, crap." She pinches her lip between her teeth, her face cast down, guilt radiating from her. "I wasn't trying to—"

"Anna," I say, stopping her words with a finger beneath her chin to lift her gaze. "Heat of the moment. I was ready to let you."

Anna nods sheepishly. "Okay."

My dick pulses between us. "Now hop on and ride me, yeah?"

She nods again, more certain this time as she leans up, and I line up my head with her wet slit.

I can feel how swollen she is as she lowers herself, swallowing me up inch by inch, making sure I feel every bit of her cunt sliding over me.

"Goddamn, Mama," I pant into her neck when she leans closer, bracing her palms on my shoulders. "Is this payback for last night?"

She chuckles but it's throaty. "Maybe."

I hum and trail my lips down her throat, her head arching back for me. "So you like taking me slow, don't you? Feeling my dick take you."

Anna whimpers and lowers, taking the final few inches until she's completely impaled by my dick. "*Yessss*," she hisses out in response, her hips grinding into my pelvis.

She's so much closer this way, with her arms snaking around my neck and my tongue dancing over her salty flesh.

It's hot and sexy and everything I didn't know I needed.

"That's it," I growl out. "Take my dick and make it yours."

Anna lifts, sliding me almost all the way out, and then slams her hips back down on me.

"Toby," she whimpers out. "Why do you feel so good?"

I take one of her rosy-colored nipples between my teeth. "Because you like being stuffed full of my dick, Mama."

She gasps when I thrust up to meet her. "It is pretty big. Stretches."

"Uh-huh. Stretches that juicy cunt wide open, doesn't it?"

She nods with a breathy *uh-huh* when I rise my lower half and meet her once again. It makes the thrust hard when she lowers, deeper, and pulls the most glorious sound from her perfect mouth.

"Toby," she moans, her nails digging into my pecs.

I grab a fistful of her hair as she grinds against me, chasing that orgasm until it crashes into her and she explodes around me.

The way she holds onto me, clenches around me, comes while I'm inside her has my abs tightening and my balls drawing up.

I ride her from the bottom so fast and hard that all I can hear is slapping flesh and heavy breaths. All I can feel is her pussy milking me. All I can focus on is that delicious high she brings me.

And I lose it all inside her perfect cunt as she clings to me for dear life.

"Anna…"

# Chapter Thirty

## Anna

Seven days.

Of heaven and hell wrapped into one stupid trip on the mountain. Including constant calls from my boss where I have to pretend that Toby and I haven't been sleeping together every other minute I'm not working.

Which is beyond wrong and going to cost me my job at some point when it catches up to me. I know this, and yet, cabin fever has taken its toll.

*Temporary insanity is what I'll call it.*

The snow has taken over the town, claiming the trees, and wiping out the driveway. My car is still buried, the doors still basically barricaded shut, and yet …

I'm not ready to face reality.

Because the reality outside of these four walls does not include getting bent over the back of the couch by the one man that I absolutely should not allow being bent over by.

But that's exactly what is happening right now.

"I swear, Mama," Toby pants behind me, his bruising grip on my hips, his erection pumping with punishing thrusts. "I'm gonna fuck this cunt in every room. And you'll let me."

"*Yes.*"

"Such a dirty fucking girl, aren't you?" I nod and arch my hips up, meeting his thrusts.

We don't have much time. There's a call scheduled I have to be on in less than twenty minutes and today happens to be the first day I've caved to him while the sun is still up.

It's risky. It's chaotic.

*It's urgent.*

Because my need for what he gives me has become unbearable.

"Mmm, you're so desperate for this dick." He pounds his erection into me, the position hitting all the right spots and making me see stars. "Look at you, so fucking wrecked for me."

All I can do is hang on to the cushion and moan.

I'm so close to the edge that when Toby lies over me, his palm cupping around my neck, his husky voice in my ear, I almost explode. "Look at that reflection, and tell me that isn't ruined perfection staring back."

I follow his direction and lift my eyes to the window in front of us, and just as promised, I'm staring myself right in the eye with a backdrop of snowcapped mountains.

*Is that me?*

My lips are parted, my cheeks flushed, my hair loose in sex-craved waves that bounce with each of Toby's thrusts.

But when I meet his feral gaze in the reflection, I lose all control.

"Yesss, come on my dick," Toby grunts and groans and pitches forward, burying himself deep inside me as he comes with me.

It's the hottest thing I've ever seen.

He hums, thrusting a few more times, making me shudder. "You're so fucking perfect, Mama." He lifts his hand to his mouth and wets his thumb. "My perfect little slut." That same thumb lowers from my sensitive flesh to the only part of my body that he hasn't been in. His smirk is downright evil when he circles the tight ring, and I yelp.

*Am I okay with that? Who does that?*

"Reach between your legs," he demands, his deep voice leaving chills across my ear. "Rub your clit while you're stuffed full."

Toby has possessed me, mind and body, because I listen to his every word and reach down to rub my fingers over the bundle of nerves. His thumb circles, matching mine, and his hardness pulses inside me.

"It's too much," I cry out, overwhelmed with the sensations, and yet I feel another wave of wetness coating him.

"All you gotta do is let me in. In everywhere." His grip on my neck tightens and I lose focus on all things that aren't him. His touch. His breath in my ear. His grip on my throat. His length buried in me.

Him, him, him.

"*Toby*," I whimper, the sensations building higher, the stars returning to my vision full force.

"Such a filthy fucking slut," he coos and my stomach flips. "All for me."

"Uh-huh," I breathe and it must be exactly right because his digit slips inside my back entrance at the same time his length moves inside me. "*Oh God.*"

I moan like the dirty girl that Toby keeps calling me, my fingers flitting faster over myself as his thumb breaches me over and over and his length takes me again and again.

"I'm gonna be inside this ass before we leave here, dirty girl. You're gonna take me raw right inside this needy hole." His digit thrusts to punctuate his words, filling me completely, taking me to a whole new plane of toe-curling euphoria.

The idea of him raw inside me anywhere is enough to have me on the verge of begging.

*Yes, please, take me now.*

"Yes. Yes. Yes."

I'm wholly and irrevocably *consumed* by Toby Jeffers.

"Prove it, Mama. Prove that you want my dick up your tight, needy asshole," he pants out with grinding hips.

"H-how?"

"*Come.*"

One word. One command.

And even my body listens.

Everything in me tightens around him, my jaw dropping open as my eyes roll back, my entrances clamping onto him as I crash headlong into a climax that feels like it's ripping me in half.

Two halves of one person.

*The version before Toby.*

*And the one that comes after Toby.*

"That's fucking it," Toby strains.

Yet, I don't stop my hips from grinding, my hands from gripping, my mouth from moving, my body from searching for the last little morsel only Toby can provide until I'm wrung dry.

Which he gives by releasing my neck, stuffing his fingers between my lips, and finally fills me in every possible way as he ruts against me.

I'm helpless to stop this freight train.

I always was.

# Chapter Thirty-One

## WHERE IS TOBY NOW?

FIRST, IT'S KNOCKING UP *his fans.*

Next, it's knocking out *his fans.*

Reports say that an inside source has scoured all known hangouts for the rock star and yet, no one has seen him.

Is it possible that Toby has finally fallen completely off the wagon?

Or is his manager hiding him in rehab again?

Let us know what you think!

# Chapter Thirty-Two

## TOBY

"**W**HEN LEO SAID HE sent you to the cabin, I didn't expect you'd be gone so long I'd actually *miss* your ass."

Mac's snicker comes across the line and almost makes me feel homesick.

"I *knew* you liked my ass," I say with a chuckle.

"*Pffft*, nice try, limp waffle." He snorts into the receiver. "Got me checking the weather like an old-ass man. Feeling like I gotta eat dinner at four so I can be in bed by eight."

I laugh at that and the tapping I hear coming from the background. I lounge on the couch, right where I ate Anna out for breakfast this morning. "You are old, Mackie."

"You're older than me," Mac huffs, unamused. "I'm not old."

Snorting, I run my hands through my beard and stare up at the ceiling, my phone pressed to my ear.

"You're quiet. That's weird. Has Anna given you a hard time?"

The mention of her has my eyes narrowing and my chest tightening. "Why?"

"Because you two are like fucking badgers," Mac comments, unmoved by my clipped tone. "Constantly badgering each other."

*Oh. Right.*

"It's fine," I mutter.

The line goes silent. Even the tapping of Mac's drum stick against whatever nearby surface pauses and I feel a nerve twinge in my gut.

"Dude. Spit it out," Mac says into the phone.

I huff. "There's nothing to spit out."

"Ohhhh, but there is. I can tell. So tell me. Tell me, tell me, tell me."

I roll my eyes and shift so that I'm sitting back up, my hands rubbing across my face. "She spends all day in the fucking room." *Not a lie.* "That's weird, right?"

"So weird that woman has to work." It's like I can hear his eye roll over the line. "Maybe if you weren't such a wet noodle, her job would be easier and she'd hate you less."

I sigh and swipe my damp hands over my thighs. "Someone's gotta be the actual rock star around here," I comment on a scoff.

It's not lost on me that I'm deflecting most of his questions with humor. I may be as close to sober as I have been since I was fifteen, but I'm still me under all the bullshit.

The me I know is an asshole.

"Pretty sure acting a fool on a regular is *not* what makes us rock stars." The tapping on his end is back, the sharp tick echoing over the line. "Some of us wanna live past forty."

"You're just saying that because you want some dick outta life."

Mac snorts. "You'd be correct, good sir. Maybe even being *official.* Exclusive. One and only. *Someday.*"

An ache blossoms inside my chest. "Whatever the hell that means."

"You don't wanna know." Mac laughs, but it's tight. Almost humorless. "It's a thing."

Rambling is what I would consider the next few minutes of the call with my bandmate, but I spend most of the time only half listening to the man tell me what his perfect life partner would be like. His ideal proposal. His destination dreams.

"Oh! Tyro just walked in. I gotta go."

Because the other half of me is so focused on the gnawing pang in my chest that—

*No.*

"Call you tomorrow, bro."

Happily ever afters and all that other bullshit that Mac's dreaming about is nowhere in the cards for me. Not my thing. Not my desire.

I literally shake my head to wipe away the thoughts and stand, the call long ago ended.

*That kinda shit requires a relationship first and I don't know how to do those.*

But what I *do* know how to do is fuck.

And I know exactly where I can find a willing participant to work out my frustrations on.

"Anna!"

# Chapter Thirty-Three

## Anna

*U*<sup>GH.</sup>

I hear my name shouted across the house and shake my head.

Leaning into the bathroom vanity, I brace myself up on my arms. There are cramps so severe in my lower stomach that it feels like my insides are trying to barrel their way *through* my skin instead staying put.

But am I going to let that stop me from finishing this conversation with Aria?

*Nope.*

"So, I have this super cute pic of Rex with the twins." Aria's chuckle echoes over the AirPod jammed in my ear and it's like I can just *feel* the pride and love this woman has for her family through the phone. It makes that cramp going on in my stomach just a little bit harder to breathe through. "He's got one in each arm and they're both wearing band onesies."

I can hear the smile in her voice and cringe inwardly. "Aria, that sounds exactly like the last one you sent me." I snicker when I want to wince at the pain and pull in a deep breath.

"But Rex has his hair down in this one and both the babies have a handful."

"Ouch," I mumble.

"I tried to fucking warn him about that." Aria laughs, and I wince, forcing a smile anyway.

*God, is this ache going to let up any time soon?*

"Sounds perfect, then," I say through clenched teeth and double over the sink until I'm resting my head on my forearms against the cool surface. "Thanks for offering to send them to me."

"Of course," she chimes, way too chipper and happy for me. "Anything I can do to make your job easier, I'm here for it. Can't be all that great being confined to that small of a space with Toby, of all people."

I huff. "It's something alright."

"Yeah," she drawls over the line, going silent for a moment before asking in a tone completely different than the last. "How is he?" It's quieter, more reserved.

*She sounds worried.*

"He's … coping, I guess."

It's the only answer I can come up with considering I don't know how much she really knows about the man, and it's not my place to tell the world his secrets.

"Good," she breathes. "I was hopeful that spending some time with you would help him out."

"What do you mean by that?"

"Well…" Aria snickers. "You're not the one to cave and give in to his stupid sh—eet."

I laugh at her coverup of the foul language and immediately regret it. "You literally dropped two f-bombs since we've been on the phone already."

"I'm trying, okay!" She giggles. "It doesn't help when everyone else around me doesn't seem to care that my kid's first words might be *fuck*."

Snorting, I force myself upright with another wince as a knock sounds against the bedroom door. "Send me those pics and go back to your babies. I'm sorry to bug you."

"Pssh, don't worry about it. Rex is pulling diaper duty because I took the call. I got as long as you need."

"Oh," I mutter. "That's not necess—"

"So how are you, Anna? Anyone ever ask you that?"

I'm too caught up by the question to react at first. The echo of Toby's fist rings from the bedroom, once again distracting me from a reply.

*I'm not one of the girls. We don't chat like this.*

"Really, that's not necessa—"

"Anna." Aria's tone sounds every bit of the mom she is. "You've done nothing but work and deal with Toby's bullshit for weeks now. You gotta be starved for contact from another human."

"Uhhh …"

"Besides, *I'm* starved for human contact that isn't Rex. I love the man, I do. But I need some girl time."

I snort. "I haven't had that since I was a teenager."

"Honey," Aria chides over the line. "We're going to fix that the night you get back. You're one of us now. Until then, answer my question."

I can't help the laugh that bursts past my lips. "Fine, just give me a moment."

"The longer this call takes, the better. Take your time."

I tap the mute button on my phone and stride across the room with my hand to my stomach. I answer the door with a flourish that Toby ignores.

Because the man barges in before I can even get the panel all the way back, his hands grasping my face, his lips crashing against mine.

His tongue dives between my lips, his feet moving us backward into the room.

"Toby, wait," I manage to breathe out when we come up for air, his lips trailing down my jaw.

"Done waiting, Mama." Toby nips at my neck, his breath hot against my skin, his hands migrating to my loose hair he fists and tugs on.

A mewl inches its way up my throat and it takes everything in me to hold it back. "*Jeffers*," I say like a demand, my voice too thick, my breath too … breathy. "Stop."

He listens.

In fact, Toby freezes.

Tongue against my neck and all.

I roll my eyes and plant my hands on his pecs, pressing just enough that he pulls back to look at me.

If I were a weaker woman, I'd dive headfirst into those amber pools staring at me with a pinched brow and concern etched into his features.

"Five-day hiatus."

"Why?"

"I said so."

He rolls his eyes, and I feel nerves battle the cramps going on in my lower belly.

I've had the man inside me, say filthy things to me, *do* filthy things to me. So, why can't I just say that we've been here long enough that I've started menstruating?

It's normal. It's natural.

It's … gross.

"I need a better reason than *I said so.*"

I can feel the heat taking over my face. *Why is this so hard?* "Fine." I square my shoulders and step back from him, my hands planted on his pec to keep him at a distance.

"Anna, you back yet?"

My shoulders fall, the voice in my ear stealing all of my courage and reminding me I still have another completely different conversation to finish.

"I just can't," I tell Toby and reach up to press against the little sensor on my earpiece that unmutes the device. "Yeah, I'm back."

I don't look at him when I return to the bathroom, the woman in my ear chattering on about a girls' night plan she came up with while she was waiting.

*We should start creating distance—*

I should start creating distance. There's no way that Toby Jeffers will be willing to keep any of this up once we get back home.

I'll be lucky if he keeps his sobriety.

And that is more important than any tryst going on between him and I.

"There's this new coffee place I've been dying to try," Aria says into the phone. "I hear they have amazing hot chocolate there. How's that sound?"

My smile is weak when I answer.

"That sounds perfect."

# Chapter Thirty-Four

TOBY

*W*HY DID I DO *this?*

Blowing out a breath, I knock on the panel separating me from Anna before I talk myself into turning around for the fourth time.

I have no idea if I did it right. I also don't know if reheating it made it any worse.

*Why the fuck did I do this?*

"Go away, Toby," she calls back, and I snort.

"I, uh … did something."

It's something alright. Something that I was hoping she'd come out and find me in the middle of doing so I wouldn't have to stand here and explain.

I hear her tiny growl and her mumbled words moments before the door swings open, and I thrust my filled hand out to her.

She stands there in a baggy tee shirt she tied off on the side and a pair of yoga pants, staring at me with parted pink lips and a furrow to her brow.

*Fuck, she's sexy.*

"What is this?" She doesn't take it, just stares at it, so I lift higher.

"I made it."

Anna's brows furrow so deep, they meet in the middle, and yet she still doesn't look away from it.

*Like it's going to jump out at her.*

"Is it poisoned?"

*Or that.*

I chuckle. "No. Here," I lift the large ceramic mug to my lips and sip, letting the chocolaty flavor coat my tongue. "See?"

She watches me wearily through narrowed eyes until I shrug.

Her eyes refuse to leave mine even when she lifts the mug to her own lips and takes a swig.

It's not until the taste registers that she looks taken aback, her wide eyes landing on the cup in her grip.

"You made ... hot chocolate?"

"Uh." I brush my hands down my beard. "Yeah. Is it terrible? We were out of the packets, so I figured something else out."

"You made hot chocolate ... from *scratch*?"

"Yes."

"Why?"

"It sounded like a better idea than microwaving Bailey's."

Anna sputters out a laugh and nods her agreement. "It's pretty good, Toby." Her cheeks heat, but her smile is fucking radiant when she aims it at me.

I grin, too, my stomach warmed over, my senses filled with her ocean scent. "C'mon. Work's over for the day."

Holding out a hand, I wait for her to slide her pale skin against mine, her hand soft to the touch.

*Delicate.*

It's what comes to mind when I wrap our entwined hands around her until my arm drapes over her shoulder and I'm pulling her in the direction of the living room.

The woman is anything but delicate, though. She just feels that way in my arms, in this moment, all tucked up into me.

*It's the perfect fit.*

"What's that smell?"

"You saying I stink?"

She snickers. "No, it smells delicious. What did you make?"

I chuckle and release her so that she can plop onto the recliner part of the couch. "The biggest plate of nachos ever."

Bending to the coffee table, I remove the overturned cooking sheet. The scent of fresh taco meat and chopped onions wafts through the air, and I hum in appreciation.

"Holy crap." Anna scoots to the edge of her seat. "That looks amazing."

"It is. Cause I made it." I grin at her when she rolls her eyes and drag the table closer so we can both reach from our seats.

The woman surprises the hell out of me by snagging a blanket and draping it over both of our laps. She lifts the cooking sheet from its pot holders, tests the bottom to make sure it's not too hot, and lays it directly on the blanket spread across us.

Her feet are up before I can even register what she's doing, her hands armed with the fork I left there for her to eat with.

"Remote?"

I'm unable to tame my smile as I produce the remote for the TV over the mantle and hand it over.

She chooses some show about a group of friends all hanging out at a coffee shop together and we settle into the cushions with only an occasional snicker from her and the crunch of chips between teeth.

There are moments that I would swear she's mouthing the words right along with the actors on the show, but when I sneak a look over, she's focused on the TV with her lips pressed together.

The silence between us is comfortable. It's easy.

So easy that when the food is all gone and Anna goes to relax into the couch, I lift her feet into my lap and cover her legs with the blanket.

"What are you doing?"

I shrug and work my thumbs into the socked arches of her foot. "I listen to you pace all damn day. It's like a stampede in that room while you work."

She huffs and closes her eyes.

They stay that way, even when I switch to the other foot and knead the tense muscles there long enough that the episode clicks over to the next one.

Convinced she's passed out, I rest my hands on her shins and drop my head back against the couch.

I stare at the ceiling, questions rolling around in my head.

I can't catch any of them long enough to find an answer before my thoughts are wandering off to the next one that flitters away in the wind of my mind. All of them fly away except one.

*Is this what it feels like to give a fuck?*

God, I'd kill for a shot right now. If only to calm the racing thoughts for just a minute.

# Chapter Thirty-Five

## Toby

"**F**UCK!"

I slam the axe down against the log for the third time, the wood finally splitting down the center enough for me to wedge my fingers between and rip it off.

"Well, that was eventful." Mac snickers into my ear, the earbuds echoing his voice around my head. "Did you hit your target or your hand?"

"The log," I answer, my breath rushing out before me in the form of a fog.

I told myself I came out here because the stash was getting low and the sun was at the perfect peak to get the temp high enough that I would only slightly freeze to death.

What I wasn't expecting was the draw to stay out here long after the lights came on in the cabin and to watch Anna disappear into the bedroom to work.

I'd snuck out from under her before she woke up, cleared the mess from dinner, and just … came outside.

The jonesing has been too much to consider anything else.

Being inside only made it worse.

"I thought splitting wood was my thing," Mac chimes in, and I can't help the chuckle that bubbles up before smacking the axe down on the next piece. It goes flying, splintered in three, and lands among the rubble.

"In the literal sense of the statement, I know damn well the only wood you know how to handle is dick."

Mac laughs. "I got tons of experience."

It's as if I can see the man in front of me, suggestively waggling his brows and grinning.

It almost makes me smile. "I'm sure you do."

*I shouldn't hate that he's in a good mood.*

*Right?*

"So," Mac drawls, the tapping on his end of the line changing to a lower pitch, as if he's moved to beating up the couch instead of the table. "What happened with you last night?"

I sigh, dropping the axe on the larger log and fish the pack of smokes out from my torn pocket. "Nothing."

Mac sighs back. "Right. The dreaded *nothingness*."

The way he says it has my lit lighter pausing midair, my cigarette poised between my lips and waiting. "What's that supposed to mean?"

I light the cigarette and drag the smoke deep into my lungs as he speaks. "Means what you want it to mean, fizzlefuck."

"Wait," I say as I blow the smoke out and pinch the cigarette between my fingers. "Fizzlefuck?"

Mac snorts on his end of the call, the rustle that follows indicating the shaking of his head.

"Yesterday was all *it's fine* and *she spends all her time in the room*. But today, you're calling me—after not talking to me for almost a month!—to bitch about doing *nothing*. C'mon, Tob."

I shake my head and take another drag, letting the nicotine calm my system. "Still don't know what you're talking about."

"Let's see," Mac mumbles. "Toby spent yesterday fine with Anna taking the only bed for the last few weeks. And today, he's called me moping about doing *nothing* last night. What's that sound like to you?"

I hear another voice muffled over the phone, and I growl into the receiver. "That better not be your bodyguard you're talking to."

"Oh, it's not." His resulting chuckle tells me he's lying out of his teeth. "He's not on duty until I leave this house in ten minutes."

"Why the fuck did you answer the phone, then?"

"Um, because my brother, who's stuck on a mountain with a witch, called and demanded my attention."

"Watch it, Mac." The growl is automatic. The defense is like a stronghold I can't hold back the moment my best friend calls her a witch.

"Ohhh," Mac calls over the line. "I fuckin' knew it."

My stomach flips.

"You were so expecting the *prune* to sleep with you and she didn't. Now you're moping."

Mac's laughter only fuels the anger building in my chest. Because while he's not entirely correct, he's not fucking *wrong* either.

"Pay up, Tyro!" he calls into the background of his side of the phone.

"Goddammit, Mac."

"Okay, okay. I'm here. Tell me what happened."

"No," I growl into the phone and lean back against the tree a few feet from my chopping station.

I should just hang up. Disconnect the line and move on with my life.

But the thought triggers a gnawing in my gut, an urge that's too hard to ignore on my own.

"No?" Mac seems taken aback, and I hear a rustle that leads to a groan before his end of the line falls silent except for a light tapping. "Okay, it's just you, me, and my sticks, Tob. Promise."

I grumble into the phone, toss the cigarette into the snow, and then light up a new one. "Nothing to talk about."

"Bullshit," Mac responds.

"If those fuckers hadn't gone all fucking domesticated on me, this wouldn't be happening," I snarl into the receiver, and that feeling in my gut churns some more.

*What the fuck am I doing?*

The leather hanging off my shoulders becomes too hot, the sweat on my brow beading up all over again despite the low temperature around me.

"Toby," Mac starts, his tone too calm. Too collected. Too much for me to hear. "There's nothing wrong with—"

"Just fucking *stop*, Mac. Not everyone can be like Rex. O-or fucking Fin, okay?" I know I'm attacking the wrong person. Deep down, I recognize it. But I can't stop the train from rolling right over me and barreling out of my mouth. "Leave me the hell out of it."

My breath is heavy and my feet have pushed me from my lean on the tree and into a pace around the little clearing.

"Toby, I didn't lump you in with anyone."

The realization has my boots halting in the snow and my stomach rolling over itself.

I hate this. I don't want to feel this feeling of my guts twisting and my chest collapsing in on itself.

In fact, I want to go back to not feeling a fucking thing.

*Being drunk makes life easier.*

It numbs the pain. The confusion. The ache of guilt so damn deep in me that I don't think I'll ever get rid of it.

It all hurts so damn much.

Why does it have to hurt?

"Toby." The whisper of my name is desperate and thick. "Tell me where you are."

"At the cabin, dipshit," I lash out, and my gaze goes skyward, regret washing over me like a flood. "Shit, I'm sor—"

"Don't you dare." I hear the rustle of Mac shaking his head. "Don't apologize."

"I'm sick of being stuck here, man."

Mac's sigh flitters over the speaker and has me shaking my head. "I know, Tob. Should only be a few more days."

"I know, I know," I breathe out. "Cabin fever is getting to me."

"I believe it. Even if it wasn't *the* cabin."

My chest tightens at the mention. The fact that he remembered something I haven't talked much about in years.

When Leo offered to buy the place, I got drunk and told him off.

But then when I sobered up for a few hours, heard his rationale behind the idea, and I couldn't stomach the idea of this place being in the hands of anyone else.

It went to shit after my pops died. I just couldn't bring myself back here without feeling like I might find him hiding in the woods, avoiding me, ignoring me.

*Most days I wish that were the truth.*

Leo has done so much to the place that it's almost unrecognizable. Except I spent most of my childhood in these woods, carving trees that still hold my initials, that I'd find my way back to the cabin blindfolded if I had to.

*I couldn't let it go.*

"You know you don't have to pretend with me, right?"

I blink against the blue sky. "Why do you think I called you?"

Mac's snicker is weak. "Knew I was your favorite." He blows out a breath, one I think is more evident than even *he* realizes. "Then don't pretend."

The statement is so easy to say. So easy to ask.

And yet … it's loaded. Heavy.

Because pretending is what I've done since the night of our first big show.

# Chapter Thirty-Six

## Welcome to the Wagon, Population: Toby Jeffers.

*K*NOWN ALCOHOL AND DRUG enthusiast has been reported to be hiding in a mansion along the coast to dry out. Have you seen him? Do you know where Toby is?

Send us all the info!

# Chapter Thirty-Seven

## Anna

"Jesus Christ, Jeffers. Are you *trying* to catch hypothermia?"

I can tell his fingers are numb from the way he fumbles with the zipper of his jacket that he's zipped for the first time ever, and his lips are a serious shade of almost blue.

It concerns me.

Almost as much as the ice currently melting from the ends of his hair.

"How long were you out there?"

He shrugs, his gaze unfocused as his jacket slides off his shoulders. "Dunno. What time is it?"

I draw in a deep breath with a shaking head. "Well past noon. You were gone when I woke up. I would have never guessed to check outside. Where it's freaking freezing." I walk to the stove, fetch the kettle, and fill it in the sink.

"Didn't wanna wake you." His jacket lands with a *thwap* against the back of the recliner. "You were out cold."

Toby doesn't look at me as he drags the little cart to the fireplace with a protesting creak under the weight stacked on top.

"Shit," he grumbles. From my spot at the stove near the heating kettle, I watch him kneel at the hearth, jabbing the poker into the nearly spent logs. "You didn't put any on this whole time?"

I shrug. "I didn't know I was supposed to."

He growls, and I swear I see his jaw tick through his beard from across the room, his eyes going to the ceiling. "You have to keep something on the fire, Anna. There's no other heat in this place," he says through gritted teeth and jams two logs into the fireplace.

*That would be why it got so cold in here …*

I'm so used to him taking care of it that I didn't even think to check it.

Toby pokes, waits, and when the logs don't do what he's expecting, he curses some more. "Would you like a lighter?"

"Matches," he growls, and I roll my eyes. "Top drawer between the sink and fridge."

"Okay." Popping open the kettle so that it doesn't scream at me—because the noise is terrible but the water is the best from a kettle—I rummage through the drawer that's in desperate need of organization and come up with a pack of super long matches.

Toby's holding out his hand when I turn around, but he's not looking at me.

So, in an attempt at levity, I throw them at his head.

The box pings off his shoulder instead and falls at his feet, explodes open, and the sticks all fly around the stone surrounding him.

I snort, my hand coming up to cover the noise and the grin when he looks up at me, completely unamused. In fact, he almost looks angry, those deep brown eyes landing on me for the first time since he stepped back in the cabin.

My stomach flips in response.

"The fuck?"

"You're being weird. So, I thought …" My grin slips. *God, he's so confusing.* "I was trying to be funny."

Stone-faced, he stands from his crouch, and crooks a finger in my direction. "Come here."

A chill races down my spine, my fuzzy-socked feet walking me straight to him.

"What?" I half snap, hands to my hips.

His brow raises as his arm does, his rough fingers curling around the back of my neck and yanking me forward. So close that my chest meets his, and his eyes darken.

"Do not ever let the fire go out again." His breath caresses my lips as he speaks and desire pools low in my belly.

*Which fire?*

"Why?" I squeak out.

"Because." Voice low, his grip curls tighter around the back of my neck. "You're not freezing to death on my watch."

With that, he releases me so fast I stumble back a step.

"The bedroom is going to take a while to get warmed back up," Toby says like I'm not standing here trying to collect myself. "'Til then, you should stay out here."

I'm nodding, but I'm not even sure what I'm agreeing to as I stumble back another step and drag in a cleansing breath. Except even that is filled with all things Toby. That citrusy-tobacco scent mixed with campfire and leather and I'm fairly certain my brain cells are scrambling even farther.

"Do you know how to start a fire?"

"Um." My tongue feels too heavy to answer. Too ready to flop out of my mouth and pant instead.

*Get it together, Anna.*

"Take care of the damn kettle, then get your ass back over here."

Nodding again, I scramble my way across the cabin, returning to his side with two mugs of hot tea.

*Why does being this close to him turn my brain to mush?*

"You have to build a teepee with the sticks like this," Toby explains, stacking the smaller logs on top of the ash pile so that they come to a point. "The bottom needs air."

"Okay." I bite my lip.

*I should not be this horny—*

*Oh my God, what is he doing to me?*

"Kindling goes in the middle. Smaller sticks, paper, whatever will catch easy." He wads up some stuff that looks more like dead pine needles and shoves it into the opening left between the upright logs. "Now you need to light it."

My brows shoot up when he looks over his shoulder at me expectantly. "Oh, crap. Okay." My hands freeze with the mugs still stuck to my palms until he chuckles and takes them from me.

Scooping up a match from the floor, I find the box on the other side of Toby's crouch and strike the stick against the sandpapery side of the cardboard.

I immediately toss the small flame into the fireplace and gasp when it bounces off a log and lands on the stone.

"Crap!"

Toby's quicker than I expect.

He snags the match before it can catch another one on fire and throws it into the mess of stuff at the bottom of the peaked wood. "It's not gonna burn you if you take the time to aim."

Huffing, I shove the box at Toby. "Here. You do it."

"Nah. Needs another one." His gaze catches and holds mine long enough that he tilts his head at the fireplace. "One more."

Growling, I swipe the remaining matches from the hearth and keep one to light. This time, I take a moment before flicking it into the small flame, the stick landing on the opposite side from Toby's.

It doesn't take long for them both to catch the kindling on fire, the flames rising to meet the logs.

"If I hadn't already put those other logs in there, you wouldn't need the peak. Not in a fireplace like this." I bob my head, but I'm too focused on watching the flames take over. "That's what that metal rack in the bottom is for."

"Okay."

The fire builds, catching the bark of the logs and transferring to the two already in the bottom. Heat blusters out, licking at my face. I reach out, feeling the heat take over my extremities and lick at my skin.

"Mama."

I'm slow to glance over my shoulder, and when I do, I find Toby's hand held out in offering. There's still a slight chill to his skin when my palm slides into his, but it still sends a swirl of warmth through me at his touch.

He pulls me to my feet and his arms envelop me, holding me close to his chest. "Why the hell didn't you come get me?"

I shrug against his torso, my nose buried in his chest, his scent intoxicating. "Didn't really think much about how cold it got in here. We're in the dang mountains."

His grip moves to my biceps and pulls me back enough to look down at me with a grit to his jaw. "I'm gonna need you to not get so damn distracted."

"Wasn't distracted," I argue but tilt my head forward, seeking him out.

A lazy smile spreads across my face when he does exactly what I want and wraps his massive arms around me. My cheek squishes against his pec, my arms sliding around his trim waist.

It's so tender, his touch at the back of my head, that it makes my heart pound.

*So unlike Toby.*

We've been intimate in all the physical ways one can when it comes to sex, but this feels like a whole other level of soul-deep connection.

There's no dirty talk. No foreplay.

Just us. Here. In front of a fire, in a cabin, together.

"Fuck," Toby rumbles on a rocky whisper, his fingers threading into my hair and tugging my head back. "What are you doing to me, Mama?"

Those deep brown eyes of his bounce between mine, so clear and soulful.

*He really is beautiful.*

All thick hair and a sinful smile …

I stifle my groan by biting my lip, my gaze clashing with his heated one. "Probably the same thing you're doing to me," I admit on a loaded whisper.

His other hand moves from my waist to my jaw, the roughness of his calloused fingertips scraping over my skin in a way that I feel it down to my curling toes.

When the move has me sinking my teeth further into my lip, his eyes darken. And when he backs us up to a wall and a gasp escapes me at the contact, he slams his lips against mine.

A burning kiss that sears me straight to my core as his tongue takes everything I'm willing to give and then some.

*What* is *he doing to me?*

# Chapter Thirty-Eight

## Anna

I'M NOT SURE EXACTLY when Toby fell into my bed along with me, or why I never threw a fit about it all those weeks ago, but tonight is no different than it has been.

He stayed awake to mess around with his guitar while I retired some time ago, alone, yet am awakened by the man climbing into bed with me.

He doesn't touch me, like most nights. Doesn't scoot close or even steal the covers.

Pretending I'm still passed out, just like I do every night he comes in, I resist my protesting huff when a chill flutters beneath the covers.

*He was right, it's definitely colder in here tonight.*

It's quickly replaced when his body heat takes over, the radiator of a man sealing the heatwaves in with us.

"Mama," he whispers so quietly into the night, it almost sounds like a plea.

Biting my lip, I wait.

It's so quiet, save for the pulse beating in my ears, that I hear his long exhale and his growled words. "Fuck it."

The duvet rustles with his movement, the mattress dipping moments before I feel his arm dive between my legs and hook around the one I keep bent as I sleep. I gasp when his hand flattens over my butt, and he hauls me into his bare chest, his leg wedging between mine. I release that groan when I instinctively drape my thigh over his waist, sinking more into his body.

He lets loose a satisfied hum when my body finally touches his from chest to knee, his hand diving beneath my sleep shirt to flatten against my lower back where his fingertips feather over my skin.

"Perfect," he mumbles into my hair, the arm he has beneath me tightening its curl around me, holding me as close as possible. "So fucking perfect, Mama."

I huff out some kind of agreement and settle into him, my nose buried in his neck.

Sleep threatens to claim me, and while I try my best to fight it, to keep enough consciousness that I can remember this in the morning, I feel myself slipping into the depths of unconsciousness.

*"God, I think you broke me, Anna."*

# Chapter Thirty-Nine

## TOBY

"**I**T'S BEEN five days."

I lean in the doorway of the bedroom and stare at the woman I'm basically frothing over with my arms crossed over my chest.

The arched brow thrown in my direction from the bed where Anna works looks almost as vicious as the wait has been.

*Pure torture.*

My hand has not been enough.

Drowning in her ocean scent all night, her body pressed into mine …

Absolute torment.

Do I plan on stopping?

*Hard no.*

"My balls are aching," I murmur and push off the door frame, stalking straight to her side. "Help me empty them."

Anna's face turns the same shade of red as a beet as she sputters out a laugh. "Jesus Christ, Jeffers. Insatiable much?"

I hum and hike a knee up on the mattress. "Always."

She just shakes her head and goes back to typing on the laptop taking up the space of her thighs. "We're heading home tonight. What do you plan to do then?"

Shrugging, I snag the computer, eliciting a gasp from the surprised workaholic, and toss it across the bed. "Sounds like a problem for later."

Lifting so I'm on the bed the rest of the way, I brace one hand on the comforter that smells just like her and wrap the other around her waist, dragging her under me.

"Jeffers," she yelps, the embarrassed redness to her cheeks fading into an aroused flush. "We have stuff we gotta do and I'm working!"

I hum through a gritted jaw and ignore her protests, dipping low so that my nose drags over the column of her throat.

Inhaling, I let the ocean of her claim me, swirl around inside of me until it's settled low in my gut. "Just means we gotta make the best of our time." My tongue darts out to taste the soft skin of her neck. "Not much time to christen the rest of the cabin."

"Toby," Anna half whimpers, half protests, but her hands are on me, gripping the fabric covering my torso. "Since when do you wear clothes?"

I chuckle. "Since someone had to clear the damned driveway."

Pushing up to my knees, I reach a hand back between my shoulder blades and grasp the shirt, pulling it over my head.

"That's better," Anna mutters before bolting upright, her hands back on me, her lips finding my pecs and leaving hot kisses in her wake.

"Huh," I rumble out and lick my lips when her teeth latch on to an already hard nipple. "Who's insatiable now?"

"Your fault," Anna growls out, her lips tracing their way across my chest.

"If you weren't so fucking sexy, I would've kept my hands to myself." I hiss when her teeth clamp down on my other nipple, the pain throbbing down to my hard dick.

"Right," she mumbles against my skin, her hands warm against my hips. "It wasn't because it was just convenient or anything."

I grip her shoulders, pushing her back down to the bed. Her startled stare finds me and my jaw ticks beneath my furrowed brow. "That's all you think this is? Convenience?"

She shrugs.

*Shrugs.*

The center of my chest pinches at her response as I stare down into her intense green eyes, glistening with concern.

*Isn't it, though?*

Pitching forward, I brace most of my weight on an arm, the rest of me settling between her thighs. I grind into her, my body too desperate to feel her feeling me. "You're not a simple convenience, Mama, fuck."

My lips find hers when she goes to speak, cutting her off as I claim her tongue with mine. She melts against me, her hips lifting to meet my grinds, the rest of her putty beneath me.

"That's it, Mama," I say when I pop my lips free and suck in air. "Feel what you do to me. How fucking hard you make me."

She whimpers, her nails digging into my back as my head hangs into the space between her shoulder and neck. "Need you."

"Yeah? Need me inside that wet cunt, do you, dirty girl?"

"*Yes.*"

I hum and free my dick. "Then touch me. Feel what you do to me, Anna."

Whimpering, the woman does as she's told and wraps a hand around my dick. My hips jut forward, a gasp ripping from my throat.

"God, you're so hard."

"Uh-huh," I breathe out as she strokes me, her grip the perfect amount of tug and tightness. "You're not the only one who needs something, Mama."

Anna snickers. "I think I like this."

A groaning snigger escapes me. "Torturing me?" I breathe into her neck. "Figured that out already."

"No." She sinks her teeth into my shoulder, and I hiss, "This."

I'm not prepared when she twists her wrist as she strokes me all the way to the base and back up, the nails of her free hand scoring into my back.

The duality of pain and pleasure leaves me throbbing in her palm.

"*Fuck*," I moan into her skin, my eyes rolling back. "Do that again and I'm gonna ruin this pretty little outfit with my cum."

Anna snorts. "Then back up so I can get my pants off."

Humming when she releases me, I flop onto my back beside her, my dick landing heavily against my abs. I drag in a breath, desperate to calm my racing heart.

"You're so big." I swear I feel her words in my dick, whispering over my skin and making it jump.

"Oh, fuck," I call out and nearly climb up the bed when she envelops me in the warmth of her mouth. The head of my cock hits the back of her throat, and I fist the sheets in a death grip to keep from blowing too fast. "Fuuuuck me."

Anna drags her tongue over me, coating me, and it takes every ounce of my restraint to let her taste me.

I'm covered in sweat, my jaw so tight I can feel my teeth protesting, when she finally sits back and stares down at me.

*Completely naked.*

"Fuck, you're so damn sexy." I'm gasping for air as she pats the pockets of the jeans still around my waist.

The grin she releases when she finds the foil pack and fishes it free is downright evil.

"Were you expecting I'd say yes, Jeffers?"

I don't get a chance to answer. Because she rips it open as she speaks and takes her sweet-ass time rolling the rubber down my shaft.

"Fuuuuck," I groan, my hands aching with how hard I hold onto the sheets. "Come sit on my face. It's my turn to taste that juicy cunt."

Anna blinks at me, her hands stilled on my dick. "What?"

I swear I see a flush cover her pretty face. "You heard me."

"Oh, no. I can't—"

I shoot upright so fast, I have to ignore the way my head spins. "You can. And you will." I cup her face in my palms and press my lips to hers. "Cover me in you, Mama. I'm dying for a taste."

Flopping back, I grab her hips when she remains still, working her body up my chest and over my shoulders. She comes to me slowly, carefully, but moves until she's hovering right over my chin, her knees on either side of my head.

I hum at the sight of her, spread open and so close to my tongue that I dart up to give her a teasing lick.

"Toby," Anna yelps, her chest fluttering with her racing breath.

"What?" I smirk when she stares at me with wild eyes.

"W-what if I smother you?"

I chuckle and run my tongue over my teeth, tasting the remnants of her sweet cunt clinging to my tastebuds. "I'd sooner drown in you."

Adjusting my grip to her hips, I pull Anna closer until she's seated over my lips. I suck the little bundle, and she bucks off me.

"Toby, I can't do this," she gasps out, those pink lips parted.

"Mama." I wait until her eyes collide with mine. "Sit. On. My. Fucking. Face."

Anna shudders. "O-okay."

She lowers all the way this time, that peachy ass planted on my chest, and I waste no time diving back in to lick and lap at her.

"*Oh God ... Toby*," she moans, her hands finding mine and latching on. *Fuck.*

The sight of her towering over me, her head tilted back and that long hair of hers teasing the tips of my fingers that dig into her hips, has both my dick and my chest throbbing. My pulse is through the roof when she shudders, her mewls releasing with each pass of my tongue, her breathy rasps calling my name with each swirl over her clit.

*God, she's fucking beautiful.*

I'm hard as steel when she arches her back, those perfect tits of hers pushing up into the air with peaked nipples, and I reach up to roll one between my roughened thumb and finger.

"T-Toby!"

It's enough to set her off, her orgasm coating my tongue as she rides out the wave with grinding hips and gasping moans.

I hum into her core, and she shudders, her body slumping.

"My turn," I growl into her, lifting her from my chest and planting her beside me. I roll on top of her and settle between her thighs, my dick achingly stiff.

"Wait," Anna breathes out, her hand flattening on my abs. "I wanna …" She licks her lips and sucks in a breath. "I want to be on top."

Quirking a brow, I grin. "Yes, ma'am."

I settle on my back, my hand finding hers and threading our fingers together.

I tell myself it's to help her to her knees. To assist her in getting back on top of me.

*It's nothing.*

But she doesn't release my grip when she climbs on top of me, her thighs spread over my hips, and she lowers that delicious cunt I can still taste over my pulsing dick.

"Anna," I growl out as she envelops me, her tightness stealing my breath almost as much as our joined hands going over my head where she braces herself. Her other hand finds my chest as she rides me, taking all of me.

*Consuming me.*

I feel her in my chest. In my bones. In each breath that gets me closer to that edge.

"Fuck, I'm not going to last."

I curl my entwined fingers around hers, my free hand going to her hip and guiding her movements when she shudders.

"Oh God," she whispers, her muscles tensing, her body pulsing over me. "I'm gonna—"

Her words cut off with a scream that rips from her chest, her cunt fluttering around me, her back arching.

I hold onto her, my grip keeping her hips close to mine as she grinds out her orgasm on me.

I couldn't stop mine if I tried.

It rips through me, devouring me to my core as I fill the condom.

"Fuck, Mama. Fuck."

My breath heaves, my vision of Anna blurred as she slumps over me.

"Same," she utters, and I glance down at her to find her cheek smooshed against my pec, right over my racing heart. Her lids are half closed, her fingernails scratching through the hair on my chest. "That was intense."

I chuckle, the sound deeper than normal. "I'll take that as a compliment."

"God, I love that."

I'm too far gone to put meaning to the words when I lazily trail my gaze from her lips to find her eyes already studying me. "What?"

"The way your voice sounds after—y'know."

"My sex voice?"

She nods, her hair rustling against my skin. "Yes, that. Keep saying the words."

I snort. "Weren't you the one giving me shit about having shit to do?"

"Doesn't matter right now."

"Okay." I chuckle and rest my hand against her smooth skin. "What do you want me to talk about then?"

She shrugs. "How about me?"

I aim a cocked brow at her. "You? What about you?"

"Say something … dirty."

*That's not at all what I was expecting.*

"I think someone's dick drunk."

"It's me. I'm someone," Anna says with the straightest face and I can't help the laugh that bubbles up.

"Okay, now I *know* you're intoxicated."

She pushes up, her red hair falling over her shoulder on one side, and I groan.

*Goddamn, she captivating.*

"So?"

Humming, I lift my torso until my chest meets hers and thread my fingers through her hair, tightening my grip at the base of her skull as I wrap my other arm around her waist. Our lips are only a breadth apart, her gasps feeding down my throat, my heated gaze colliding with her green one, my dick still buried inside her. "I could spend all night buried in this cunt." I flex my hips and capture her gasp against my lips. "And it *still* wouldn't be enough."

Her eyes roll as her body shivers in my arms. "Oh, crap," she mutters.

*"Toby … Anna!"*

Anna freezes, her eyes going wide, her lips barely moving as she squeaks, "Oh, no."

"Shit—" I lift Anna from my lap and roll from the bed, tucking my dick back into my pants as I go. "I'll hold him off." I swipe my shirt from the floor as I walk, my hands going through my hair once they're free.

The door snicks closed behind me as I hear my name again, the call of an irritated bodyguard echoing through the hallway.

*I'd recognize that tone anywhere.*

"Do you not know how to answer a fucking phone?"

I roll my eyes at the prickly man now towering in the kitchen, his coat and boots covered in snow.

I would say his hair, too, but the man has recently shaved it all off—to the scalp—where no snowflakes had a chance.

"Well fuck you, too," I mutter and blow past Lugh, straight to the stove.

*Anna's gonna need some hot chocolate for this mess.*

"Seriously, what have you been doing for the six hours it took me to get up here?"

I ignore the question, because mostly it's been me waiting for Anna. Clearing the driveway. And then fucking Anna. Playing some tunes to myself and watching another episode or two of that show she picked. Basically, just … wondering what the hell she's doing.

I start a pot on the stove, slowly heating the last of the milk while I fish the chocolates from the packaging.

"Since when do you cook?"

"I'm not cooking," I toss over my shoulder at the bodyguard as I shave small flakes off the little blocks and scrape them into the pot.

"Looks like it to me," he grunts, the thumping of his boots echoing as if receding from me, not coming closer.

My gut twinges when I register where he's going, my jaw clenching with the words that want to rush out of my face. Words I have no business thinking, let alone *feeling* straight to my tightened core.

Things like … *don't you dare go near her* and *if you see anything you shouldn't, you're losing an eye.*

I clear my throat and settle on a simple statement, growled just loud enough for him to hear. "I wouldn't do that."

"Why?"

*Good fucking question, Lugh.*

"She's a fucking savage when you interrupt her." *Open to interpretation* … Mentally, I pat myself on the back for not saying anything to the contrary.

"Well, if *she'd* answered her phone …" The man trails off, his insinuation clear, and that jaw clenching comes right back.

"She's been back there all day." *Not a lie.*

My back heats with his gaze and that twinge in my stomach becomes a full onset of nerves flipping the organ all over itself.

*Why does it feel like I've been caught with my hand in the cookie jar?*

*Oh, right. Because my face still smells like Anna's actual cookie.*

"Listen," Lugh starts, his gruff voice coming closer to me, easing the guilt and possessiveness threatening to build higher inside me, possibly even choke me until I figure out how to keep him from her. "I don't care what you two have been up to while you've been here. None of my business. But she's Leo's sanity."

*Is this going where I think it is? Is Lugh really about to hit me with* the *talk?*

"So, keep it to your fucking self," Lugh finishes.

*Almost went where I thought it would.*

"I like you better when you don't talk," I mutter on a sigh that I hope sounds irritated, while stirring my actual pot and not the metaphorical one at my back.

Grunting, he knocks on the bedroom door.

I hang my head on a strained neck, my utensil hand still steadily stirring with a grip too tight on the wooden spoon, and just wait.

I wait for the Jenga tower to come crumbling down around me, burying me in its blocks until there's no light left.

Life is officially going back to the way it was.

*Except, I'm not ready for it to.*

# Chapter Forty

## Anna

W HEN THE BODYGUARD STARTLED us by showing up to escort us home and essentially ruined any chance Toby and I had to discuss our … *situation*, I did not expect a whirlwind of crap to be waiting for me when I arrived.

Crap that Leo apparently forgot to mention each time the two of us ended up on the phone while I was stowed away in the mountains.

*Which was literally every day.*

He's still getting the cold shoulder from me for it, which is why he's staring bullets at the side of my head while I ignore him.

*Again.*

Keys tap on my laptop, my fingers stuttering over the emails I've been forwarded from my *oh-so-wonderful* boss that include so many inquiries that the band's schedule is about to be booked for the next two months straight if I agree.

*Which I don't.*

They need a break. Time to be with their growing families. Deal with their *affairs* before embarking on yet another tour, even if this one is strictly just to interview, record, and meet with fans.

There's a way to do this without burning them out, and I'm determined to figure that out, despite what my boss is demanding of me, and essentially, of them.

And I'm not thrilled about the idea of throwing Toby into the mix of this crazy schedule when we haven't had a chance to talk in the last three days, let alone *discuss* what his plans are with his sobriety.

Because while I know it shouldn't matter what my personal wishes are, and that this is all about the band as well as the individual, I need to see him. See how he's doing now that he's back in the same places that lead him to drink.

*Around with the same crew that enabled the demons without even knowing it.*

I need to know I can trust the man not to fly off the deep end without supervision.

*We won't talk about how in knots my stomach is over not seeing him with my own eyes. Nope, we don't need to talk about that.*

"How long do you plan to ignore me?"

Pushing back from the screen, I rub my eyes. "As long as it takes."

Leo heaves a hearty sigh and picks up his phone, the screen reflecting in the readers perched on his nose. "At least tell me what takeout you want."

I shake my head when he glances at me over the devices and stretch side to side, easing the tension in my neck that's built up from spending so much time leaning over this dang laptop.

"Seriously?" he huffs, the local delivery app illuminating the lenses. "Just give me something, Anna. I'll have it here in twenty minutes."

"Sounds more like a you problem to handle, boss." Closing the laptop, I push to my feet and stretch. "Unless you'd like to order my dinner for me and leave me alone with it."

He sighs and swipes away the app. "Fine. I'll send something up and be on my way." He closes his own computer and finally stands. Pops sound with each inch that he gains, finally stopping with an ache-filled groan off his lips. "Jesus, I'm too old for this leaning over laptop shit."

"Uh-huh," I mutter knowingly, my brow cocked in his direction.

"Don't start with the *I told ya so* BS."

"Oh, I wasn't. Your body was doing it for me. Just like the—" I gesture with a pointer to the readers still clinging to his nose. "Old man look you got going on."

Leo scoffs. "I'll have you know, some chicks think it's hot."

I snort out a laugh. "I'm sure they do."

He shakes his head and reaches for the readers in question with a small grin. "These guys are the culprit. They're aging me."

"I don't think it's *all* of them."

"I thought you were ignoring me. Can we go back to you ignoring me?"

"Sure. Now get out."

Leo chortles, nodding. "We definitely should stop using your apartment as an office."

"Yes. We should." He's still shaking his head when he lifts his bag to his shoulder and walks to the door.

"I'll send up Chinese," Leo mutters, the door open, his foot already cresting the hallway. "And have a good night."

"You, too, I guess," I call to his back. I catch his half wave flail into the air moments before the door closes behind him, finally shutting me in my own place.

It's the first time in months I've been *alone* alone, without a ringing phone in my palm or a looming bossy presence taking up my couch.

The sudden silence feels almost … eerie.

Void of clanging dishes I'd end up rewashing, TV show reruns over the crackling fire, or the soft strums of a guitar.

It's too quiet.

One would think, after dealing with Toby and working endlessly, I'd want a piece of the quiet life. That I'd be dying for the peace and complete lack of continued auditory stimulation.

But tonight … it just feels empty. Hollow.

Looking around my studio apartment, with all its tall ceilings and exposed brick walls, I feel more lost than ever.

*It's so quiet that it's* loud.

There's a small voice tickling the back of my brain, telling me to pick up my phone and dial a particular bassist's number, even if it's just to see what he's been up to.

Wheeling around, I locate the device sitting silent on the arm of the couch and nibble at my bottom lip.

*Did he eat anything?*

Nonsense. I'm not the man's keeper. He can take care of himself.

*But would he come over?*

I shake my head because why would Toby Jeffers want to come over to my apartment? Why should I care what he's doing? He's back home, with his band, and probably raising Cain in all kinds of ways that I'm going to have to deal with in the morning.

Maybe it would be best to check in, at least …

*Does he miss me?*

My eyes go wide as I suck in a breath.

"What am I doing?" I ask aloud and shudder against the chill raking over my own skin, the idea absolutely ludicrous.

I do not do this. I do not chase after anyone that does not wish to be caught.

I do not fawn over men with baggage bigger than their equipment, and I especially don't violate my own rules by sleeping with anyone I work with.

*Except you already did that, Anna.*

I growl into the open space and abandon the phone for the fresh linens in my bedroom. I slip into my pajamas, the comfy, stretchy kind, and stomp my way to the fridge in my open concept kitchen. It reminds me too much of the cabin with how easily I can see my couch from the counter, the breakfast bar the only thing separating me from the furniture.

I release my frustration with another audible sound and toss the water bottle onto the counter.

*Wine. I need wine.*

With stiff fingers, I retrieve the bottle and opt to skip the glass for drinking straight from the bottle. After the first long pull, I stare at the liquid swishing around inside, leaving long legs of droplets down the smooth surface.

Liquid I've now contaminated by drinking straight from the source without a single second thought.

*Who am I?*

Counting my shaky breaths, I walk to the sink and tip the bottle until the red splashes against the metal and swirls its way down the drain.

*I have no idea who I am and I don't know when that happened.*

Retrieving the backup wine I've had in the cabinet just as long, I uncork the bottle. It, too, finds its way to the sink where I empty the contents down the drain.

I'm elbows deep into scrubbing the sink clean with a prickling to the backs of my eyes when the beeping of my phone breaks the unbearable silence.

A wave of relief washes over me as I scurry across the tile to the device, my thoughts finally silenced.

But then the name flashing across the screen twists my stomach up so tight I'm pretty sure I'm going to see that drink of wine all over again.

I swipe to answer with shaking fingers, my heart in my throat. "Hello?"

"Anna? It's Denver."

*Oh, God, please no.*

"I'm gonna need you guys to come get him. I don't wanna have to blacklist him from my bar."

"O-okay," I mutter from under the weight pressing my chest in, threatening to cave in on me. "I'll call one of the guys."

"Uh-uh. He's asking for *you*."

# Chapter Forty-One

## Anna

PEOPLE TOTING CAMERAS BIGGER than my torso line the street, their vans and tinted cars taking up the majority of the parking, including stopping in the middle of the road.

Lights dance across the night sky, each flash attempting to catch a crazed rock star in the act, the moment that it happens.

*This is a whole freaking mess.*

I would have been here a few minutes earlier, if it wasn't for throwing up.

*This can't be. Not already.*

The denial is the only thing keeping my feet moving as I slink passed the lenses as big as my head and sneak down the alley to the back of the bar Toby's known to frequent.

*I've been here before.*

Too many times have I gotten the same call, and yet this one stings so bad that I'm sick over it. After all the work he did at the cabin, talking about his demon, and asking for the help.

All the days he spent without taking a single drop.

Kicking the withdrawals so quickly . . .

*Did he just use me to forget?*

Shivering from more than just the cold, I hug my coat closer and prepare to pound a fist against the metal in hopes of being heard over the thumping music echoing from inside.

*Was he even sober?*

The thought jars me, freezing me in my spot with my hand lifted, and I blink the burn of tears threatening my eyes.

"Anna? I've been trying to call you." *When did Denver open the door?* "He took off. I didn't want to draw attention, so I didn't watch where he went."

My head hangs, and my fist falls limp at my side.

"I'm so sorry about this, Denver," I breathe because anything else feels like it'll just push me over the edge of the pending breakdown. "How bad was it?"

The man's feet shuffle in my line of sight, his hesitance drawing my attention to his pinched brow and knowing eyes. "Bad, Anna. He was real bad."

"Thanks for calling me."

"Listen," Denver says and holds out a hand to stop me from advancing, "I'd send someone with you, but my guys are barely keeping the door up. Do you want me to call someone?"

Sighing, my shoulders pitched inward, I nod. "Give Lugh a heads up, please. I have a feeling I'm going to need the hand."

"Sure thing." Denver steps away from me, his body half inside his bar before he speaks again. "I would check the liquor store just two blocks down."

Again, I nod, my voice quaking before it even rises up my throat to form the words that come out next. "If you see him again, Den, call the cops."

*I don't know what else to do.*

He nods solemnly, his clean-shaven jaw ticking with the severity. "Yes, ma'am."

I don't wait for him to go back inside before I move down the street and locate the store he'd mentioned.

I'm not even to the front of the barred windows and I know he's here.

Because all I hear is yelling … glass shattering …

And I'm *angry*. Vibrating with the lead in my veins as my rage flows easily through my system.

The storefront is lined with more cameras. Phones and tablets aimed at the chaos going on inside.

*There's no way out of this now.*

So I run in, headfirst.

And what I find, amidst the chaos of destroyed bottles and tipped over displays, is the last thing I ever wanted to see.

# Chapter Forty-Two

## TOBY

Somewhere between meeting up with the guys and now, I've managed to acquire a four-ton anvil that's parked itself right on my head.

While someone uses it to do blacksmithing.

Because all I hear is *ting ting ting* and all I feel is the reverberation of each hit inside my skull.

"Ugh," I mumble, a mouth full of sand, eyes too heavy to open.

*Maybe five more minutes …*

The surface my face nuzzles against is cold and hard, but my limbs feel too heavy to do anything about it. In fact, I'm certain my hip bone is bruising with just the weight of me pressing into the unforgiving rigidity beneath me.

*The cool feels nice.*

And as long as I focus on the smooth chill my cheek is pressed against, the longer the *why* takes to settle in.

*Who knows why I'm on the floor?*

*Not me.*

Unlike most people, I actually enjoy waking up disoriented.

It's like I get to go on the adventure all over again, rediscovering all the things I got up to before I passed out, possibly even doing them all over again later—but for the *second* first time.

*First time experiences are cool.*

It feels like a rift in time that only I have the power to redo.

*Some superpower, huh?*

If only it would stick around long enough to combat the fact that I *do* know why I'm on the floor, and I recall exactly what put me here.

*Traitors.*

# Chapter Forty-Three

## Anna

THE PROBLEM WITH EXPERIENCING the highs of life while under the influence is that there's always a dangerous *low*.

Even without having to imbibe to get through the day, life has its way of throwing you to the wolves, only to bring you back again.

Except, you never know how far, until it's so bad that you find yourself trapped in a room full of people that helped you get there ... only for them to say you've gone too far.

*That they want a backup for your position.*

Looking around the room now, at all the downturned faces and solemn glances while we wait for the man of the hour to finally wake up from his bender, I gnaw at my bottom lip and send a prayer out to the universe that an intervention is the right answer for Toby.

It'll be better for him in the long run, I know this.

*But will he hate me for it?*

Part II

"The journey of a thousand miles begins with one step."
—Lao Tzu

Seven weeks later

# Chapter Forty-Four

## Leo

"A NNA," I DRAWL INTO the phone that has become even more of a permanent fixture to the side of my head than my five-o'clock shadow and grin. "This working remote shit has gotta stop. You're killing me."

Her scoff echoes over the speaker, and I snicker.

"If *you* hadn't sent me up here to get you more crap for *your* label, we wouldn't have to deal with this now, would we?"

Shaking my head, I bite back the snort from her snark and sigh. "No, I suppose not."

I wait a beat, the levity a nice break from the seemingly constant turn of negativity that's been dumped on us, and then ask her the question I already know the answer to. The reason I called her to begin with.

*Good news first.*

"So didja get 'em?"

"You know I did."

"Hot dayum," I call out and throw a fist into the air. "Communications Officer *and* Signing Agent. I fucking knew they wouldn't say no to you, ma'am."

"I am not old enough to be a ma'am. Can you not?"

I snort and relax back into the couch cushion, my feet kicking up onto the coffee table next to my to-go cup. "I'm telling you. Age gap is all the rage now."

Anna mutters something unintelligible into the phone, but I can't even begin to make it out over the laugh I'm desperately holding in.

"Some of us are considered *seasoned*."

"Wow," she deadpans, unimpressed. "Did you need those readers perched on your nose to tell you that one?"

I don't bother holding back the laugh on that one. "How'd you know?"

"Because you are old, Leo."

I reach for the coffee cup and take a sip. It's still lukewarm enough and hits just right.

"I'm just glad for some fucking good news for once," I mumble against the plastic lid and the dead silence that greets me has my stomach dropping.

"So you haven't heard then?"

Returning the cup to the table, I run a thumb beneath my nose and purse my lips. *Because that's the* other *reason I had to call.* "I … have, actually."

*Guess it's bad news time.*

"And it's not good news." Anna doesn't even have to ask to know. She's already sighing a breath of defeat over the line.

"He's not ready to come home yet, Anna."

A sound that's awfully familiar to a broken heart fills the line only moments before she covers it up with a clearing of her throat.

*She thinks I don't know, but I do.*

"As long as he's getting what he needs," she mutters, but it's forced. Just as it was the last time I told her that Toby opted to sign himself up for another program at the rehab clinic he was court-ordered to attend.

He was only supposed to be gone a week. Get a detox. Come home.

The man fought us tooth and fucking nail the entire way there, to the point where his mug ended up on the front page of the tabloids for being a drunk on his way to rehab.

*Least creative headline ever.*

But as of this morning, he's enrolled himself in the facility's most immersive program available.

"How long?"

"Ninety days."

For so long, I thought Toby was just like the rest of us. Having a drink, a good fucking time, no big deal.

I *still* don't know all the demons that hide in his closet, possibly never will, but if I'd been able to put two and two together without Anna having to basically threaten me to see it …

It took her breaking down in front of me while holding a phone that played yet another viral video of our dearest troublemaker destroying the inside of a liquor store with his bare hands and only little Anna there to stop him.

*I'm still raw from it all.*

That the biggest demon hiding in one of my best friend's closet was alcoholism.

*And I had no fucking clue.*

In fact, I *encouraged* the shit on more than one occasion. And for that, I don't know if I'll ever forgive *myself*, let alone ask for Toby's forgiveness.

*I know I don't deserve it.*

So when the man from the clinic that's sponsoring Toby called and gave me the news … I knew the only option I had was to agree.

*Give him what he needs.*

"That's … a long time."

Clearing the lump from my throat, I blink a few times to break myself out of my thoughts and come back to the phone. "Yeah. The guy said he was going to email me the itinerary for the program. I guess they have already mapped out a few things."

"That's … good …" Anna breathes into the phone, barely audible.

I sigh and switch the phone to my other ear. "I know it sucks, Anna. You don't have to pretend with me."

"I'm not," she shoots back quietly, but I hear the sniffle on her end of the line. "Not pretending. His healing is his and I want him to get better. Whatever that means."

"Even if it means he never comes back home?" The question coming from my own lips engages an ache so deep, I feel it in my soul.

*I hope that's not the case.*

"That's … up to him to decide. Not any of us. And definitely not me."

"He's going to get better, Anna."

Her scoff feels like a gut punch.

"Things have to change, Leo." She all but sobs into the phone. "*You* have to change. Or he'll never make it out alive."

"I know. Fuck, I know." I scrub my hand over my face. "I already talked to the guys. As soon as he's willing, we're all going to see him. And they've all promised to be there for him after."

"No, not just them. *You.* He looks to you most of all." The weight I was already feeling doubles. "*You* need to do better."

"I … I know."

I sheltered him too long. Out of guilt and shame. Partly because of fear and wholly because I care.

But I ignored the things right in front of my face because it was easier than accepting that any one of the men I protect on a daily basis was still hurting.

*Still breaking.*

Chasing the fix over and over again.

I see it now.

And I have a lifetime of regret to go right along with it.

# Chapter Forty-Five

## TOBY

"How have you been today, Toby?"

"Tired," I grunt and fall back into the couch that's supposed to be comfy and inviting, but it's almost as stiff as the doc watching me over her glasses. She's so prim and proper that it reminds me of Anna, and now, I'm just angry. "Pissed."

She nods, her pen perched between her fingers, hovering just above her notepad like she might need to record something at any moment. That's what I've learned since coming to rehab: they like to listen to you talk, only to write down every damn word.

And everyone has a solution to every problem you bring up.

Even if they *aren't* certified in whatever brain degree is required to therapize someone.

"How have the cravings been?"

I snort. "I don't feel shit, Doc. Other than tired and pissed. Like I said."

"That's fair," she scribbles on her page, her eyes finding me once again. "And more than likely the medication you were put on when you arrived."

"You mean the drugs they gave me to stop wanting drugs? Sure."

Still doesn't make much sense to me, but I guess the dosage can be reduced in two weeks. Then again two weeks from that until I'm completely sober for the remaining time I'm here. It was a temporary fix to the extreme condition I showed up in, or something like that.

*And I thought alcohol made me numb until I started smashing shit.*

I'll be glad to have my head back. This shit just feels weird.

And not the good kind of weird, the high kind of weird.

Just … wonky.

*Quiet.*

Because while my mind's been silent for the first time in over a decade … my heart has started screaming in its place.

*Aching* after all the mistakes I've made. Demanding I accept the beating for all the wrongs I've done.

*Like surviving the night my dad died.*

*Destroying that liquor store.*

*Ruining my best friend's lives.*

*Getting fucking arrested.*

*Lying to the one person that's realized how deeply fucked I really am …*

"It didn't feel like a lie then. It felt like I was doing my own thing, dealing with myself all damn day long while she kept herself locked away in the castle."

"And this would be Anna, right?"

Startled, I shake my head and blink at the doc. "I said that out loud?"

She nods, jots something down, then crosses her ankles next to the leg of her chair. She's wearing one of those skirts that get smaller around her knees, just like some of the ones Anna wears.

It's even beige and now I'm digging the heel of my palm into my aching chest.

"Yeah. I …" I sigh and lick my cracked lips. "I tried quitting then. At the cabin."

"But you didn't?"

My hand goes to my hair and my fingers stutter against the missing length, the shorter strands slipping through.

*Will Anna like it?*

I clear the lump building in my throat and shake my head.

It's not gonna matter if she likes my hair.

"When you first walked in, you said you were pissed?" My gaze shoots to the doc, my brow raised at her flippant ability to curse. "Tell me why."

"Well, first, I need to get over the p-bomb you just dropped, Doc."

The woman snickers and returns a lifted brow. "You think because I'm on this side of the chair that I don't understand the language?"

"Just surprised is all. I wasn't expecting that."

"Well? Why do you feel that way?"

Pulling in a deep breath even though my ribs feel like they're toting around bone-deep bruises, I run a hand down my face. "It's hard to explain."

The doc is quiet for a moment, her gaze on me expectantly as I work through the feeling in my head.

"I'm pissed that I made it." I sigh, staring at the ugly rug between us. "I'm pissed that my *family* hasn't come to see me." I gnaw at the fleshy inside of my cheek for a beat. "And I'm more mad at myself."

"Is it really anger that you're feeling towards your family?"

The way she says it, the way she says *family* like it's an absolute and not a question … it lands like another hit to my tender ribs.

"No … because it's really my fault."

"Toby, none of this is your fault."

"No, I know—that's not what I meant." I sigh, dragging another hand down my face, the stubble scratching against my skin. "I did choose this. So it is my fault, but that's not what I meant when I said the thing about my family seeing me."

"Okay, so explain."

The truth is another jab against my rib cage. "I never filled out the release forms for them. I never agreed that they could."

The doc waits, her pen hand hovering over her notepad, forever at the ready. "And why not?"

"Because I … I don't trust …" The words get caught in my throat, the weight of them so damn heavy. Weighing me down in the ocean of uncertainty and shame.

"Toby, if anyone in your life is a means for trouble, there are other ways to get help."

I shake my head. "No, they aren't the trouble. They just didn't know. Hell, *I* didn't know until I fucked it all up."

"That you were addicted to alcohol."

The bluntness of the truth nearly knocks the wind out of me. "Jesus, Doc, way to go for the jugular."

"It's the truth, is it not? The sooner the truth is accepted, the sooner you can accept the steps needed to leave it in the past. Let go of the baggage, if you will."

This session is easily becoming the most draining.

I don't think my heart can take more pummeling.

"Who don't you trust, then, Toby?"

"*Myself.*"

And there goes that pen again, flying over the lines of her page and documenting the moment that I accepted myself as the problem, even though I feel like I'm dying on the inside.

"Care to explain?" The cap of her pen taps the doc's lower lip and perches there, her gaze searching me.

"I caused a lot of headache in my lifetime, Doc. For a lot of people. My choices. *Me.*" I don't realize my arm has raised until my thumb is jamming into my own chest. "*I* lied and *I* trashed that store and *I* made everyone else clean it all up. I may have even fucked that girl, and I don't *remember.*"

"Did you?" Doc asks with a raise to her brow as her only reaction to my words.

"No."

"Toby, the choices we make while under the influence are not always our own. Any choices we make, whether sober or not, don't have to define us, either. It's up to you and you alone, on how you want to be perceived." She glances at her paper, only to toss it to the side as she leans forward, bracing her elbows to her crossed knees. "How would you define yourself now? Without the press in your face, no brothers calling the shots, no expectations for you as a public figure. Tell me … who is Toby Jeffers without the fame?"

I purse my lips, and blink at the doc's manicured hands. They're smooth, and yet too tan, with a bold color tinting her nails, several rings lining her fingers.

Somehow … it just looks weird.

"I'm not … really sure."

"Who do you *want* to be?" doc presses, leaning closer still, her top showing just enough non-freckled chest that I catch a glimpse of a necklace and avert my eyes.

"I want to be a guitar player. I want to be at peace. I want to live a life my pops would be proud of … and I want …" I trail off, that pain sinking deeper in my chest, its aching almost unbearable as I consider the real answers to the questions I never wanted to ask myself. Yet here I am, being asked them anyways, because I lived that day and my pops didn't. I kept on breathing every damn day after, even though it felt like my lungs stopped and my heart gave up, just like his.

I went and made a fucking life without even realizing it, only to fuck most of it up along the way.

*No, that's not entirely true.*

I didn't entirely *choose* this life I got. It's the one I always wanted—at least, it feels like it's close to it—but it's so damn *empty*.

Lonely and isolating.

Trailing the gales of my chosen brothers while someone else made the calls on what we did next. Where we went. Who and how and why was up to everyone except me, because I was too out of it to decide.

*Until Anna showed up.*

"I want to trust." The words are barely a broken whisper, their magnitude settling in my scratched throat. "And I want to *be* trusted."

The doc nods somewhere in my periphery, but I'm too stuck on staring at the wall instead of looking her in the eye. It makes it too real if I do.

"What's the first building block of trust, Toby?"

The question is supposed to be rhetorical, I think, but the word leaves my lips on a shattered pain-filled sound anyways. "*Honesty*."

With that word, that realization, comes the flash of a face. One lined with wavy red hair and filled with enough anguish to last a lifetime.

*Will she ever forgive me?*

Six weeks later

# Chapter Forty-Six

## *Toby*

"LAST DOSE, MR. JEFFERS."

I accept the tiny cup with the little pill inside with a cock to my brow as I swallow it dry. "I thought I had another two weeks on this shit?"

The nurse smiles at me. "Doc said to make this it. Says so in your chart."

*Huh. I guess that's good news.*

"And don't forget," the nurse continues as she fiddles with things around the room, going about her normal checks to make sure no sharp objects or substances have been stashed. "Group was moved to the next morning for you."

I nod.

"I'm so excited for you," she continues, oblivious to my internal turmoil, replacing the throw pillows on the little couch in the corner and dusting off the cushion with her palm. "You have family coming for the first time tonight! How long has it been?"

Sighing, I run a hand down my face, the fingers itching to grow back the length that's been trimmed down. "Thirteen weeks."

"Wow." The nurse straightens, her eyes wandering over the space of my room, still in search of something out of place, something that might cause alarm, before finally settling on me. "That's a long time. Only a few more to go, though." She nods with a smile, as if reassuring me, though it doesn't settle the nerves battling their way through my stomach.

*These meds fucking suck.*

"Five weeks, six days, and ten hours. Give or take."

"Not that you're counting." The nurse snickers, but nods knowingly. "Well, I'm off. Let me know if you need anything."

A simple jut of my chin sends her on her way, leaving me alone with my thoughts for the next few hours.

I could have gone down to the game hall, got lost in some gaming system, or a movie playing on the projector, but my nerves keep me planted in my safe space.

Here, I'm surrounded by muted colors. Easy textures. A room that looks similar to many a hotel suite—minus the extravagancies—that I would have destroyed in the past for being just too damn … bland.

*Like the singular painting hanging on the wall above the bed that looks an awful lot like the view of the cabin from down the mountain.*

That one little painting almost didn't make it when the staff led me to this room, convincing me to sleep beneath it each night like it wasn't a sordid reminder of all the things I'd done wrong.

An exact replica of the place I'd fucked up the worst.

*All the lies I told.*

"Toby?"

I turn away from the painting at the sound of the knock accompanying my name, and square my shoulders. "Hey, Lugh, are they here?"

Nodding curtly, he steps back and closes the door once again, granting me a moment of reprieve.

When I got here, Lugh was not my first choice to be the one sticking around. I would have rather he left along with the rest of them, leaving me to rot here alone, and in peace.

But that's the thing about being a rock star. You never really get to be alone once everyone knows your name.

Even some of the patrons here knew me, not to mention the staff, and my anonymity flew out the window on the second day.

I guess having the bodyguard not too far away wasn't such a bad idea, after all.

Whoever decided that should get a fucking medal, and I'd bet my ass I knew who it was, too.

The second knock on the door has my head snapping up and my jaw clenching, my fingers trembling.

*Showtime.*

Steeling myself, I roll my shoulders back and reach for the door.

It's been weeks since I've seen any of the men I call brothers. The guys I talk about with the doc. Months since I spoke to any one of them.

I know it'll take a lot on both our parts, but they're all I've got left.

The walk to the main house where visitors are allowed is long and winding, but lined with plants coming to life and a few clients of the facility that prefer to stare.

I used to think they watched me walk along the path because they *knew.* Because they could see my addiction painted on my face, and in my gait, and there was never a time where anyone would look at me and think anything different.

*I'm just an addict. An alcoholic. A man with a problem.*

*A liar and a fool.*

*A man without a father.*

But now … their eyes avert out of wonder instead of fear.

*All they ever saw was a rock star in their midst.*

A rock star with a rather large and imposing shadow that followed everywhere I went.

*Thanks, Lugh.*

Tossing a glance at the man looming just behind me, I smile.

"Quit looking at me like that," Lugh murmurs, keeping his sights trained ahead.

"Like what?" I spin toward him, my feet carrying me backward along the path I could walk blindfolded.

"Like you're about to say some shit that's nice or something. It's weird."

I snort and spin back around, my muscles stiffening as the main house comes into view. "Fine, I'll bottle that up with the rest of my bullshit."

"Tell your bandmates that shit. Not me. I'm just here for a paycheck."

"Liar."

A grunt rumbles out of my bodyguard.

My heart pounds in my chest as we reach the stoop of the main house, and I swear I feel like I'm about to puke with the nerves that only resemble those I got before I walked on stage for the first time.

*Weeks.*

*Months.*

It might as well be years since I've been in front of anyone from my band. My friends.

*My unknowing enablers.*

I nearly stumble when Lugh pushes me into the building and rests a directing, but reassuring, hand on my shoulder.

I force a breath just before we enter the visitor room, my hands set on vibrating out the anxiety flowing through me as he keeps me walking

Straight to the tables set up for just this occasion, with only one body taking up space.

One set of shoulders.

One head of perfectly styled blonde hair.

My heart sinks.

With a desperate gaze darting around the room, I lift up on my toes to see the window in the door that leads to the outside of this place, only to come up empty.

*I was expecting all of them.*

"*Toby …*"

The air of the room thickens when my band manager stands and offers a hand in greeting.

It's not the handshake I leave hanging that has my stomach prepping to evacuate once again.

No.

It's the sadness in his normally brilliant blue eyes. The band tee in place of his pressed button-up. The five-o'clock shadow highlighting his jawline. The knowing way his mouth *doesn't* lift in a grin at the sight of me.

Leo's hand drops back to his side. "I'm so glad your sponsor called me, man. It's been too fucking long."

I nod with a clench to my jaw and a flare to my nostrils as a wave of anger settles itself into my blood like it's in for the long haul.

*Doc was right.*

Because while I'm pissed the rest of the crew isn't here, I'm even more angry at the man standing in front of me.

As if he can sense the change in me, he hangs his head.

"I'm sorry, Toby. I'm so fucking sorry. I had no idea." His blonde head shakes, some of the pieces of hair falling loose around his forehead. "I should've known and I didn't."

I know I need to say something to the man, but instead of rushing the words, I busy myself by pulling out the chair across from him and plopping my ass in it.

"No one is being replaced. In the band," Leo continues as he sinks into the seat across from me. "That's not at all what I was going for when the guys brought it up all those months ago."

"Then what were you going for?" The sound of my voice seems to shock him, and to be honest, it comes out pretty thick, even to my own ears.

"I … I wanted everyone to have a touring backup. It was about burnout and the media. After all the shit we've all been through, I wanted to make sure that each of you could get a break when you needed it."

"Like this?" I cock a brow and gesture around us. "Having to send one of us to rehab?"

His gaze sharpens, his shoulders squaring. But the voice that responds is anything but angry.

"If this isn't what you need, then tell me."

I shake my head. "You made the decision. You and whoever else, while I was out, to add more people to the band. To our *family*. And didn't bother to tell me you were even thinking about it. Just like *you* decided to medicate me when I was too weak to make the decision myself."

Leo's torso slams back in his seat like I gut punched him.

A thick silence falls around us, and I would swear I could see the bags under his eyes darken in that moment, just as I feel my stomach drop against the weight of the words.

It hurts. So damn much. And yet, it needed to be said.

*Honesty.*

"I know that now," he mutters, that icy gaze slamming to mine and refusing to leave. "I made a mistake. Actually, quite a few. And I know that an apology will only go so far. So instead of saying *I'm sorry* again"—Leo's throat bobs with a swallow before he leans forward, bracing his forearms on the table—"I'll ask for your forgiveness and hope that I can actually earn it someday."

A lump forms in my throat at his declaration, and I nod.

*I don't want to be mad at him forever.*

*I don't want to be mad at them at all.*

*I just want my family back.*
"Let's go for a walk."

# Chapter Forty-Seven

## TOBY

Dusk has quickly given way to night since I walked the path to find Leo waiting for me, an apology at the ready for his transgressions.

I know he means it.

And I believe him, believe that he's sorry for his part in things. Just like I am.

"I'm sorry, too, Le," I mutter into the cooling nighttime air, my steps slow along the path, one of my best friends keeping pace at my side.

"You're here. You're getting help. That's what matters, Toby."

I nod, my fists shoved in the pockets of my leather jacket, my anger vacating my veins like a cleanse of all the bad shit between us with each pull of fresh air in my lungs.

"So what have I missed?" I ask, desperate for a change of subject, ready to move on from the heartfelt shit that's making my already broken chest ache. "Where is everyone?"

Leo sniffs, his head bouncing on a nod as if accepting the conversation between us is what it is. "Well, we've got fan events and shit lined up once you're sprung from here. Shows if you're up for it."

"That's always what's up." I give a snicker. "I didn't miss that shit. What's up with the guys?"

He snorts. "Well, Mac came with me. Fin and Rex'll be in sometime tomorrow. I thought it would be best to go slow with them."

Some of that weight lifts off my chest. "So they didn't avoid me like the plague. Cool."

A laugh bubbles up out of Leo's mouth, and I have to admit … it feels good to be the source of someone laughing for a change.

Leo shakes his head, a small grin lightening his features. "Didn't wanna throw the whole pot at the wall, just to see what stuck. We know shit has to change and we're all in."

"I don't want things to change for you guys."

"We're not the same guys we were when we first started this, Toby. Rex has a fucking family now. Shit, Fin's got a partner." He says the last word like it tastes weird on his tongue, but he's still got a lift to the corner of his mouth. "We're not teenagers anymore. It's time we act like it. Starting with having backups for *all* parts of the band. Being adults. Making big boy decisions."

"What about you?" I ask, my heart too hopeful that he'll include Anna in his answer, because asking outright just feels too raw. Too much.

*Too soon.*

"Actually," Leo sighs heavily, his boots kicking at a pebble along the path. "I've gotta find some hands."

I bob my head, silently encouraging him to continue.

*Does that include Anna? Is she getting some hands, too?*

"Things are delicate right now," Leo continues. "We've had events cancelled because of the rumors around you being noticeably absent to the point that As Above has gone completely radio silent. There's been a lot of damage control to keep names out of the media as much as possible." My jaw grits, knowing that's all my doing yet again. *Anna's gotta be so pissed.* "And then Anna gave me her three months' notice."

*There it is.*

*The shoe.*

Leo's too busy kicking that little pebble along the path to notice my head whipping in his direction, my breath sticking in my throat. "How long ago was that?"

"Two fucking months ago," Leo murmurs, shoulders sagging inward.

If this were a movie, this would be the moment that the scenery around me suddenly becomes never ending, and Leo would fade into the dark laughing mass that floats about and triggers terror in the viewer. Where the lead realizes that what they knew to be real, in fact, wasn't.

*Reality as I know it has changed. Again.*

At least, that's how it feels when my heart pounds on an irregular rhythm behind my ribs, threatening to crack out of its prison for good.

My muscles tense.

My mind reels.

"No. She can't," I choke, barely above a whisper, filled with the desperation I feel down to my bones.

I bite off the rest of the words lashing at my tongue, begging to be said aloud for anyone to hear. I keep in the phrases that might damn us. The ones that broke open my scars, only to become my sole motivation for sticking it out here.

Because loving her is the only truth I've believed in.

And if she's not part of the band, part of the crew, then … I'd never have my chance to tell her. To show her. Have her by my side. To make up for all the fucked up things I put her through.

*After the look on her face that night … I can't ask her to sacrifice another moment for me.*

"Leo, do not let her go until I get out of here." I grab his shoulder, stopping him. "Promise me you won't let her leave us yet."

He shakes his head. "I've tried everything I can think of, man. She's still convinced."

"Not good enough." I give him a squeeze, dipping to make sure his defeated sight meets the conviction in mine. "Tell her …" I lick my lips. "Tell her I need her to try. To stay."

His eyes shine with an intensity that throws me off, almost as much as his next words do.

"Why don't *you* tell her."

"What?" His suggestion jolts me.

"Call her," Leo mutters, his gaze darting between mine, his lips set in a firm line. "I know you needed time to screw your head back on, but please, talk to her before we all lose her."

"I'm not … wait—*how?*"

Leo shakes his head, more of his blond locks falling around his forehead. "I didn't know it was two-sided, Toby. Not until right fucking now."

I huff, my hands dropping back to my sides, another wave of guilt rushing over me that has me pacing along the path next to him. "Shit."

"Here," Leo interrupts, and I spin to find his phone held out. "It's already dialing. Might as well take it."

I snag the device the moment the call connects, stepping just far enough away from him to get some privacy.

"Leo, I swear to freaking God, if you're calling me just to tell me about your trip, I'm gonna commit murder. You'll be victim number one."

The sound of Anna's voice has my lungs inflating for what feels like the first time in months.

"Murder, Leo. Freaking Murder."

I chuckle darkly, and the line goes silent.

# Chapter Forty-Eight

## Anna

The silence that greets me is so unexpected that I feel like I can't move. I can't breathe. I can't speak.

If I do, then this becomes real, and reality and I aren't on speaking terms right now.

*No way.*

I would recognize that sound, that husky chuckle almost anywhere, even if it hadn't shot straight to my groin and made my heart ache simultaneously the second it came over the line.

*But it can't be…..*

No. It *won't* be is more appropriate, because I will not fall into the trap all over again. I will not dive headfirst into the emotional damage set to take me out. I won't fall prey to the antics of a spoiled and damaged rock star.

"Hey, Mama."

And when he breathes that crap over the line—clear, sultry, and sober—my poor heart *weeps*.

"Toby," I breathe out on a weighted whisper, my middle all twisted up. Torn between what I want and what I know that I need. "I—"

"Stay."

That one word could have enough power over me had he uttered them months ago. Before I put myself through the hell of finally shutting out every piece of me that wants him. Misses him.

But the *way* he says it into the phone …

Like it's everything he could need wrapped up in one giant pleading demand.

*For me.*

"I can't," I mumble into the phone, the backs of my eyes burning.

"Try."

I swallow.

"For me, Anna."

I choke back a sob.

"*Please.*"

Breath ragged, heart pounding—yet somehow breaking at the same time—I lick my dried lips and switch my grip on the phone.

"Toby, I'm sorry, but … I can't."

"Anna, please don't walk away. Not yet."

Biting my lip, I swipe away at the tears staining my lashes. "Why not?"

"I … There's so fucking much I wanna say to you, baby, but I didn't wanna do it over the phone like this." I hear rustling, like maybe he's shaking his head. "I had this whole fucking plan …" His voice muffles, thickens. "I'm sorry, Anna. I'm sorry for all the bullshit I put you through. Especially the shit you don't know about. And I swear I'm gonna say all this again to your face as soon as I see it. Just, please, wait five more weeks."

"It's more than five weeks, Toby." I sniffle.

"Five weeks, five days, fourteen hours. I promise, I'm counting them by the second."

"It's not that simple. It will never be that simple."

"Why not?

His question, loaded and aimed right for where I'm weakest for the man, has me hanging my head. "Toby, I've seen what substance abuse does to people."

"I know—"

"You *don't*," I cut in, more gusto to my voice than I thought I could muster. "You have no clue what happens *after*."

"Then tell me," Toby begs into the receiver. "You never talk about yourself unless it's negative and maybe if I know what you know, I can make sure it doesn't happen."

"No."

Another stretch of silence falls over the line.

Until finally, he asks the right question. The one I don't want to have to answer, but I'm going to.

"No to what?"

Dragging in a deep breath, despite the splintering of my heart, I say what needs to be said.

"No to this, Toby. No to you and I hooking up. It shouldn't have happened to begin with."

*Because to him, that's all it was between us, anyway.*

"Fine."

One word. Smashed into a single quip rolling off Toby's talented tongue and my heart splinters a little more.

"Right. Okay, then. Good talk."

With a shake to my hands and a grit to my jaw, I force back the emotion building behind my eyes and pull the phone away from me, preparing to hit the big red button on the screen.

"It's not hooking up if you're mine, right?"

*He's out of his mind.*

My eyes slide closed, and I ignore the quake that rakes over my entire body at the prospect.

*He's not in his right mind.*

Sighing, I blink back the collection on my lashes and tap the edge of the phone to my temple. "I don't know what that's supposed to mean, and I'm pretty sure I shouldn't want to know, either."

"That sounded like a roundabout way of saying maybe."

"I can't with you. You're so freaking exhausting."

"C'mon, Mama," he coos into the phone, his voice traveling over my skin like a caress that I shake off. "Say yes."

My thighs clench, and I scrub at my eyes. "No. Now I'm hanging up."

"Wait, I know I've asked a fuckton from you, Anna. Shit that I didn't even know I was asking. Or realize it, I guess. Shit I had no right to ask for and technically I'm asking more from you, but all I'm really after is a chance."

My heart splinters a little more, more tears sliding past my defenses. "Chance for what?"

"To make it up to you. Be with you. To show you. Feel you, earn you, trust you, and lo—"

"Toby, stop." I tighten my grip on the phone, my throat threatening to choke me. "It can't and won't happen, okay? I'm leaving the label for me, and I am *not* changing my mind."

"But, Anna—"

With tear-stained cheeks and an unbearable ache I will never be able to fill, I pull the phone away from my ear and finally hang up.

*Fool me once …*

# Chapter Forty-Nine

## TOBY

I T ONLY TOOK A minor bit of convincing and a way-too-long discussion with the doc about boundaries and habits and blah, blah, blah …

Once she said it was cool, I stopped listening.

Because I am now holding a brand-new phone that's shiny and black and currently ringing.

*I get to call Anna. Text her whenever I want.*

I don't expect her to answer an unknown number. I expect even less of a hospitable reception once she finds out that the new number spam calling her is me. After the way things were left yesterday, I'm not sure she'll ever actually speak to me again.

But I don't care. I plan to reach out to her until she makes me stop.

"Hey, Mama," I whisper into the phone once the voicemail picks up. "I'm totally not supposed to have this, but I guess I've been doing decent enough that the doc okayed it." I keep my voice low. "Guess who punched me today?" I chortle, the sound whistling through my swollen nose. "That's right, it was Fin. Of all fucking people! I told him that he's a stage hog, stealing my spotlight and things, and … well … he was mad I never told him. I think I deserved it, because I also said something about his award belonging to me. He didn't like that much, either." Licking my dried lips, I roll over in the bed and stare up at the ceiling. "Anyways, I don't know how long a message I can leave before it kicks my ass, but that's my update for today." I clear my throat, my hand brushing against my jaw. "I hope yours was decent, too. Only five more weeks, four days, six hours, and thirteen minutes."

With a stiff smile, I end the call.

# Chapter Fifty



"Y**OU'LL NEVER GUESS WHAT** happened in group today." I chuckle; the urge to rush it out before the voicemail stops recording knocking at the back of my mind. "We had to share today, talk about our experiences as an addict, and some guy said he was so hard up for a hit one time that he cut chocolate chip cookies and sniffed them. Like the shit you dunk in your hot cocoa sometimes! Fucking *cookies.* I almost wish I'd tried that, just out of curiosity." I laugh, rolling over against the cool side of the pillow beneath my head. "Anyways, that was the highlight of my day aside from being able to call you." Pushing to a sitting position, I lean back against the headboard and sigh. "I miss you, and I hope you had a good day." I glance at the calendar atop the desk beside me. "Only five more weeks, seven hours because I couldn't wait until lights out to call you, and twenty minutes."

Unwarranted hope blossoms in my chest.

"I'll call you tomorrow, Mama."

# Chapter Fifty-One

## *TOBY*

I STARE AT THE dimmed screen, its blankness mocking me.

No missed calls. No returned texts. No notifications begging for my attention.

And still … I hit the phone icon, the trail of Anna's number filling every spot in the log.

It rings, just as it has every night for the last two weeks, with no answer.

Part of me sours with each call that goes unanswered. Like a niggling in the back of my mind that maybe Anna doesn't feel the same way I do. That maybe her chest doesn't ache at the distance like mine does. That her heart doesn't speed up with each ring that cuts off, only to play another one.

Yet … I can't pull the phone away and hang up without leaving something for her.

*Doc says that communication is the key to basically everything …*

*So here goes something.*

"Today was not a great day. I'm not really sure why it's different, because it's just another damn day, but it's clung to me so bad that I'd love nothing more than to drown in a bottle right about now. I miss whiskey and you and my—" My throat clogs with emotion. "Shit, Anna…" The heel of my palm rotates over the ache so deep in my chest that I don't think any kind of medication could tame it. "I miss my pops so fucking much. I want to tell you all about him, everything I remember, and probably some shit I've made up over the years. You two would have been a blast together if he was still around." I gaze at the crossed-out squares sitting next to me for confirmation. "Four more weeks, Mama. Three days. Four hours. I know I'm a mess, but I'm all yours if you'll have me."

# Chapter Fifty-Two

## *TOBY*

"**M**AC BROUGHT UP MA's cookies today," I say to the phone wedged between my ear and shoulder, munching on said cookies. "They're so fucking good." I chew and swallow the mouthful muffling my words. "He totally traded them like it was a drop and security got pissed." Snorting, I pop another one between my lips and seal the baggie up. "They only found one, so I get to keep this one."

Tossing the plastic bag onto the desk, I settle against the far wall with an arm across the headboard, my legs stretched out across the mattress.

"We're gonna see how long this thing goes before it cuts me off. Sound good to you, Mama?"

I know I'm talking to her inbox like she's going to respond, but whatever.

*It makes me feel better to talk to her. Even if she's not there.*

"I think there's something going on with our drummer. He was normal but totally not. The bags under his eyes were dead giveaways. What do you think? Have you seen him recently?"

I roll an errant crumb between my finger and thumb.

"I guess he'll say something eventually. He's always been better than me at a lot of shit like telling the people he cares about that he cares about them. Doc says I need to try it out more."

I clear my throat and toss the crumb into the trashcan beside the desk. It's dark in here, so I'm not quite sure if it makes it or not.

"Anna," I almost whisper into the receiver, my voice more gravel than I intend. "God, I wish you were fucking here with me." My eyes slide closed and the memory of her ocean scent fills my nose. "Wish I could see your beautiful face. Touch your soft skin …"

A soft sound escapes me, and I bite my lip.

"Tell me I'm ridiculous for still wanting you, Mama." My hand slides down my ribs, my fingertips teasing the waistband of my shorts. "I'm crazy, I know it."

The same shorts I was wearing the night she gave me head for the first time and started this whole *situation*.

"Wanting those plump lips wrapped around my—" I cup my stiff dick over the material, squeezing, humming. "Fuck, I need time to move faster." I grunt against the pressure of my hand, my breath coming in ragged puffs. "Three weeks," I breathe and shove my hand beneath the material. "Six days." Groaning, I stroke up and down my shaft. "Four hours."

It's been too long. My balls are already aching, my abs clenching with the idea that Anna might actually listen to this message and it might make her as hot as it's making me.

"Thirty-nine—*unnng*—minutes."

There's no stopping this train wreck of a voicemail or the orgasm that's barreling through my system.

"Anna," I breathe out, stroking my dick faster. "I'm gonna fucking come. I'm gonna—"

"*If you'd like to delete this message, please press one. Or, hang up.*"

"Fuck!"

My cum paints my chest and the tops of my thighs, my heart beating wildly in my chest.

*Did I just come on voicemail?*

With a trembling limb, I lift the phone from the side of my head and stare at the screen, the little voice reminding me to delete the message or end the call.

I shudder with an aftershock and hang up.

# Chapter Fifty-Three

## Anna

ANOTHER NOTIFICATION DINGS ACROSS the screen of my phone, and yet, it hangs in the limbo of my hand, my eyes trained on the other device in front of me.

I can't take my sight off of the headlines lighting up my laptop, my stomach jumping up to stick in my throat.

After all the long hours and months spent, the stories fed to the tabloids, and the payoff of one pesky person, I am staring at a leak of As Above's personal life, live on the screen for everyone to see.

I swallow thickly.

Twenty-five thousand dollars went to Toby's accuser, in exchange for her disappearance from the media. Enough cash to get her life started somewhere far away from them—him—and a promise of more if she kept her silence.

It didn't matter that the baby isn't his.

It didn't matter that the paperwork she possessed was forged.

It didn't matter that she never actually had any contact with Toby at all.

None of it mattered.

Leo and I both agreed that it was for his peace.

His protection.

And yet …

Conveniently, less than twenty-four hours after the transfer of funds, Tobias Jeffers is once again the top story of not just the vultures of media, but every news outlet I can think to check.

My phone pings, and I absentmindedly thumb my way through the screens until the voicemail plays in a low voice.

It's another one from Leo.

He's begging me to stay.

*I can't.*

Deleting the voicemail so I have the space for others, I remind myself that I'm down to one more week. Seven more days of carrying the burden of protecting the band at all cost, deceiving the world, and myself, in their honor. Seven more days of fake narratives, pushy reporters, and terrifying camerapersons.

Only seven more days until I can move on to the next chapter of my life.

I have a new place in a new town, a job far away from here, a new everything waiting for me.

Just one more week.

My phone spits out another notification and I hit the screen without looking to silence it.

I'm too tired to do much else.

So damn tired of all the calls, seeing the hateful words spewed across the internet.

The stress and loneliness left in its wake.

Letting the phone drop next to me to free my hands, I set up a blast email I've already had to utilize for these situations and send it out in hopes of overshadowing the negative headlines about Toby and his current stint in rehab.

*Maybe the baby rumor would have been a better pill to swallow.*

The man is so ingrained into my subconscious, I swear I hear him speaking. His words muffled as he tells me all about that same rehabilitation spell, just as he does in every voicemail he leaves me.

Every night he calls.

And every night, I listen.

Ever since the cabin, I've taken up torturing myself like it's become my new pastime. My new favorite hobby.

Especially when it involves the bassist of the band I have failed to keep pieced together.

*It's exactly why I have to leave.*

"Anyways…" Toby says as if dismissing my internal dilemma and preparing his defense of my self-deprecation, boosting me up in his own way while I tear myself down.

*It's one of the things I miss. Hearing what he thinks about things.*

"You clearly haven't blocked this number after last week's jerk-off message."

*That is not what I was expecting from my subconscious.*

"Did it make you hot, Mama?"

Realization has me shooting up off of my couch, tossing my laptop to the cushion in the process and wheeling around the room.

*Am I losing my mind?*

A faint groan interrupt the otherwise silent space and my wide eyes land on the spot I just vacated.

The spot between my laptop and my phone.

*Oh, no.*

"Did you touch yourself to the sound of my voice?"

I can barely hear his words over the rushing of blood pumping around my ears and the racing breaths escaping my lungs.

*Crap, crap, crap!*

"I don't wanna get cut off this time, but—*uhhng*—just the thought of you listening feels too good."

My thighs clench and my hands go to my hot face.

*What the heck do I do?*

*Why am I sweating?*

My mind, the smarter of the two organs controlling me, screams to run back to the couch and hang up the phone. Separate myself from him and never listen to another voicemail he leaves me. Maybe even block the number.

My heart, though, begs me not to cut off the real time connection with the man that it yearns after.

It's what has me sinking to my knees next to the couch and flipping the phone over.

The screen lights up with his name, confirming the connected lines.

I bite my lip.

He shutters out a breath.

I don't pick the phone. Instead, I run my finger along the edge of the cream-colored case that has golden sparkles imbedded in the back.

It's new.

The second I saw the flash of gold, it reminded me of the light in Toby's eyes.

I've never added something to my cart so fast.

And now … here he is … on the line for real. Tucked inside the case I bought because of him, and creating sparks inside my stomach from just his ragged breaths.

"I don't want you to miss it this time, Mama. So, I'm going to make it fast."

*Would he rush if he knew I was listening?*

"*Fuck*, it's like I can hear—*ahh*—your little breaths in my ear … taste your—*ahng*—cunt on my tongue."

He exhales and it's like his body is begging me to say something. Acknowledge him.

*Encourage him.*

I don't. In fact, I pinch my lips between my teeth and shove my hand between my already clenched thighs. I wiggle my warm and eager fingers closer to my aching core.

My hand slides closer, pressing against myself over the material of my pants, wetness soaking through the thin fabric.

The pressure alone is enough to send my eyes skyward and my teeth biting down hard on my lips.

"Anna," Toby breathes. "Me stroking my dick … while thinking of you … wrapped around it." He lets loose a choked noise. "Buried inside that tight cunt of yours … It's gonna make me come." He grunts, and I have to work to hold back the sound bubbling up my throat. "Gonna make me paint my chest all over again."

Turning my head away from the phone, I shove my mouth against my bicep to hold back the gasps I can't control.

He hums. "There it is, Mama."

Toby's rugged gasp drowns out mine and ends with my name from his lips.

Chills flood my skin, and my body clenches in response, my teeth sinking into my arm to hide the noises.

"Two weeks," Toby reminds me in his deep voice. "Three days. Four hours."

Before he can say anything else …

I disconnect us.

# Chapter Fifty-Four

## TOBY

THREE DAYS IN A ROW, the line connects, but no automatic recording plays.

No demands to leave a message. No robot voice greeting me.

"Hey, Mama," I say into the phone with a smirk and a tingling palm.

*Silence.*

"I know you've been answering me." My grin grows, my dick filling.

*More silence.*

"I could stay on this phone all damn night. Just stop hanging up on me when I come."

She thinks she muffles the snort, but I hear it.

I've heard it all.

All the way to my balls.

"What would you do if I waited 'til later to rub one off for you?" *No response.* "Or *didn't* touch my cock at all?"

I tsk into the mic. "My pristine little Ms. Prune is a voyeur, isn't she?"

I growl into the phone, and Anna squeaks out a tiny sound in response. My heart pinches. My dick thickens.

"Get horizontal, Anna," I rasp, and a heat blooms behind my ribs. "I'm gonna fuck you with my tongue through this phone."

A whimper, small and almost non-existent, feeds over the line and my dick throbs.

I don't bother tampering my fast breaths as I tug down the waistband of my shorts. There's something that's just so fucking hot about hearing Anna try so hard not to react to me. To this.

*To us.*

It's inexorable.

We're inescapable.

"You and me, Mama," I breathe into the phone and fist my hard-as-steel dick. "There's no stopping this."

Her tiny gasp nestles its way into my ear and my eyes roll back.

"Now shove those fingers in that cunt and let me hear how juicy it is."

For a moment, it's quiet. So quiet that I pull the device from my head to make sure she didn't hang up on me.

Sure enough, the screen lights up, her name and a picture I found online of her illuminating my face.

*Still there.*

And that's when I hear it.

The sound of flesh on slicked flesh, and I groan.

"*Fuuuuck*, Mama …" My balls draw up. "That's me. My dick sliding in and out of that wet cunt."

Anna can shove her face in a pillow, or bite down on her shirt all she wants. Do whatever she thinks stifles the sounds coming from her.

I hear every fucking bit of it.

I stroke my dick, matching the noise.

"Taking you. Fucking you. That's me inside you, Anna." I grip my swollen head to tame the orgasm threatening me too soon. "Making you feel so, so good."

My neck arches back, the muscles taut as chills rack over my skin. "Making you *mine*."

Anna makes a sound that's somewhere between a gasp and a moan and I know she's close.

"Spread those legs, Anna," I choke out, my dick's pulse beating against my palm. "Let me come in that cunt and make it mine. Only mine."

There's no mistaking the dampened mewl on her end on the line, no mistaking the way my words do exactly what she needs.

*What no one else has done for her.*

I gasp out. "Squeeze those fingers with that tight cunt like the dirty girl I know you are."

I'm leaking. So close to busting all over my fist that goosebumps rise over most of my body.

"Toby," she sobs for me in that perfect orgasming cry, and I lose it.

All over my stomach, my chest.

"Tell me you're mine, Anna." I'm dragging ragged breaths in and pushing the negative voices out. "Tell me you'll stay."

The quiet descends upon me once again.

*She's going to say no.*

Yet, there's five little words that are strong enough to ruin lives and start wars that sit on the tip of my tongue.

"Anna," I breathe out, the weight settling into this silence getting heavier with each second that passes without a response.

I want to tell her.

But there's another four words I've yet to say, ones that stick in my throat like the betrayal that they are.

*I lied to you.*

She may never forgive me for what I did at the cabin. She may never trust a word I say ever again. May never be able to see past what I've done.

*That* is what has an ache blossoming in my chest, one that grows with each day that I reach out to her and *don't* say the words.

I pretend, for her sake, because I want the connection only she can give. I don't want her to stop. To lose her.

I don't want her to hate me.

*But is this any better?*

"I just wish I could see you," I whisper, the thoughts spoken aloud for her. "Trace the patterns of your freckles with my eyes when you're not paying attention. Feel the strands of your hair slip through my fingers."

Biting my lip, I snatch up the tee I left beside me on the bed and swipe away the mess.

"Hear your voice ... tell me how ridiculous I'm being." There's a faint chuckle that escapes me, but it comes out thick. "Tell me I'm an idiot. Fling that attitude in my direction, shoot fire from your eyes, even though they're as green as precious gemstones. The way they light up ..."

I shake my head.

For the rest of what I have to say, I need to be in front of her for. Need to see that light in her eyes flare at me in person for the things I've done.

And for that, I'd be willing to wait a lifetime.

A lifetime of groveling and making up. Building. Learning. Trusting.

*A lifetime, nonetheless.*

"Two weeks, Mama," I say into the phone, my voice a graveled murmur. "One hour. Fifty-two minutes."

# Chapter Fifty-Five

## Anna

"So wait a second."

I whip my head from one side of the table to the next, my hair floating all around and ending up stuck in the lipstick Aria swore I should wear tonight.

It's a soft pink that's super pretty and not at all what I'm used to.

"You're still leaving?" Aria asks over the bass of the heavy music drowning out most other conversations, hence the head on a swivel.

*Not to mention the showpieces on each table.*

"Of course I am." I shrug and bring the glass back up to my lips, careful of the color as I sip the fruity concoction Cedar brought to our table. "Leo will be fine. So if he put you up to this, you can stop."

Aria snorts and Cedar's shoulder bumps into me when she shrugs.

"It's just us being nosey bitches, is what it is," Cedar responds as she raises her glass and sways with the beat of the music, her eyes lifted to the space above us.

"She's not wrong." Aria says on a snicker and shoots back the rest of her drink. "We are nosey *and* thirsty."

I tip my head back and laugh, the warmth of the liquor I've already consumed loosening my inhibitions and swirling around in my chest.

I can even feel it in my face already.

"At least you two have thirst-quenchers at home," I mutter low enough that I hope they don't hear, but Cedar's guffaw is a dead giveaway that at least she did.

"A tallllll drink of water in the desert, baby!" Cedar exclaims with a grin and downs the rest of her drink.

"So why are we watching dudes shake their stuff in our faces?" I motion with my cup-holding hand to the rather attractive men taking up several tables, including ours, with nothing but strings covering their groins.

Literally nothing has been left to my imagination and the guy dancing all over our table is *blessed.*

"It's the closest we'll ever get to another cock," Aria explains around the straw between her bright red lips. "*You* on the other hand …"

I feel the flush hit me before she even finishes her statement, the look in her eyes screaming mischief despite my shaking head. "Nope. Absolutely not."

Aria's grin mirrors in her best friend when I turn to her for help. "Drink up, buttercup. We already bought you a show."

I'm still shaking my head when Aria tips my elbow up, the glass meeting my lips and as soon as the liquor is gone, I'm being pulled by my wrist to another part of the club.

Colored light dance across the walls, highlighting the people, only single spotlight illuminating the dancers at their stations.

Thankfully, we're heading *away* from the thick of the people, but that just means that Aria wasn't kidding at all.

Because back here are the private rooms.

The bouncer at the hall's entrance doesn't even check our ID's, just nods the two of them along despite my protests and clearly restrained nature.

Had I been sober for any of this, I probably would have given it some more fight. Some resilience. But I'm not and I don't.

In fact, I'm laughing when the two women push me into the single seat in the room sat directly in front of the small, lifted platform and step back as if to flank me.

"What if he's a serial killer?" I call after them, too loudly now that the closed door has cut off some of the noise.

"Oh, honey, we're not leaving." Cedar's snicker has me turning around in the chair, her hand extended with another glass that she's offering to me.

"We came to fucking watch," Aria adds and I wrinkle my nose.

"Ew."

Aria snorts and shakes her head. "You don't get to have sex in here, Anna, Jesus."

I plop back down in my chair, my smile amped up, my pits too sweaty. *That answers that.*

"But if you want to," Cedar adds, her hand finding my shoulder. "You gotta wait until his shift is over and we will totally wait with you."

I snicker, but nod to Cedar's receding form as the lights change in the room and the stage illuminates.

A deep beat fills the space, one of those that's so bassy that I can feel it's reverberations rattling around in my chest, and a figure darkens the far corner of the stage. It doesn't take long for him to make his way front and center, his caramel skin and dark hair lit up perfectly, his hips rotating to the music.

Slinking back in the wing-backed chair seems like the wrong approach to this situation, but that's exactly what I do when the stranger comes to the edge of the stage and grips the tight tee shirt covering his clearly defined torso.

It should be tempting when he rips the shirt from his frame, exposing his sculpted muscles, the shreds of material hanging from his arms.

Just as it should be attractive when he fists his pant legs and yanks the tearaways in a move that leads him to his knees.

Knees he crawls on towards me, his bare bottom on full display, until his hands find the arms of my chair and his body lifts right in front of my face.

The heat of his bare skin skims my knees and I clench my already crossed thighs even tighter when he stands, naked as the day he was born.

I'm single. I have been for a long time.

*So why does this feel like betrayal?*

The man is beautiful. His moves alluring as he twists and grinds in the air around me. He's even got a sheen of sweat coating his skin that makes it look like he's glowing in the light.

But when he leans down to me, hips gyrating in my direction, and his lips ghost over the shell of my ear, I instantly wish I could sink into the cushion beneath me and disappear.

Anywhere else but here, because while I might be single, my heart is clearly still stuck in the past.

*If this enticing stranger can't catch my attention, will anyone else ever?*

Those lips, too hot against my ear, lean close enough that skin makes contact.

"*Aye, mami,*" he mutters in a thick accent, and I freeze. "*Eres tan hermosa.* I get off in two hours."

I push on his sweaty shoulders.

"No, thank you," I mutter, the edge of my voice shaking as he leans back with his brows in his hairline and it's just enough for me to bolt from the seat.

With my heart in my throat and the women I came with hot on my heels, I sprint from the private room and out into the wild mass of gyrating bodies.

All the colors flashing, the musky scent of sweat mixed with booze thickening the air, makes it hard to breathe.

*I shouldn't be here.*

"I shouldn't have come," I say the thought out loud, my heeled feet refusing to stop despite the hands that grab at me and the voices that ask things like '*are you okay?*'.

My lungs feels like they're working overtime, through a sludge of guilt that rolls over me violent enough that it churns my stomach.

When I break out into the humid night air, a sense of relief washes over me and I pull in the first deep breath since that man took the stage just for me.

"Anna," Aria murmurs, her voice soft and close as she lays a hand on my shoulder and helps guide me down the sidewalk. "Just breathe, honey. You're alright."

"Tell me if he did something weird and I'll go get my bat," Cedar adds strongly, her thin frame taking up my other side. "But after you breathe, like Ari said."

Nodding, I do just as the women advise and focus on calming my wild heart.

It takes a moment, possibly a few, before I feel confident enough to raise my sight from the passing sidewalk, and for my stomach to stop threatening to evacuate its contents.

"Where are we?"

"Still in downtown," Aria answers, her grip still steadying on my shoulder. "The boys are behind us, so don't worry about it."

I nod, thankful in this moment that security follows both Aria and Cedar around when they appear in public because the park we're approaching is dark and intimidating.

*And probably filled with all kinds of riff raff at night.*

"I'm so sorry." The words are shaky when they leave my lips. "I didn't mean to ruin your guys' night."

"Nonsense." Cedar shakes her head, her raven-colored hair flowing around her shoulders, the thin stripe of red peeking out from behind her ear with the movement.

"You didn't ruin anything, Anna," Aria adds, her brows pinched, creating a vee between them. She uses the hand on me to pull me to a stop just in front of one of those little benches most parks have right at the entrance of the greenery, and gives me an encouraging push. "I ran out on a concert once."

Cedar snickers as I settle into the seat and try my best not to think about the number of germs transferring from the wood to my butt.

*The number of germs in my ear from that stranger …*

"And I had a panic attack right in the middle of a tattoo festival." Cedar slides into the seat beside me. "Not sure if that's what happened with you just now, but it's totally cool if it was."

"I'm honestly not sure …" I shrug and brush away invisible lint from my skirt, my sight trained on the grass beneath Aria's feet. "It was fine until—"

I cut myself off and bite my lip.

"Until what?" One of them ask and I feel the heat rise on my face.

Sighing, I shrug.

Because how can I explain that the man called me a name way too close to the one that Toby does without giving everything away?

There's no way I can tell either of them that *Mama* and all its variations prompts all kinds of thoughts in my head about a man that they know and I want, but can't have.

It's not for me to tell Cedar or Aria about the tryst that happened at the cabin, one that's over with for good, without giving it away that at some point, the playing around became serious for me.

*That just makes me sound pitiful and no different that the woman that blackmailed him to begin with.*

I shrug again when I feel both of them just staring at me. It's all I can manage when it feels like my heart is breaking all over again.

For the man that Toby could be.

For the version of him that I fell in love with anyway.

Neither of which are mine to keep.

"So, I just want to say something." Aria crouches in front of me, her head dipping until her green eyes meet mine. "Both instances C and I just mentioned, the panic attacks? They were both because of other people and the uncertainty that comes with exposing yourself to them."

She nods encouragingly, her eyes so soft and understanding that I feel tears prick the backs of my eyes.

"And sometimes," Aria continues as Cedar's hand finds my shoulder and rubs soothingly. "It helps to talk it through with someone else."

The woman's perfectly sculpted brow arches expectantly, almost knowingly, and my heart swells for a moment. A beat.

"Just say his name," Cedar snarls next to me. "And I'll go get that fucking bat."

*Is it possible to feel both heartbroken, and loved at the same time?*

I snicker, and it comes out thick. "It's really no … big deal."

"That's it. I'll be back," Cedar leans up from the seat like she's leaving for real and I grab her arm, stopping her midair.

"Seriously, it's fine. No one needs the Slugger."

"Aw," Aria coos, still crouched in front of me and snickers. "She even knows his name."

Cedar snorts but drops back into her seat. "Fine. *For now.*"

"So. Since I've literally never seen you with anyone else, you wanna tell us what Toby has done?"

I jolt back in my seat.

Breath has left me, eyes have gone wide, and if she didn't know before, I'm certain my reaction has given me away.

"How in the—"

I swing my startled gaze to Cedar who shrugs. "There's only two people you spend all of your time with."

Aria still has that arched brow aimed at me. "And you didn't mute the phone that night."

My furrowed brow swings back to Aria and I blink at her. "Mute—what?"

"On the phone," Aria says easily, like she's not tearing apart every denial I've built up over the last few weeks.

*Months.*

"When you called about the pictures to cover up more of Toby's mistakes. I heard him call for you and that phone did *not* mute when you answered him."

"The only other option was Leo," Cedar adds like she's been in on the secret the whole time. "And he's just too …" Her lips purse in my peripheral and a laugh bursts past my lips.

"Corporate," I answer for her, and she nods, Aria snorting her agreement.

"You'd run circles over him, all day long."

I sigh. "Leo's great at his job. He just needs to meet reality for a dang second."

Aria's eyes roll, but she nods as if she understands and I realize that some of the weight bearing down in my chest has begun to ease.

These women … they're here with me, accepting of me, and comprehend more of what I'm going through than I thought possible.

The pieces of my heart inflate a little more.

"Do you guys like hot cocoa?"

# Chapter Fifty-Six

## Anna

"HOLY *SHIT*," CEDAR CALLS as soon as we walk through the glass doors of the twenty-four-hour café that's just two blocks away from my apartment. "They've got *books!*"

I grin when a flash of black hair brushes past me and disappears somewhere near the few shelves the owner keeps stocked with some of her favorite romance novels.

By the time Aria and I order fancy hot chocolate and make our way to a table, Cedar emerges with an arm full of books that she slams onto the tiny table and beams around. "I've read all of these."

Aria shakes her head. "I knew you were a nerd."

Cedar smacks her lips and snags the cup from Aria's lifting grasp. "Like you haven't benefited from a smutty book or two, woman."

The resulting snicker has my own grin amping up. "How are you two not related?"

"Oh, we are." Aria cocks her head at me. "It's called *found family* and you're our newest member."

My mouth drops open, then slams shut when the words evade me and warmth blossoms in my chest.

"Now," Cedar interrupts, peeking at me around her stack of already-read treasures and sips from the stolen cup against her palm. "Either we talk about books, or we talk about boys. Spill the deets."

A flush takes over my face and I shake my head. "This was a terrible idea."

"Never," Aria exclaims. "Now spill about Toby. We can talk about books later."

Dragging in a deep breath, my eyes dart over to the bodyguard taking up most of the front window, his back to us.

"Don't worry about him," Cedar says, waving him off with her cup holding hand. "Jon doesn't listen to shit unless Squirt is around."

I nod and drag my sight away from the buzzed head that's just far enough away, but lean closer into the table anyways. "So what do you wanna know?"

Aria snorts and mirrors my pose. "Is he good?"

My eyes go wide.

"Does he eat out?" Cedar asks over the stack of books and I can *feel* the heat take over my face.

"Okay, so both of those are a yes, if the redness is any indication." Aria leans back with a knowing smirk. "Is it dickmatized or for real?"

I blink.

And blink.

*What have I done?*

"Right," Cedar adds, oh so helpfully. "Well, if we're still not cool with lap dances even though he's been gone this long, then it's gotta be for real, Ari."

"Have you seen him? At rehab?" Aria asks.

I force out a breath that moves the hair near my forehead. "I was with Leo when we took him."

"Oh," Aria states, her brows dipping. "You haven't been to see him?"

I shake my head and feel my shoulders drooping. "No, I haven't."

"Why?"

It's a simple question. Easy to ask when you're on the outside like Cedar is, easy to want to know when you haven't seen the things that I have.

I lick my drying lips, then take a sip from the to-go cup in my hand to give myself a moment.

I'm slow to swallow the scolding mouthful, thankful for its distraction while I set the cup back on the table between me and the women dead set on knowing me.

When I look up to find concern lining both of their features, Cedar's blue eyes blazing in a different way than Aria's, I decide to speak the truth.

*My truth.*

The reason I'm here. Why I took a job like this to begin with.

How I already knew about addiction when I interviewed with Leo.

And why I can't stick around any longer.

I clear my throat. "I—"

A ring cuts off my words and my brow furrows when neither woman in front of me reaches for their pockets or bags.

"Oh, crap." I feel the color drain from my face as I pull the device out with trembling hands from my tiny clutch.

"Hey, Mama," Toby's gruff tone greets me like a calm to my internal storm, a salve to my aching heart, and I stumble off the stool and away from prying ears. "You watching TV?"

*Crap, crap, crap.*

When I answered, I forgot that I was leaving Toby hanging most nights.

We've talked on the phone, but I haven't *talked* at all.

*What do I say?*

The heat rises up my chest, and I pinch my blouse away, using the material to fan my face.

If I say nothing, he touches himself. If I speak, then I've broken the promise I made to myself to move on, leave him be.

Shaking my head, I push out of the little café, past the bodyguard, and into the thick night air.

Except, the sounds of traffic echo around me and I still don't find the answers I'm looking for.

"It's like I can hear you thinking too loud," he mutters into the phone, and I stop, looking skyward.

"Talk to me about it. Maybe I can help."

*What if it's you?*

"What's going on?"

With every night I postpone the inevitable, I lose another piece of my soul.

"Look, I don't have to keep calling like this. I'd love to, but I understand if you don't."

His solid breathing fills my ear despite the world crashing in around me.

A truth I know all too well. A pain I refuse to live with a second time.

*I'm in love with an addict who will never put me first.*

"This is goodbye, Toby."

# Chapter Fifty-Seven

## *Toby*

FOR EIGHT DAYS, I have called a number that claims it's no longer in service.

No more voicemails to leave, text messages bouncing back as undeliverable.

And for just as long, I have held on to hope that the woman holding my heart will still be present when I finally take the first steps out into the world as a sober man.

So when Leo greets me with a wide grin and we walk to the town car he scheduled to pick me up, I can only half match his enthusiasm.

It's the same when he rambles on about new projects on the plane ride home, speaks of the new lyrics Rex and Fin wrote as we cross the tarmac to yet another car.

By the time we turn onto the street that houses Rex's penthouse, my smile has completely fallen.

Because not once in the last several hours has the man even hinted at Anna or her replacement.

When we pull into the open level of the garage, I direct him to pull over so I can get out of the car.

The air feels fresher out here, despite the residual fumes from the vehicles, the city itself, and yet it feels heavy as fuck and unlike what I remember.

Leo bumps my shoulder. "Talk to me, man. How are you doing?"

"That's a loaded fucking question."

He just huffs and stares at me as if expecting me to answer.

I want to seal my lips, swallow the disappointment down to where no one can touch it ever again.

I want to scream in his face that he's the last one I wanna see right now.

I do neither.

"It's different than what I was expecting," I admit and turn toward the elevators.

"How so?"

"Is everyone inside?"

*Diversion.*

*Doc wouldn't approve.*

*But I can't handle anything else right now.*

"The band, yeah," he answers. "Everyone wanted to see you when you got home and I thought here would be easier. Then you could escape if you needed to."

My head bobs with a nod as I knuckle the call button. "Thanks."

The dings of the elevator indicating each floor we've passed feels like my head is stuck to the speaker that amplifies Mac's drum kit, hitting too hard and too fast this close.

*She's not up there.*

The elevator still opens to the correct floor and Leo still strides right up to the door he opens without pause.

*She's not in there.*

I follow him even though all I want to do is turn around, find Anna's apartment, and bang on her door until she agrees to at least acknowledge my existence.

That we had something.

At least, if I knew that she felt *something*, at any point in our time together, then I might be able to stomach an existence without her.

*As long as she's happy.*

I could live with that. Anna being happy.

So long as no other man lays a hand on her, I think I could live with that.

Rounding the entryway into the main living space, the faint noise of people conversing over the sound of music playing hits my ears like static.

"Broby!"

Mac vaults over the back of the couch and tackles me around the torso, knocking me off balance. We tumble to the solid marble beneath us with a thud I feel in my bones.

*Hello floor, I've missed you, too.*

"Ow," I growl out, but he just uses my shoulders to leverage himself back to his feet.

A chorus of greetings echo around me as my family fills my vision, most of them snickering at me.

"Who does that?" I ask from the floor with my arms spread out wide, causing Rex to shrug and Fin to shake his head.

"Me, duh." Mac rolls his eyes, drawing my gaze to the dark bags still present beneath them, and holds a hand out in offering. "Someone didn't work out in the yard like the rest of the inmates."

Grasping his hand tight, I yank myself to my feet. "Har har, Mackie."

The drummer snorts, his face now level with mine, and that's when I smell it.

The sweet serenity of liquor coating his breath and clinging to me with each moment he sticks close by.

I drop his hand and step back.

Thankfully, he uses the release as means to push my shoulder, spinning me in the direction of the kitchen. "C'mon, there's mac and cake."

My stomach rolls.

My hands go clammy.

A plate is thrust into my trembling hands, filled with shit I only pick at when I finally take a seat, and dismiss completely when seats are rotated and Mac ends up back beside me.

He's perched on the back of the couch, cradling a plate filled with nothing but mac and cheese that does nothing to cover the scent of alcohol clinging to my senses.

Rex drones on about his kids, all the milestones they've had since I've been gone.

Fin fills everyone in on the updates to his place, the parlor Cedar now owns, which entices the guys to talk about the ink they want next, but I sit silent, hearing none of it.

Because while I've missed these men, the ones I call brothers, I can't stop the churning of my stomach or the impulses threatening to surface.

Ones that scream for me to head to the kitchen and check to see if Rex's liquor cabinet is fully stocked. Or lean closer to Mac, if only to catch the scent.

Just one …

*I miss it.*

My mouth goes dry.

The fiending is too much.

Thoughts circling, I thrust to my feet. "I gotta go."

"Go? You just got here," someone grumbles but I'm already moving across the room, my mostly full plate in my hands and prepped for the trash.

"Yeah, there's …" I shake my head, hoping the movement will clear it enough. "Someone I need to see."

*Anna. I need to find Anna.*

She's the only one who matters right now.

Not me, or this demon inside me, or the shit that's happened in the last few months.

I'm at the elevator when Leo catches up to me and spins me, his hand landing on my shoulder.

The despondent look in his eyes says it all before his words do. "Toby … she's not here."

"Then tell me where she is." My heart hammers, my breathing ragged. "I have to know, Le."

He shakes his head.

"She's gone, man."

Part III

"If you own this story, you get to write the ending."
—Brene Brown

THREE MONTHS LATER

# Chapter Fifty-Eight

## Anna

"Y'KNOW, JON, IT'S BEEN months."

The bodyguard who was assigned to follow me just shrugs, a single calloused finger holding back the gauzy curtains I just got hung up. "I'm contracted for at least five, ma'am."

"Ew." My nose crinkles. "Don't call me that."

Jonathon nods and turns his attention back out to the fire escape attached to the side of the building and just so happens to have a little terrace right outside my third-story window.

"I hate this thing," he grumbles for the hundredth time since I found this place.

"It *does* look like a tetanus shot waiting to happen, doesn't it?" I snicker when he leans closer to the glass and assesses the alleyway beneath, his breath fogging up the glass.

"I'm going to put both sensors on this one."

I shrug and pull more items from the box accompanying me on the hardwood floor. "If that'll get you out of my house, then fine."

"You'll need to remember to arm it when you're not present."

"Thanks for that," I mutter and roll my eyes.

"I'm serious, Anna." Jonathon turns to me on booted feet I try not to stare at because they remind me of the person I've managed to avoid for the last three freaking months, and narrows his eyes at me. "I only have a few weeks to make sure this is a safe place. That is, if you don't move *again*."

I point a finger in his direction. "It's not my fault that the job fell through and the housing with it. Those hotels were *not* ideal for me either."

Jonathon's hands go to his hips like he doesn't believe me. "The job you had was perfectly fine."

I shake my head and swipe a hand through the air between us, dismissing the sentiment. "That's done with and not for me anymore. So *stop*."

"Uh-huh. Sure," he mumbles, and I swear I catch his eyes roll before he goes back to his security duties.

Like attaching sensors to each of the windows and doors inside this place.

It wasn't my idea. I've never had them before.

But this side of the coast is a completely different animal that terrifies me at times. A place I've only visited a few times.

Yet it's the capital for artists, labels, and people who need people like me.

It just happens to be on the other side of the country from the man I refuse to think about.

*It hurts less that way.*

So the sensors and security systems Leo demanded I put in, go in, and I get to rest in peace from the outside world when I'm home.

*Sounds like a win to me.*

"Have you called him back yet?" Jonathon calls from the guest bedroom I'm planning to make my in-home office.

"Wh—"

"Leo would not let me off the damn phone," Jonathon continues as he swaggers back into the living room with needle nose plyers in one hand

and cut wires in the other. "Not until I swore I would get you to return his calls."

I slump back into a completely unladylike, cross-legged heap on the floor. I sigh out and flip through the picture frames in my lap. "No. And I'm not going to any time soon."

"Why?" He stops beside me, his looming presence requiring me to lean all the way back to catch his eyes.

"Because *noneya*. I'll call him when I'm good and ready to." I huff, narrowing my sight on him.

Jonathon holds his full hands up in surrender. "Just the messenger, *ma'am*."

He's already moving when I growl at him, halfway down the hall when I dart after the couch and find a throw pillow to lob in his direction. The soft material plops against the door he slams closed, his laugh echoing from inside the room.

"You're as bad as the rest of them!"

Sighing when Jonathon doesn't emerge from his fortress, I let my attention drop back to the photos discarded on the floor in front of my open cardboard box. It's the last one to unpack, all of my furniture and knick-knacks in their rightful places, leaving this box.

The one I didn't want to have company for when I opened.

The one I'd rather have left in the storage unit, all on its own.

But apparently Jonathon's not leaving anytime soon and paying for a unit that houses only one box seemed ridiculous. Plus, leaving a singular box unpacked in my apartment was unacceptable to my quirky brain.

I force my feet to move back to the box, dropping to my knees.

I drag in a deep breath and shove my hands inside, grasping at the contents and pulling it all out at once.

Photo albums hold the stack steady from the bottom as I pull it from its cardboard prison and lay it all out on the hardwood beside me.

The albums are old school, probably purchased in the nineties when my mother used to think photographing everything was her life's work, and could use replacements.

But it's not the books themselves that have me questioning my sanity and desperation to keep the pain in my chest at bay.

It's what's housed between the covers, attached to a spine that crinkles when I open the first page.

My fingers feather over the glossy surface, touching a face I haven't seen in nearly twenty years. A face too young and precious for a world that she entered, completely unprepared for what she'd find when she got there.

Slamming the book closed, I toss it back to the floor and push to my feet, swiping at my teary eyes as I go.

"Anna," Jonathon calls out, and I sniffle back the emotions.

"Yeah?" It's weak and waterlogged, but enough to get a response from the oblivious bodyguard.

"I'm starving. You mind if I order something?"

I tiptoe over the pile of devastation laid out on my floor and approach the closed bedroom. Swiping at my face one last time, I try my best to suck in a modicum of steadiness before pushing the door out of my way.

"Egg rolls good?"

"Nah," Jonathon says, his face still trained on the device he's tweaking in his grip. "I was thinking chili dogs."

I freeze.

"Burgers, maybe," he continues. "Something to hold me over."

"O-okay, I think I saw a place nearby. I'll look it up."

*Eventually things won't remind me of him, right?*

"Aw, thanks," the man answers with a small smile, his attention never wavering from his task. "I was going to do it."

I wave him off even though he's not paying any attention to me and head back to the kitchen where I left my phone.

"If I don't let you get distracted, then you can get out of my house."

He snickers. "Cuz across the hallway is so much different."

"It very much is."

After several more hours, a disappearing sun, and another meal delivered for the clearly starved bodyguard, I finally sit on my couch alone for the first time.

I didn't eat. The takeout containers mock me from their perch on my countertop, the smell of grease permeates the air enough that I consider opening the infamous window Jonathon ensured was locked before he stalked his giant butt across the hallway.

My hand is in my hair, my legs curled beneath me in the soft glow from the lamp, and my apartment is put together. All except for the pile of memories laid out on the hardwood floor that I abandoned.

For now, I plan to keep it that way.

At least until the chaos of an untamed mess drives me madder than the thought of looking through them.

Knowing all this, I should be settling into my seat, pulling up my favorite sitcom, and calling it a night.

*So why do I keep staring at my phone and hoping it rings?*

# Chapter Fifty-Nine

## TOBY

"**I** SWEAR TO FUCKING God, if you don't fucking tell me, I'm gonna tie guitar strings around your fingers until they fall off."

Leo stares at me from across the seat of the rental I'm driving with an arch to his brow.

"You're the one that let it slip she's here. Now spill your guts, or I'm pulling over."

"And do what?" His eyes roll. "Make me cry *uncle?*"

I nod, dead ass serious.

The man stays silent.

"For fuck's sake, Le. I did all the bullshit you asked," I growl. "I gave it time, kept my shit under control, *and* participated in all your *marketing bullshit.*" I switch my grip on the wheel when it creaks in protest. "If I don't get my girl, and my axe in my hands, I'm gonna fucking choke you."

Leo snorts and brushes his hands down his pressed shirt. "I can give you the latter, but the rest is not up to me. And it wasn't *marketing bullshit.* It was your transition."

"Well, I'm transitionized, okay? All good. Got a sponsor, go to meetings, and I haven't touched a drop. Now call my woman."

"Pretty sure you need to stop claiming her without even talking to her about it first."

"If she'd answer my call, I would have already."

"You understand what just came out of your mouth, right?"

It's my turn to snort. "Yeah, yeah." I release the wheel with one hand and smack at his elbow. "Pick up the phone."

"You gotta turn here!" Leo jolts up in his seat, his arm stretched out to point at a street I drive by.

"Seriously?" I growl and readjust my grip on the wheel. "No warning?"

"If you'd get out of the Stone Age and use a fucking GPS like the rest of us, I wouldn't need to give you damn directions."

"Give me a break, dick. I spent most of my life *not driving*."

"Clearly," Leo enunciates, leaning back in his seat and perching his elbow on the window. His fingers tease the *oh shit* handle before grabbing the thing like his life depends on it when I bank a U-turn that's probably illegal. "*Dude.*"

I chuckle and straighten the car out into the traffic. Only a few horns blare in my direction, and I signal to switch into the lane closest to the street Leo told me to turn down.

With the roar of the engine beneath me and a grin, I reach over and blindly smack at his arm again. "Send her tickets for tomorrow, at least."

The sigh that comes out of the man is borderline hysterical with how deep and intense it is. "Fine. But it's not my fault if she doesn't come."

I chuckle, a warmth I haven't felt in months blooming in my chest. "It's gonna be all your fault."

"Goddammit, you're never gonna let this go, are you?"

I shake my head and hit the gas. "That would require letting Anna go." A somber wave rushing down my spine has my soul feeling like it might be swallowed up in an endless void. "Can't do that."

Leo makes some kind of sound that's a mix of irritation and distress, and I shake the thoughts out of my head.

"You're starting to sound like the other two," Leo murmurs. "All that time talking shit, now look at you."

I huff, but shrug. "I guess I understand now."

I can't see the band manager roll his eyes, but I feel it. "Understand what exactly?"

"That I would rather see her, know her, be with her. That over everything else in my life, she's the one that matters most. Anna makes the most sense to me when the rest of the world doesn't."

"You're giving me diabetes."

The laugh that bursts out of me is cathartic.

"I take it back," Leo mumbles with a shake of his head and a raise of his phone wielding hand. "You *are* worse than Rex and Fin." He makes a fake gagging noise in the back of his throat that has more laughter bubbling out of me.

"One day, you might get it."

"Jesus, now you sound like Ma." His phone makes a pinging noise when he taps at the screen. "There, man. I sent her two VIP tickets. Now, will you shut the hell up?"

My eyes bulge. "Why the fuck would you send two?"

"Maybe she's got a friend—*Turn here*!"

"Oh, motherfucker."

# Chapter Sixty

## Anna

MY PHONE TAPPING AGAINST my thigh is the only noise in my otherwise dead silent office. It makes my mouth dry and my heart pound.

*I miss all of them.*

Leo has called me nearly every day since I left As Above, claiming he's just checking in. Making sure I've settled. Wondering if I'd ever come back. Asking what it would take to bring me back.

Sighing, I open the invite that's plagued me for the last several hours.

*I'm going to decline.*

It's the only logical answer.

*Right?*

Thumb hovering over the button to send it back, I jump clear out of my skin and let loose a scream when the device rings against my palm.

"Holy smokes, get it together, Anna."

I don't even get a chance to speak when I slide over the answer button, Aria's voice filling my little speaker as soon as the line connects.

"You have to come! Oh, my god, it'll be so much fun if you come, too."

"Hello Aria. It's nice to talk to you, too."

The woman in my ear snorts, another voice rising in the background. "Cut the shit and tell us yes, lady."

"Hello to you, too, Cedar."

"It's been too long," Aria drones out, the words on the verge of a whine that makes my heart fill. "We're in town and totally would rather crash with you. Send me your address and we'll make it a girls' night."

I blink and take a look around my small apartment. "Is that a thing? An actual slumber party?"

"Yes, it's totally a thing. As long as you're cool with it."

"Yes, okay."

The squeals on the other end of the line make me jerk the phone away from my head, but I smile nonetheless.

"C will bring the booze and the makeup. I'll bring the ice cream and the clothes!"

"O-okay." My heart swells inside my chest. "Okay. I'll text you my address."

When Aria finally disconnects the call sometime later, I sit in my office and just stare.

I'm not sure when the homesickness settled in, but now that these women are voluntarily coming to spend their time with me, I feel its effects waning.

Eventually, it won't feel like this.

*Right?*

# Chapter Sixty-One

## Anna

Not only did Aria and Cedar show up with an entire wardrobe of clothes for me to try on, but they also came toting a fancy charcuterie board and enough ice cream to feed an army.

I pull my office door closed and shut the women in with the white noise of a comedy movie on the small TV.

*So glad I kept a guest bed in there.*

There's a lightness to my steps, and I'm fairly certain I'm going to need anti-wrinkle cream in the morning from all the emotions displaying on my face.

*I wouldn't take back a single second.*

In fact, I'm not sure how I'm going to keep on once they leave come tomorrow, but that sounds like a problem for the Anna of tomorrow to think about.

I head to the small kitchen and fill a glass of water from the filtered tap that I down to prevent the hangover I know is going to come if I don't. I didn't drink much, but the wine Cedar picked was perfect with the little cubes of cheese.

Leaning into the fridge, I pull out the leftovers and pop a few of those same cubes into my mouth.

*There's just something about eating cheese at night in the dark.*

With a little jiggle, I bump my butt back against the barely lit counter, the Tupperware perched beneath my chin, and glance out at the mess of clothes and makeup containers left strewn about.

My eyes twitch with the need to tidy up, but the memories outweigh the need to fix it.

*Aria on the floor, clipping and trimming material. Sharp threaded needles pinched between her teeth.*

*Cedar sitting cross-legged in the chair next to the window with her gallon of mint chocolate chip …*

My smile falls straight off my face and I squeeze my eyes shut against what I think I see.

*I've been drinking. That's all it is.*

When I reopen them, a scream lodges in my throat, and I drop the container to the counter to make space in my hands for my phone.

A tap has me freezing, Jonathon's speed dial stuck on my screen, unengaged.

"Oh, my God…"

Another tap and I know the person standing on the fire escape, just on the other side of the glass, can see me.

I'm shaking when I risk a glance through my lashes, hoping that staying still will prevent the stranger on my little terrace from busting through, and that's when I see it.

A face, lit up by the screen of a phone, is staring right at me.

A face I'd recognize in my sleep.

Even though his beard is trimmed back and his hair is tamed.

*"Jeffers?"*

I take a tentative step around the breakfast bar and squeeze my eyes closed again.

Sure enough, when the darkened view of my living room comes back into focus, there most certainly is a rock star standing outside my window.

With his phone screen facing toward me, playing a Papa Roach song just loud enough that the melody barely bleeds through the pane separating us.

I'm stuck in my tracks, eyes darting between the screen showing what's playing and the face behind it all.

Every nightmare and every steamy dream.

The one taking up more of my memories, my waking thoughts, than I'd care to ever admit out loud.

*The beat of my heart.*

I pad across the hardwood floor and reach the lock of the window.

The thing slams open, probably triggering the stupid sensor Jonathon insisted on, and clears the way for As Above's bassist to climb through.

Music fills the space, and Toby stretches to his full height.

"Hey, Mama."

Even if he hadn't spoken *that* phrase, his grin would have done it for me.

*He's here.*

Before I can respond, he wraps his arm around my hips and moves into the apartment, hauling me to his hardened body.

"Your damn bodyguard wouldn't let me in the front," he mumbles, his face going to my neck and drawing in a breath. I snake my arms around his neck to hold some of my weight.

The first thing my mind suggests is that he's out of breath from carrying me across the floor.

But then my calf hits the arm of the couch and he perches me on top of it.

The man buries his face against the skin of my neck and inhales so deep that I worry his lungs might actually burst.

"Jesus Christ, Mama," he growls, his lips moving against the sensitive spot behind my ear. "I could eat you right here, right now. Drown in this ocean. *Fuck*, I missed you."

He scrapes his teeth along the same trail his lips just crested and it takes everything in me not to moan.

"Wh—what are you doing here?" I croak out as Toby's hands wander all over me, leaving goosebumps in their wake. He's grabbing my hips and pinching my butt, smoothing down my spine and hooking around my knees.

"Taking the next step in my journey," he says in that deep voice that does things to me as his hands migrate to the sides of my neck.

Toby's sight slams to mine, all amber brown and clear as freaking day, and my breath catches in my throat.

With my heart stuttering in my chest, I meet his gaze head-on. "What step is that?"

The smirk that crests the man's face is somehow both devilish and soothing. Damning and downright sexy.

"The one with you next to me."

I only have half a second to think about his words before he's leaning in. I manage to wedge my hands between us, when his lips press against my knuckles.

"Wait!"

Our breaths mingle through the cage of my fingers, his darkening eyes only millimeters from mine.

"I've been drinking," I rush out and lean back, dropping the defense I threw up. "I don't want ... I mean, I do *want* to kiss yo—"

I don't get a chance to get the rest of my rambled thoughts out or throw up another blockade.

Because my bassist slams his mouth against mine.

# Chapter Sixty-Two

## TOBY

I COULD HAVE LET her go.

Had her brush her teeth or chug a gallon of water.

But once those approving words left her lips, I no longer had a choice.

With her … I've never had a choice.

Because Anna kisses me back with those plump lips and I tease her tongue with mine and the rest of the world officially disappears.

Just me and her.

I lean into her until she falls back onto the cushions, and I follow her down, my hips wedging between her thighs.

Anna lets out a sweet little grunt when my weight settles atop her, wrapping her thick thighs around my waist.

*This is not what I intended to start the night with.*

"Fuck," I breathe out against her lips and nip at the bottom one.

Lowering my chest so that Anna's tits press against my pecs, I trail my lips across her jaw and down her delicate neck.

It smells better than I remember.

"Jeffers," Anna half moans, half whispers. "I have guests in the other room." She wiggles beneath me.

"Guess you'll have to keep it quiet then," I murmur and sink my teeth into the junction where her neck meets her shoulder, and she whimpers. "Or don't, I don't give a fuck."

Anna settles her hand in my hair. "This is a terrible idea." She grips the strands. "*You're* a terrible idea." Then yanks my head back until the fire in her emerald eyes meet mine.

I slide my hips forward, my stiff dick hitting the juncture between her thighs.

"That feel like a terrible idea?"

Her eyes somehow roll *and* roll back when my hips keep the momentum up, dragging my bulge over her clothed pussy.

The sight of her below me again, slowly sliding into that euphoric state because of me, makes my heart thunder. I salivate for her taste.

Pulling back, I shrug off my tee and then curl my fingers around the waistband of her pants and yank her legs free.

She yelps.

I grin.

"Jeffers, what are you doing? We should—"

I stop her with a palm to her belly.

"Let me eat…" I drop my chin between her legs, my words flowing over the little cotton panties. "I'm starved."

Anna shivers.

I trail the outline of the panties with one finger, dipping the pad beneath the fabric.

"Fuck, Mama," I groan at her wetness, and I'm not even inside her yet. "Let's play *how quiet can you be.*"

With that, I push the barrier aside and dive headfirst between her legs.

"Oh *God*," Anna moans deep, her grip finding my hair again and yanking. "T–th–that's so *good*."

Swirling my tongue, I hum against her and lap up every bit of her.

Her legs shake when my fingers find her entrance, her cunt quivering when I slide them inside.

"So close, aren't you, dirty girl?"

Looking past the mound of her tits, I catch her nod.

"Then come on my tongue. Show me how much you missed me."

Two pumps of my fingers and she's clamping down on them; one swipe of my tongue over her clit and she detonates.

"That's it, naughty girl. Soak my fucking face."

"Oh God, *Toby*," Anna cries, her hips rotating into me as the orgasm wrecks her body. She whines, her hands slapping over her reddening face.

"What?" I can't help but chuckle. "I know I'm outta practice, but it couldn't have been that bad."

She grunts behind her coverage and hikes a leg over my head until they're crossed, but her ass is now in my face and my fingers are still buried inside her.

I bite her cheek, the digits pumping.

"*Oh*," Anna calls out and swats my hands away. "What is wrong with you?"

"Oh," I mumble with a grin. "So much." Snorting when all she does is grumble, I sit my ass back on the couch beside her and throw an arm over her shoulders, tongue darting out to lick her taste from my fingers.

She's stiff at first, but when I jostle her a bit, she huffs and leans in to press her head to my chest.

"Is this considered cuddling?"

I snort and make grabby hands at her knee with my free hand. "Hell yes, Mama. Now gimme that leg."

The heat that radiates from her face settles into my chest like ink, but then she lifts that bare leg, and I lay it across my thighs.

My dick is still hard and restricted in my pants, but with her in my arms like this for the first time in fucking months and her smell stuck to the hair on my face, I don't care.

It weeps a little at the prospect of ignoring it, adding to the collection of pre-cum dampening my boxers, and yet the thought of letting Anna go is unfathomable.

Borderline painful.

*Even if I got off because of it.*

Pressing my lips to her hair, I remind myself that there's plenty of time for that later.

*After she tells me when the hell she's coming home.*

"So …" Anna drags out the word, her breath tickling the hairs on my chest. "How long has it been?"

"You wanna know if I'll remember this tomorrow?"

She tilts her head in affirmation.

And my heart aches.

"Anna, look at me," I demand, lifting her chin and guiding her gorgeous eyes up.

Except … she won't meet my gaze.

Her face is beyond red, yet not the shade I recall, and that grin I was clinging to for her drops. "Anna …?"

"You can't just—" She plants a hand to my chest, pushing herself away from me.

I let her.

"I can't just what?"

"Waltz in here!" Her arms fling up. "Through the damn *window*." She bolts to her feet. "And eat me out." She jams her legs back into her pants. "Like it's nothing!"

"You forgot the cuddle." I bite back my smile when she whips around and stares daggers right at my head.

She says my name like she's chastising me, but it just makes my dick jump in my pants.

"Anna," I murmur back, and she flings those arms out again, letting them slap back down against her thighs.

"You didn't even say *hi* first."

When she punctuates her statement by crossing her arms over her full chest, I hop to my feet.

I raise my hands and cup the side of her neck. With my thumbs beneath her chin, I angle her face until her gaze slams to mine.

Smirking, I cock a brow at her.

"Hey, Mama."

# Chapter Sixty-Three

## ANNA

TWO WORDS AND MY body wants to melt like there hasn't been *months* separating us. Like there isn't a disease that's kept this version of him from me. Like I haven't been lying to myself for over half of a year about my feelings for Tobias Jeffers.

Is it possible to be both turned on *and* infuriated?

I scoff. "*Now* what?"

His amber eyes are so clear, striking a contrast against the whites and the dark, that I see the little specks within them.

*Just like the golden sparkles.*

His eyes dart to me biting my lip and darken.

"It's been two hundred and twenty-nine days," he says to my lips. "And yet not a single moment, before or after, has been as intoxicating as this one."

Toby leans in, and just when I think he's going to kiss me again, he slants his forehead against mine.

"Men have fought wars over women like you, Mama." The words ghost over my lips, snake their way behind my ribs, and burrow into my heart. "And I will gladly fight my own, every day, just so I can drown in *you*."

His lips slam against mine, his hands gripping my butt and lifting me until my legs wrap around his waist.

There's not a part of me that wants to stop this as he carries us down the short hallway and through the only open door—my bedroom.

Him.

*Us.*

And it's this moment, as Toby lays me on the bed and settles atop my body, that I accept he's *it*.

He'll only ever be *it* for me.

The one who undoes me.

My own personal *fix*.

# Chapter Sixty-Four

## Anna

"That's it," Toby rumbles into my breast where his face is buried. "You take me so fucking well."

My legs are wrapped around his waist, and after another two rounds of him going down on me, taking his time with me, I'm swollen.

Which means I can feel every rigid inch of his bare erection slowly anchoring inside me.

And if sex with Toby was amazing before …

It's got *nothing* on *this*.

He presses his open mouth to my flesh and suckles.

"You feel … different." I curl my forearms around his shoulders, grasping at anything that will keep him close.

He hums. "You feel *better*. Better than my wet dreams."

My eyes roll back.

"Better than phone sex," he mumbles and sinks deeper. "Better than any high I've ever reached." He presses deeper. "I want to memorize." *Deeper.* "Every inch of this dripping cunt." *Deeper.* "With my cock."

My hips arch, my breath hitching. "Toby."

"Yeah, my needy girl?"

I shiver, a gasp popping off my lips. "Need you."

His hum vibrates across my chest and teases my exposed nipples. "Need all of me, don't you. Every bare inch of my cock inside this pussy?"

I nod frantically. "Yes, yes."

"Then that's what my girl gets."

He doesn't slam home like I expect. Instead, he hooks his elbows around my knees, breaking my hold on him, and raises them to his shoulders.

I'm squished beneath him, my chest constricted, but none of that matters when he finally sinks to the hilt and his pelvis meets my butt.

His moan echoes mine, the fullness I feel claiming my breath, stealing my consciousness, and squeezing around my heart.

There is no more me or him, only the way he stretches me. Fills me. Takes me.

His hips move, retreating and sliding home again, over and over. It makes the headboard dance, the room spin, and my vision to dot.

I swear I see the sun starting to peek from behind my curtains, but the faint light only creates a halo around Toby's profile, transforming him into the god I know he can be.

"More," I pant.

The sound of slapping flesh takes over my ears and I don't know how much more I can take.

"Tell me this cunt is mine, Mama." My neck arches back, muscles going taut. "Tell me it's mine and mine only. Mine to come in."

I clamp on to him, my hands finding purchase in anything that'll tether me to this planet. "Yes. *Yes*. It's yours."

Toby shudders out a breath. "Say it again."

"It's yours," I gasp.

He bottoms out, his body pressing all the right buttons inside me that tears spring to my eyes. "Say you forgive me."

My eyes slam to his and it feels like so much more than sex swirling in those pretty eyes. "I do."

Toby doesn't move. "You knew … how?"

My head shakes and my hips try to squirm beneath him, my body set on resuming our original pursuit, but I'm firmly pinned down.

"You needed to want it more than me," I whisper, my throat constricting against the intensity staring down at me.

His mouth falls open like he's going to say something, then snaps shut.

It's that moment that I see the puzzle pieces collect inside his mind, his eyes darkening. "I'm not your first."

"No …" My bottom lip wobbles, the memories slamming me full force, and it's no longer the weight of Toby holding me against the mattress, but the burden of my past.

The one I couldn't help.

The person I couldn't fix.

"Mama," Toby growls and grips my chin, dragging my attention up from his chest. "It's not your fault."

My heart breaks, and I sob.

"Fuck," Toby murmurs and slides one of my legs down. Gripping the other, he drops to the bed beside me, tugging me along until we're on our sides facing one another and my leg is hiked up on his hip. "Tell me," he whispers in a raspy tone, his hand cupping my face, his thumb swiping away the tears.

When I shake my head, he scoots closer. His body seals to mine, his erection still buried inside me, his warmth taking over me.

My lip wobbles when the words collect on my tongue.

*How can he make me feel so safe yet so … raw?*

I bury my face in his chest when the vigor of his gaze becomes too much. "Four years doesn't seem like a huge gap to most people." I pause to lick my lips and blink back the tears clouding my vision. "It wasn't a big deal until we got older." The mention of another person has Toby stiffening against me and my muscles aching against the memories. "The dis—" My throat clogs with the truth of where it all began for me, so

I try a different angle. A separate chapter of the story. "It started with drinking, smoking things … but then the people that supplied the stuff started hanging around far too often."

Toby's calloused fingers swipe the hair back from my temple, and I squeeze my eyes shut. "I knew about all the lies. The sneaking around. The pretending to be fine."

"Tell me what you're not telling me, Anna," he murmurs against my forehead. "Say it out loud."

"I found—" A sob breaks free, my memory of that night still so fresh that I can *smell* the bathroom soap, *see* the tainted curtain, the soiled tile floor. "It was a-an OD."

"Anna," Toby croaks, his arms circling around me and holding me close.

"I was fourteen the first time I found her."

His breath whooshes out of him and moves the hair on top of my head, his grip like steel around me.

"She survived that night … only to do it again six more times before I graduated high school. My sister broke out of rehab three times before she finally hopped on a tour bus and disappeared."

"She never stayed?"

"Once." I shake my head against him, smearing the wetness from my eyes all over my cheek. "My parents eventually gave up. Let her go. Buried an empty casket."

"And you hopped on your own tour bus," he finishes for me like the decision made sense. My parents didn't think so, in fact, they haven't spoken to me since.

*But Toby understands.*

"In hopes that I might come across her somehow. I mean, she'd managed to survive dying all those times, right?" I lift my head and look into the speckled amber eyes of the rock star that holds my heart. I told myself

I wouldn't follow in her footsteps. That I wouldn't fall in love with an artist and follow them around the world like she did. *And yet …* "She must certainly be alive still."

"You haven't found her."

I shake my head. "A few years ago, I'd heard that she was living in an encampment, but when I went, she was already gone. If it even was her, I'm not certain."

"You went *alone*?" Toby growls and cups my face. "If you ever get another lead, don't you dare go alone."

"What if—" I hiccup. "What if it's to a bar or a drug den? I can't ask you to do that."

"Anna, I'd follow you to the ends of the Earth if it meant you didn't have to live with the pain of not knowing."

I roll my eyes even though my heart squeezes at the declaration. "I wouldn't risk your sobriety for a hunch. You're also kind of famous. That might cause a few problems."

"Fine. If you won't promise to take me, then at least promise to take one the guys. Lugh or Ian."

"Toby—"

"Promise me." His hips flex, and I gasp when his erection slides deeper inside me.

"O-okay. I promise if you keep doing that."

Toby's chuckle fills my ears and my heart and I couldn't stop my hips from moving, even if I'd wanted to.

"What my needy girl needs," Toby breathes out and flips us, making me squeal, "my needy girl gets."

My legs are wrapped around his waist once again, and I moan when he drives his hips forward. "Toby … I-l—"

"You were promising me something else." He groans. "Open those gorgeous eyes and tell me you're fucking mine."

Chest constricting, I open my eyes and nod.

"Say you're mine, Mama." He growls his words, his eyes as intense as his hips slapping against mine, and a threatening orgasm swirls in my lower belly.

"I-I-I'm yours, Toby. *Oh God.*" My back arches, my body desperate to get as close as possible.

As if understanding me without the words, he leans in and shoves an arm underneath my neck, his chest flattening against mine.

His shuddering breath crests the shell of my ear, making my body shiver, and my muscles clench. "Anna," he grunts. "I'm in fucking love with you. And I promise I'll remind you every day, for the rest of my life."

I gasp.

My orgasm doesn't get the memo that my heart is bursting and barrels over me like a tsunami.

"That's it, naughty girl." He pants. "Come on my cock."

I couldn't stop if I tried.

My hips roll against him, my mouth letting lose all kinds of incoherent noises with each slam.

"Right here, Mama," he pants out. "Ready to fill this dripping cunt with my cum."

"Yes, yes."

"That's my girl." He arches back, only to drive forward and cry out.

With a swelling heart and his cries of pleasure in my ear, I let the man I'm in love with come inside me.

Claim me.

Fill me in every way possible.

*I knew I'd never be the same again after Toby.*

# Chapter Sixty-Five

## Anna

"Girl," Aria mutters with a knowing smirk.

I grumble and shuffle my way past her to the kitchen, where I snag a pan and throw it on the stove to heat up. "Need cocoa."

"I bet you do, woman, Jesus."

My feet shuffle toward the fridge, my steps unsteady from the ache Toby left behind. I gather all the ingredients to craft my morning beverage, a replica of the one Toby made for me at the cabin, which softens my already gentle smile even more.

Have I tried to remake it every day since? *Yes.*

Has it ever come out the same? *Nope.*

Will I ever tell *him* that? *No.*

"So?" she asks from behind her steaming mug, the scent of roasted beans wafting through the air, as I finally turn and lean against the countertop across her seated form. Even in the barstool, she seems taller than me and—

*Wait.*

My wide eyes land on the Tupperware of cheese left on the counter between us, a few of the cubes plotting their escape across the marble, and I feel all the heat rush to my face.

"I'm dying here, Anna," Aria whines and straightens her spine, her mug settling back on the counter. "Please tell me that was Toby last night."

"Oh God."

"Yep," she mutters with a pop to the word. "Heard you say that a bunch, too."

"Wh-what else did you hear?"

She snorts and lifts her mug to take a sip with grinning lips. "Enough to know you had a good night."

"Shouldn't you be hungover or something?" I scowl and turn away from her to stir my concoction with my achy muscles and a burning face.

*Maybe if I avoid answering the question, she'll let it go.*

"Honey, it's noon and I have twins at home. I don't know how to hangover anymore."

I whip my head in her direction when her words sink in.

"*Noon?*"

I rub my dampening brow when her grin only grows.

"I haven't … *Oh God.* I haven't slept past seven in literal decades, Aria." I feel suddenly hot, my thoughts whirling around all the things I might have missed in the last several hours while I was passed out in the most peaceful sleep I've ever had.

*We won't mention that it was in Toby's arms. Nope.*

She snorts. "Damn, girl."

"Is that coffee I smell?"

My already stiff muscles tighten at the deep sound of Toby's voice traveling down the short hallway right behind Aria.

*I mean she knows, but she doesn't* know … *right?*

When the roughened pads of his fingers touch my jaw and his talented fingers bring my wild eyes to his, my pulse calms.

My thoughts slow.

My smile appears.

"Hey, Mama," he murmurs with a smirk that makes my heart soar, and leans in to ghost his lips over mine in the sweetest kiss.

I melt on the inside at the contact. "Hey."

A clearing of the throat snaps into my subconscious, and I turn to see Aria fanning her face, her lips forming around a single word that makes my chest fill.

*Wow.*

I bite my lip.

"Don't do that," Toby grumbles, his thumb moving to the base of my lip and pulling it free.

"Why not?" I sass, and the man growls low and deep and close to my ear.

I shiver and giggle.

Just the sound alone is enough to have my stomach clenching and my thighs itching to cross.

*Am I dreaming? This has to be a dream.*

Toby's thumb feathers over my jaw, a lift to the corner of his lips. "Check your cocoa, Mama."

"Oh!" Whipping around, I take the few steps to the stove and scrunch up my nose. "Dang."

I stare down at the boiling pot, watching clumps move through the foam, the shaved chunks of chocolate still sitting beside it instead of melting into it. I nibble on the inside of my lip, the disappointment sagging my shoulders.

"Here." Hands grip my hips and spin me until my chest collides with Toby's and a gasp escapes my lips. "Let me."

Toby winks, his grasp guiding me to the side of the stove where he moves to take over redoing my cocoa, and I just stand there where he left me.

The bassist is making me hot cocoa in low riding jeans.

The same ones he wore when he snuck in through my window last night.

"Ohhhkay," Aria drags out, drawing my attention. "I knew there was physical shit, but …" She blinks at me, her pointer finger fluttering between Toby and I. "When the fuck did this happen?"

"You didn't hear?" He throws a smirk over his bare shoulder.

"Hear what?" Aria asks with a furrow to her brow and a tilt to her head.

"Last night," Toby chuckles, and Aria snickers.

"Jeffers!" I scold and tap his bare bicep. "Where is your freaking *shirt?*"

His gaze drops to my chest, that's covered in a black tee with a giant RHCP printed on the front and two sizes too big.

*Busted.*

"Where it should be," he answers easily and turns away. "There, or on the floor."

"Floor? Why would you want your clothes on the floor?"

The smirk that flashes over his shoulder in my direction is downright sinful. Add in the way his eyes rake down my body and his brow flexes, and I just …

"Oh." If I was any more slack-jawed at his brazenness, I'd be mopping the floor with my tongue. "Can you not? I have a guest!"

"Don't mind me, boo." Aria snorts. "I'm here for the show. Plus, it's nice to see someone else as bad as my husband." She flashes me a wink that has me sighing at her disappearing back. "You have an hour!" she calls from the hallway and slams the door closed before I can protest.

"Here." The scent of chocolate wafts through the air, and my mouth waters when Toby holds the steaming mug out to me.

"Thank you," I mutter and accept the ceramic, his fingers grazing over mine in the process and sending little tingles up both of my arms.

I take a sip as he watches, his eyes so light it makes my heart ache with hope, and groan aloud when the rich flavor meets my tastebuds.

"I don't understand how," I mutter and stare at the contents like it might whisper his secret.

When I finally snap out of the trance induced by the warm gift, my gaze travels up Toby's tattooed back, the muscles taut, and a wave of uncertainty washes over me. He stands in front of the coffee maker, the cabinet above it open, a mug set before him. Yet he remains still, his jaw clenching, his eyes fixed straight ahead. I follow his line of sight, only to freeze.

*Oh, God, please don't.*

Toby's hands flex as he wrenches his hardened gaze from the wine bottles next to the coffeepot and whirls toward me. His nostrils flare as if my presence surprises him, but the moment is fleeting. Within a heartbeat, he curls a hand around the back of my neck, pulling me close to him.

"Please don't look at me like that ever again," he murmurs into my hair, his arms going around my shoulders and holding me against his chest. "Two-hundred and thirty days, Mama."

I clutch at his back, a tear escaping past my defenses.

"I'm okay, Anna," he assures. "I've meant every damn word I've said over the last few months. Every voicemail. Every phone call and text message."

The strength of my own voice surprises me despite its shake. "Even last night?"

My heart clenches when I feel him nod. "I'll always choose to love you more. *That* is what I want over anything else." He gazes at me with blazing irises. "Loving you kept me where I needed to be, for as long as I needed to be there." His grip migrates to my face. "And loving you is what brought me back to you. Keep me if you want or don't. You have a choice, always. But you're *it* for me. I've never known anything more."

I swallow against the emotions collecting in my throat.

"I don't expect the trust to be immediate. Not in me, or these demons I carry. But if I could ask anything else, it'd be that you trust how much I fucking love you, Anna. How many demons I'd fight just so I could keep loving you."

My lip wobbles, tears cascading down my cheeks. "I want to." My chest pinches. "I want to trust you, Toby."

"That's good enough for me."

"But I also …" I trail off when his jaw clenches and I know he's thinking the worst. *I would be.*

"Say what you need, Mama. I'll love you no matter what comes out of those pretty lips."

*He's choosing me.*

Toby *has* chosen me.

Just him being here, in this state, with a clear mind and enough conviction in his tone that I think I am starting to believe him.

He went to rehab and *stayed.*

He came home and kept up with the things he learned while he was away. I know, because Leo wouldn't let me not hear all about when he actually got me on the phone.

The meetings. Therapy. All of it.

Toby chose to come here. To find me.

To love me.

*Just like he promised.*

Without a word, I pull at his wrist and break away from his hold. I cross the tiny space and grab both dark green bottles by their necks and tear them from the counter.

"Anna …" Toby drawls out, as I step up to the sink and uncork both bottles. Tipping them, I watch as the maroon and white liquid swirls its way down drain, disappearing beneath the faucet's spray, and with it, my guilt.

My reservations.

My mistrust.

"For months," I say to the sink, my fists gripping the edge. "I tried to forget. About the job, the guys … *you.*"

"Anna, I don't want—" He's close, but not close enough.

I shake my head. "I couldn't forget about the guys, or the job. What I could do for you that was better than whoever took my place. What Leo was doing that I could do better … I tried to let it go … Let you go." I lift my gaze to the ceiling, the heat of Toby's body burning at my back. "That's why I came all the way out here. To get away from it all. Everything that reminded me of *you.*"

I drag in a deep breath, one that's filled with sweet tobacco and citrus and warms me straight to my toes.

"Say what you're not saying."

"I'm saying that I'm not running in headfirst with you."

I spin around, and my gaze clashes with his, but he's already grinning and arching his brow.

"Doesn't sound like a no, Mama."

I shake my head to hide my smile, crossing my arms over my chest, and agree. "It's not a no, either."

Toby steps closer, so close that the smattering of hair across his chest teases my elbows. "Okay. I can work with that." He leans in when I drop my defensive stance, the tip of his nose ghosting over mine, his torso boxing me in against the counter. "Either way, you look sexy as fuck in my shirt."

# Chapter Sixty-Six

## Anna

I'M NO STRANGER TO morning routines and keeping up with myself. On a good day, I can be ready in less than an hour.

But what Aria and Cedar have done to me makes me feel like I'm on my way to a grunge beauty pageant, not standing in the center of a concert venue where my feet stick to the floor of the area known as 'the pit,' devoid of any chairs.

My empty hands tremble with excitement and curiosity about the giant black X sharpied on my right palm.

My nerves buzzing as the crowd begins to pack in around Aria and Cedar and me.

I love music, especially the kind that As Above plays, and even though I worked with them for so long, I've yet to see a single show from the listener's perspective. I'd always stand off to the side, or in the green room, with my phone and tablet at the ready to post headlines and sneaky backstage pics.

Which makes tonight even more special than it already was.

Because it's also the first time that the world sees the real Tobias Jeffers. Sober, and in the lead position as As Above's guitarist.

A spot he so rightfully earned over the last few months.

It makes my chest weep with pride and confidence in the man who's about to take the stage with his found brothers, so much so that it feels like I might burst.

I know I never said yes to the man, not officially and not outside of the bedroom, but as I look around at all the people filing in, each of them toting the same mark on their palms, I know without a doubt that Tobias Jeffers is my forever.

My demon slayer.

*My fix.*

Which is exactly what I feel zing through my system when the lights cut low and the air around me charges with an energy so palpable, I can taste it on my tongue.

"Ohhh fuuuck," Cedar mumbles beside me, her frame bouncing, her hands shaking out in front of her. "This is so fucking intense; I can't take it."

I rub my palms together, careful not to smudge the mark, and grin so wide it makes my cheeks ache.

"Are you sure he doesn't know?" Aria asks, and I shake my head.

"He's not online even now. He has no idea," I answer them both when their questioning gazes land on me.

"Still don't know how the hell you managed to do it," Cedar supplies.

"It was just an idea that I'd thrown out. Months ago, I might add. Leo and the guys did the rest."

The crowd falls silent as the lights abruptly cut out, the sudden absence of sound leaving a ringing in my ears and anticipation skittering across my damp skin. In the darkness, hands find mine—Cedar on my right and Aria on my left—and I squeeze them both when the feedback from the microphone kicks in, filling the venue with the unmistakable voice of Rex Thompson.

"*Good morning,*" Rex growls into the mic as he does at the beginning of every show and the place erupts. "*We're As Above and this ...*" His deep voice echoes over us, making my ears ache and my smile grow as the lights come up and illuminate the long-haired vocalist. "*This is called 'Demons'.*"

Drums pound out a beat, blasting us right into the first song—one I don't know—as someone I don't recognize on the stage fills the between beats with bass.

The spotlights travel from Rex to his side where it finally stops on the lead guitarist's spot.

The spot that's taken up by both an empty-handed and confused-looking Toby, and Finland, who's toting his signature candy-red guitar strapped to his back.

And a second six-string grasped in his hands.

My breath catches in my throat.

Music continues to play as Fin kneels before Toby.

The room, the fans, all howl wildly as Finland offers the instrument to Toby, my Toby, and tears spring to my eyes.

*He's sharing his throne with Toby, in front of everyone.*

Toby rolls his eyes to break the intensity, but we're so close that I can see the emotion there, the lift to his lips. The appreciation shining in his rich brown irises as he accepts the guitar from Finland and straps in.

And then … he's off, fingers flying over the strings like it's what he was meant to do, the melody filling in the blank beats of the song as Rex's vocals spill the lyrics of a man bearing his soul to the demons he intends to slay.

Toby's on stage.

Illuminated by his grin and driven by his passion.

It's so damn beautiful.

But when he finally takes in the stage and the fans beyond it, my heart surges with hope and pride as it lands on me.

He smiles big and goofy, and beyond the stage lights, when his lips work around the second best phrase to ever come from his mouth, my heart feels full.

*Hey, Mama.*

# Chapter Sixty-Seven

## TOBY

**M**y fingers throb.

My face aches.

My eyes sting.

And yet I've never felt more fucking *alive* than I do right now.

With my heart in my throat and a sweaty brow, I lock eyes with the woman I love standing in the sea of bodies, and somehow fall deeper in love with her.

*She's so fucking beautiful.*

*And so fucking mine.*

I play to her, for her, as Rex leads us into the next song that has my eyes burning even more.

Each lyric off my brother's lips, I echo back. Some into the mic when I'm supposed to for the backup. But all of them sang straight to her.

She inspired each word. Each line a moment of us. Each verse, a promise.

Because this song is the one that Rex helped me write.

*For her.*

I'm fucking flying by the time the last line leaves his lips, a growl into the void of the venue, and I drop the beat back to a soft melody of repeated strings.

It's the beginning of the next song, one of our older ones, but then Mac switches the beat of his drum to a different one.

It catches me off guard enough that I toss a look at him, but follow his lead and switch the tune.

"Tonight … is a very special night," Rex tells the wild crowd, his voice echoed in the in-ear-monitors shoved into my ears. "But you already know that, don't you?"

He pulls a marker from his pocket, one of those ones that are super thick, and uncaps it.

"Sometimes, life fucks us up," Rex says, and a cadence of agreement filters through the IEM's. "And sometimes, that fuckup … sends us to some places that we may not wanna go." The man nods along, the fans all cheering. "But what do we do with it? When we're in those places. The dark ones with seemingly no way out."

My heart pounds in my chest.

"We get the fuck back up, right?"

The mass goes wild.

Rex lifts his hand, his palm facing the crowd.

"Do you know how long it takes to form a habit?" Rex pauses as some patrons yell out answers we can't actually hear, then nods. "Thirty days. Do you know how long it takes to *break* that habit?"

I swallow hard against the emotion building in my throat when Rex lifts the marker to his raised hand and makes a thick black slash across his palm. "*Three months* … but we're not here to celebrate three months."

The yells are loud as he makes a second slash across his palm, the marks creating an X.

"We're here for *two hundred and thirty days.*"

My lungs hitch and my heart feels like it might stop.

"Let's fuckin' see 'em."

Rex raises his arm up high, palm facing out, and with it, thousands of As Above's fans lift theirs.

And each one of them, from the back to the front, all hold high the same mark on their hands, forming a sea of thick black X's.

A mark signifying that every one of them have chosen to abstain from alcohol, at least for the night.

The very same mark I put on my own hand before I showed up here tonight, as a reminder to the promises I not only made myself, but the ones I made for Anna, too. For my brothers here on stage with me.

*For my pops.*

My fingers faulter on the strings and my vision blurs.

"For Toby."

*"For Toby."*

It takes me a moment to blink my vision back, but when I do, it's aimed right at her.

*Anna.*

My Anna.

Her arm is raised just like the rest of them, her palm donning the same mark as mine, adoration shining in her wet eyes.

I know she can't hear me, but I couldn't stop the words from tumbling from my lips if I tried.

And just when I thought tonight couldn't get any goddamn better, my girl grins at me with shining eyes, nods her head, and mouths the same three little words right back to me.

*I love you.*

One year later

# Epilogue One

## TOBY

THE RESURRECTION WORLD TOUR is in full swing, and for the first time in half a year, the band is finally playing near our hometown again for three solid nights before we jet off to another continent.

Even with breaks in between and my woman at my side, it's been hard.

Venues stocking their green rooms with alcohol, stadium owners offering me drinks, fans throwing their open cans on stage during the show …

I've done it, but it's been a real bitch not to slip.

Some days are good, great even. Others make it hard to climb out of whatever hotel bed I fell asleep in.

With her, I manage.

She's my lantern in the shadowy night, the glow at the end of the tunnel.

*My sea of a thousand black X's.*

Anna has been a fucking rock when I needed it, and in the moments when her expertise, her love, hasn't been able to scrape the surface, the doc from rehab has willingly stepped in.

With the offer of a fat paycheck and the chance to tour the world with a rock band she's apparently fond of, Doc signed up to be As Above's on-staff shrink.

I probably should disclose her name, but to be honest, calling her doc just makes it more fun for me because it's begun to piss the woman off.

Not to mention the ragtag gaggle of fucks I call brothers and their undying support.

Snickering, I hike up the collar of my leather jacket—the one with the torn pocket that's been sewn back into place—and turn my face out of the chilled wind as I walk.

The path is winding and long, as has been my entire journey, but the sun is shining and my guitar is nestled in the gig bag strapped to my shoulder.

Looking out beyond the plumes of fog my exhales make, I feel the pit of my stomach twist up further with each echo of my boots amongst the salted pavement.

The rolling hills inside this place break up the stones along the way, the perimeter held back by lines of trees for just enough privacy that a fence isn't necessary, and for some reason, that sits better with me.

Fences hold things in.

And this is one of those places that shouldn't be contained.

I clear the lump in my throat and force myself forward, into the emotion instead of away from it, and finally crest the final hill to my destination.

It's the highest point of the acreage, and its view has my breath hitching in my vibrating chest. All greenery capped in undisturbed snow, with the mountains in the distance as the backdrop.

*It's perfect.*

Sniffling against the cold, I come to a stop a few feet short with numb fingers and a crawling restlessness rifling its way through my gut.

"Shit."

The urge to turn away and run back to the parking lot, to the car where I left Anna to chill with Lugh, and call this a job well done is stronger than I'd like to admit.

My hardened gaze wanders over the sight in front of me and I grit my teeth when I finally allow the carvings to register.

*Keith Jeffers.*

My eyes burn.

*Loving father.*

The center of my chest explodes with an ache so deep, it steals the rest of my breath.

*Gone too young.*

A sound of pure anguish escapes my throat, echoing off the trees surrounding me, and my knees decide I need to be closer to his grave. To examine the letters embedded in the stone. To feel the snow melting beneath my grasping palms.

"Pops."

Head dropping loose between my shoulders, I suck in a shaking breath and shoulder the cascading tears away from my face.

"I swore I wasn't gonna do this when I saw you." My voice is thick and wet as the words expel past my lips and I've never been so glad to be all alone up here. "I just … need a sec, alright? Gotta catch my breath. That was a hell of a hike to find you."

I chuckle, but it's lacking the humor.

"We both know that's an excuse," I admit aloud to the granite toting my father's name and lifespan. "Just like I know that you know I've never fucking been here."

I wince at the curse I know my pops would have thrown an eyebrow up about, but shake my head.

"Cursing is the least of your worries with me, Pops."

The snicker that escapes me is shaky, but cathartic enough that I plop on my ass in the snow at my dad's buried feet.

"You already knew that, though. Didn't you?" I spin the gig bag around so that it's settled in my lap instead of digging into my back. "I had to have her restored." I clear my throat and pat the canvas housing the guitar. "I wasn't … I haven't treated it the best over the years, Pops." I shake my head to dispel the mist forming in my eyes and unzip the bag. "She looks good though. And look," I add as I pull the instrument out and lean the headstock closer to my dad's grave, "*KJ*. Right there, so I know you're always with me."

I sniff, run a hand beneath my nose, and wrap my body around the guitar. Absently, I pluck at the strings, tweaking the tuning pegs without much thought about them, and hum.

For a moment, I lose myself in the familiar melody, my eyes sliding closed, and a calm washes over me.

"I'm sorry," I mutter to the sky. "For not visiting sooner. There's so much we need to catch up on."

A twinge of guilt tries to worm its way into my chest and snuff out the good I feel, but I shake it off and bring my gaze back to the letters marking my dad's place.

"But even as I say that, it doesn't feel right. It feels like you already know about the band—me and the guys made it, Pops." I smile. "Like you know all about the shit I got up to in the process." My smile falters. "The mistakes I made. The addiction I collected along the way …" Sitting at his feet no longer feels like the right answer, so I inch up until I've got my back leaning against his headstone. "How I went to rehab and got some help with shrinking this head of mine." I pick the melody I was playing back up. "Meeting Anna along the way … You already knew all that."

The wind picks up, rustling the branches and blowing some of the loose snow around in a swirl. It sends a chill across my already cold skin.

"Because you were always there, weren't you?" The snow flurries settle and a silence falls over the hills once again. "Making sure I didn't die on the bathroom floor somewhere. That someone always found me when I needed it."

I smile, thinking of her. My Anna.

The one that found me when I needed her most.

"You'd love her, Pops. I know you would."

A bouncing head of red hair makes its way closer.

"She's the devil, I swear." I chuckle. "That woman could make a drill sergeant quake in his boots."

Anna comes to a stop some feet away, just far enough that I can see her brilliant eyes lift and a small smile to play at her plump lips, but I know that she can't hear me.

"Do me a favor, Pops." I pause, letting the moment settle over me and turn my head toward his gravestone. "If you feel like you gotta hover around and keep anyone else from drowning in their own puke …" I bite the inside of my cheek and trail my gaze back up to clash with Anna's. "Find her sister for me. Keep her moving like you did me. Just … keep her alive and we'll figure out the rest."

Drawing in a breath, I stuff the instrument back in its case with frozen fingers and push to my feet.

"We're here for a few days, then off to what feels like another planet sometimes." I trace the letters of my dad's name. "But I promise I'll be back. I gotta take care of shit and I know you'll have my back no matter what."

My fingers brush the stone, its surface somehow warmer than the chill of the air, and though it surprises me, I let it absorb into the callouses adorning my skin.

"Just like you always have, Pops."

Sniffling, I turn away from the stone and head in the direction of my future waiting for me.

It feels like both a goodbye with an ache that I know will never go away and a greeting to what comes next.

And with a lightness I didn't feel before I showed up here, I wrap an arm around my forever girl and let her smile touch the deepest recesses of my no-longer-black heart.

"Hey, Mama."

# Epilogue Two

## TOBY

T HE CAFÉ IS SPARSE for a chilly afternoon like this, especially considering I've chosen to take up one of those weirdly unstable mesh metal tables still standing outside.

It's fucking freezing, but the brew is great and the space is wide open.

*Space is a good thing when you're trying for discretion.*

I take a steaming sip from the plastic lid reminding me that this shit is hot and let the coffee heat me from the inside out as my gaze wanders over the few patrons braving the cold like I am.

*Shouldn't be long now.*

At least, I'm hoping that my guest shows when she's supposed to so that I don't have to go through the bullshit of tracking her down again.

She had a hard enough time believing it was really me to begin with considering the sendoff she got when she received her hush money.

*Probably shouldn't call it that in front of her.*

A shadow darkens my back, and a voice I don't know whispers from behind me.

"Holy shit, it really is you."

I aim a raised brow over my shoulder at the woman wearing not much more than an old band hoodie and even darker bags under her eyes. I wait until she makes her way around and takes the seat opposite me.

"In the flesh."

"Wow," Zoey Inna murmurs and rubs her hands together to combat the cold. "I really thought that I was being set up." She shivers. "Again."

I nod and settle my hand against the icicle of a table. "Understandable."

Who wouldn't feel that way after being chased away by the most notorious rock band's entire label team?

"So …?" Zoey looks at me expectantly, though not maliciously, and I have to admit that the woman gives me pause.

Because exactly one year ago yesterday, the woman gave birth to a child that she'd claimed was mine just long enough to screw up my life.

While also being the catalyst to putting my life back together.

What I knew to be before Zoey showed up at Nitro's radio show crumbled at her feet when she presented papers containing a lawsuit and custody claim for a kid that I *knew* wasn't mine.

But what she did in return was drop Anna right in my lap for the taking.

I'm angry that she took advantage of me and mine. While also grateful as fuck that she did what she did that lead me to Anna and this life I get to live now. The peace I've gained. The spot I've earned.

*I'm in her debt.*

"So," I state with my brows still bunched and my coffee cup twirling in my palm. "How's Jack?"

Zoey shoots back in her seat, her shock flaring her already widened blue eyes. "How do you know my son's name?"

I chuckle. "You think I wouldn't? After the shitstorm you caused?"

She bites down on her lip. "I am so sorry for that, Toby. I—"

I hold up a hand and Zoey's trembling lips snap shut. "We're not here for apologies."

"Okay," she breathes out and leans back in her seat, her arms going across her chest. "What are we here for then?"

Nodding, I take another scalding sip from my cup and lean my forearms onto the table. "I have a proposition for you."

Her dark brows shoot up to her hairline and her sleeved hand goes to her mouth. "I don't think I like the sound of that."

"You might."

She stares at me, her blue eyes too haunted, and I know I'm all in already.

*As long as she agrees.*

"See, when 25k was gifted to you in exchange for your silence, the purchases made were tracked. So it surprised the shit outta me when I learned that only one was made, for a place over in Meadow's Park, in someone else's name."

Zoey freezes in her seat and those dark circles get darker.

"When I asked around, that name threw up some flags I didn't like, Zoey."

If it's possible, she scrunches further in on herself, and I would bet just as much money that the woman is hiding bruises beneath that tattered hoodie.

And that fact alone makes me wanna hide her away from whoever is putting their hands on her.

*But then there's Jack.*

"Look, I don't want any trouble," she mutters from behind her hand, her teeth working away the threads of the sleeve's already torn cuff. "I just want to raise my son and that's it."

"Funny, seeing as how that's exactly what I want for you, too."

"I don't understand what you're getting at, Toby, and frankly, I went through a lot just to get here."

I nod again and click my tongue. "Back to the proposition, then." I sit back in my seat, my gaze steady on hers. "I have a place and I have some cash that's yours if you want it."

She jolts again like I shocked her.

"No rent until you can get on your feet and a pretty damn good motherly woman in need of some company."

"*Why?*" The response comes out so fast, I think it startled even her, judging by the shake of her shoulders. "I mean … I'm sorry. I just don't understand why you would offer me *anything*."

"Because while Jack isn't mine, and I don't know you at all, I know enough to see that he deserves a chance better than what he's got right now."

Her brow furrows deep and her sight drops to the table.

"Are you saying I'm a bad mom?" Zoey whispers.

*Clearly not the first time she's thought that.*

I shake my head and dip my gaze to meet hers so that she sees the sincerity setting my jaw. "I'm saying that I know what it's like to lose a parent and I don't want Jack to live that life."

She goes quiet for a long beat, her teeth worrying that cuff of her sleeve, then shakes her head. "There's no way you care about my son that much."

I shrug. "I also owe you."

She finally lifts her distant gaze.

"How?"

"If you hadn't done what you did, I wouldn't be where I am right now. Funny how that works, isn't it."

Zoey lets out a breath that screams disappointment and my stomach drops.

*Is she going to say no?*

"If that's how life is supposed to work, then I owe a lot to a few people. And not in a good way." Her words are just shy of a whisper and muffled by that fist by her mouth.

"Then let me change that." I throw a glance over my shoulder to the woman sitting just inside the café, waiting for this very moment.

Marie Thompson throws open the door like this is *her* show, and makes her way over to our table. Except, the woman who practically raised me when my dad passed doesn't stop to greet me at all.

No.

Instead, she rushes right to Zoey's side and throws her arms around the trembling woman.

"*Ma*," I chastise, though it makes my lips pull up at the corner. "You're gonna scare her off."

"Nonsense," Ma corrects right back and gives Zoey another squeeze before throwing a cocked brow at me, then pulls out her own chair.

Zoey fidgets in her seat.

"It's so nice to finally meet you, Zoey," Ma says softly and I don't miss the way her blue-green eyes drift to the fist hiding Zoey's mouth.

"It's nice to meet you, too," she responds flatly, automatically. As if it's the last thing she really wants to say.

"Well," Ma starts. "After hearing from Toby about you, I knew I had to get to know you. I'm hoping you'll allow me just that."

She shakes her head. "I really have to get back to Jack."

My muscles tense. "Five more minutes and I'll personally drive you home."

"*No—*" Zoey shoots upright in her seat, her pale face flushing, her hands grabbing at the arms of her chair. "I'm sorry. I mean …" Her throat works down a swallow. "No thank you."

"Zoey," Ma coos and touches a reassuring hand on top of her grip. "Don't boys have the kindest hearts? The sweetest little smiles and laughs."

Her gaze trails over to Ma. "They do. My JackJack laughs *so* much." Tears spring to her eyes and she blinks rapidly against the assault.

"I'd love to meet him soon, if you're okay with that, dear," Ma continues, her voice soothing and low. "How about tomorrow?"

"O-okay. I can sneak away for a little bit."

"Perfect," Ma says on a grin even though my insides are burning. "How's noon sound?"

She nods, the action a little more animated this time.

"I'll make us some lunch." Ma raises to her feet, her hands reaching out for Zoey who meets her.

The two step closer, and I watch as Ma's knowing gaze bounces between Zoey's. "In the meantime, this is my number." Ma presses a small piece of paper in the hands that clasp hers. "Call if you need anything. Anything at all."

"O-okay. Thank you."

Ma nods and takes a step back, with a smile. "Tomorrow."

Zoey's lips lift in the first hint of smile since she arrived and I would swear her trembling has calmed. "Tomorrow."

Once she makes her way down the sidewalk on foot, alone and cold, I turn to Ma and wrap my arms around her.

"Oh!" She startles when I engulf her, but leans in and hugs me back. "Thank you."

Ma sniffles against the leather of my jacket. I pretend not to hear it, but I don't let it stop me from squeezing her tighter.

"I'm just … so glad you boys are home," Ma says on a chuckle that sounds a little thick.

"Me, too."

"Okay, okay." She leans back and swats at my chest. "Let's get out of this cold."

We're two steps away from the car, Lugh shadowing our backs, when her phone rings and she shoots me a knowing look.

"Hello, dear."

The speaker is tiny, but I can hear every word from Zoey on the other end of the line like a shotgun blast in the dead of night.

"I'm so sorry," she rushes out on a sob, her voice echoed by a man yelling in the background. "I'm sorry. C-c-can I take that lunch now?"

"Of course." Ma's lifted brows swing to me, but I'm already signaling to Lugh to drive us there. "We're on our way. Get to the street if you can." She takes on a whole new level of calculated when she instructs the woman over the phone. "Don't worry about bags or things. Grab Jack and get out."

When Lugh pulls onto the street, I see Zoey walking along, little JackJack in her grasp.

She's sobbing when we jolt to a stop at her side, her lip busted and her son barely contained in the thread-bare blanket she wrapped him with.

Ma wastes no time ushering Zoey in and buckling the kid into the seat between them.

"Get us the fuck outta here, Lugh," Ma demands.

We're off just as fast as we came, Jack calming with each mile we put between him and his old life, his mother slowly sinking into the seat beside him.

I watch in the rear view as tears track silently down Zoey's face, and I can't stop the boiling rage that tangles up my insides.

"Zoey."

Her gaze is slow to find mine in the little mirror, but when it does, I make sure my face says all the things my words don't.

"You don't have to worry about him ever again."

One single dip of her wobbling chin and I know I made the right decision coming out here today.

She gave me my life back.

It's my turn to give back hers.

*Theirs.*

**It's never really the end when they live rent free.**

# Bonus Chapter

## TOBY

"WE SO SHOULD HAVE gone to Vegas." Pulling my duffel from the jungle of bags stashed in the underbelly of the tour bus, I let the momentum smash right into Mac's gut.

He huffs.

"What? They have that break dancing crew that does shows and shit!"

"Seriously? You don't even know their name."

"Dead serious." Mac's eyes go wide and his clasped hands go out in front of him. "They got"—he juts his pelvis out, humping air—"*moves*."

I snort and hook an arm around the back of his neck, pulling him into my side.

"And they said they can't take *me* anywhere." I pull Mac along, his laugh echoing into my armpit, his feeble attempt to swat at my head easily thwarted when I can see what he can't.

At least, until his knuckles collide with the back of my skull and my steps stutter. "Jesus, fuck."

It's enough for him to break loose and snort just as the hotel's sliding doors open wide and the two of us walk right through the glass like we *weren't* just dicking around.

*All business here.*

*We're professionals.*

Just the thought has me pinching my lips between my teeth to contain my laughter from the front desk clerk handing over our room keys.

It lasts until the elevator closes us in, and a round of guffaws burst from us both.

"*I can't take you anywhere,*" Mac mocks.

"*Those break dancing guys got good moves,*" I mock right back. "It's their fucking *job*. That'd be like someone telling you that you play good drums."

"But I *do* play good drums!"

The howl that escapes me has me nearly doubling over, my grip on the railing the only thing holding me up.

*Ding!*

Mac and I snap upright, falling silent as an elderly lady steps into the car with barely a glance in our direction. With her snow white curls and a sort of hunch to her back, she punches the floor number and faces the closing doors.

Soft music fills the space, some kind of calming instrumental shit, and yet I am bursting at the seams. I hold back so tight that I actually feel a sweat breaking out on my brow.

*It's all under control. Nothing to see here.*

*Ding!*

The elevator stops on the lady's floor and before stepping out, she spins to us. "Love your music."

She winks.

And then leaves.

My jaw drops and it only takes one glance at Mac's face in the mirrored surface of the now closed doors for us both to bust up all over again.

I'm still grinning when we land on As Above's floor, which requires another swipe of the key card to let us off.

Mac goes one way, and I go the other in search of my room.

Another swipe of the card, a slam of the door, and I'm greeted with the most breathtaking sight known to man.

Anna.

In lingerie.

Laid out on the bed with the sun's rays highlighting her luscious curves and the giant picturesque window framing her in the city's backdrop.

"Fuuuuck me."

My bag drops to the floor and my shirt is off before I even get the words all the way out.

"Surprise." She grins, her legs swinging around until they're hanging off the side of the bed and I eagerly step between them.

"Please tell me this is crotchless."

Anna snorts, her pale face flushing. "You'll just have to see for yourself."

My hands roam across her skin, touching and grasping at every part of her that I can reach until they finally settle in her hair. "Sounds like a yes to me."

She bites her lip.

I lean down to run my tongue across it.

"Take my dick out, naughty girl," I say against her lips. "I wanna ask you something while you hold it."

Her fingers work the clasp of my belt, her lips ghosting over mine in the perfect tease of not-quite-kissing.

I grunt when she finally sets my aching length free and surge forward when she wraps a hand around it. I claim her mouth, stabbing my tongue between her lips and tasting her sweet flavor.

"What is—" Anna clears her throat, her chest rising and falling in a pant. "What did you wanna ask me?"

My brain short-circuits when she strokes my cock and another groan rolls off my tongue. "Um, fuck …" I gasp when her hand twists and it's like she connects the right neurons with just her touch. "You wanna move in with me?"

I claim her lips before she can answer, the motion of her hand almost too much already.

"Toby," Anna pants out when she pulls back for air. "You have couch surfed more of your life than you haven't and your address is the label's office."

"So? We've been on tour."

Her lips press against me, her breath feeding mine. "The label's office is *my* house," she breathes against our kiss. "You're already staying there when you're not touring."

I nod and grip the hair at the base of her neck. "Then I'll move in with you."

I *feel* her smile lift against my lips. "Okay."

She grips me, her strokes picking up speed and pulling a sound from deep in my gut.

"Next question," I pant out, my knees getting weaker with each pull on my dick.

"Okay," she murmurs and I'm not sure who pushes and who pulls, but I follow her as she flops back onto the mattress and I settle between her thighs. "Next question."

I trail my lips over her jawline, letting her intoxicating scent consume me. "Inside you first."

She hums her approval, and I reach between us to tweak her soaked clit.

*Definitely crotchless.*

"*Ahh,* Toby ..." Anna whines, and I line up the blunt head of my dick with her slick entrance.

Slow, so very slowly, I slide inside her until her hot pussy fully engulfs me from root to tip.

"*Fuck*, Anna. I love you." My hips thrust, my dick hitting deep enough that her eyes roll back.

"*Love you, too*," she gasps, her back arching up to meet my measured thrusts. "As-ask me."

Anna's hands find my shoulders, her nails latching onto skin, and that shining emerald stare lands on mine like she can see right through me.

My heart swells in my chest.

I probably should be nervous; I think most people are.

But with Anna … shit … I've been falling in love with her every day since she first opened that smartass mouth of hers.

She went and did what I thought was impossible.

*She made me want to see tomorrow.*

"I know it hasn't been very long," I say, my hips working in slow, sensual yet deep, thrusts. "And we can make a thing out of it if you want, but …" Groaning, I plant my lips on hers. "But I don't wanna wait anymore."

Anna's teeth sink into her bottom lip and she tugs on my hair strands. "Say what you aren't saying, Toby."

I hum and sink deep inside her.

With her tight pussy pulsing around me, her legs wrapped around my waist, I open my mouth and ask the last question I thought I'd ever speak out loud to anyone in this lifetime.

"Will you meet my pops, Anna?"

She gasps.

I thrust.

"*Yes*," she hisses with mist forming in her clear emerald eyes.

"You'll come with me?" I ask again, just because I want to hear the words on her lips one more time.

"Yes, Toby," she moans out when my hips move, impaling her on my stiff dick. "*Yes*, I'll meet your dad."

The absolute ecstasy that crosses over her flushed face has my balls drawing up. "Fuck. Yes." I grunt and pull back until only the head of my dick is still inside her. "Wanna cum, Mama?" She nods. "Wanna cum with my dick in your ass?" She nods again, and I growl. "Of course you do, my slutty girl."

Anna shivers when I lean back on my haunches and trail the head of my cock down her perinium to press against the tight ring of her ass.

It's not the first time she's let me in, and it certainly won't be the last.

But I take my time, anyway, lubing up my cock with the little packet from my pocket and teasing her open with just the tip and a finger.

When the head finally crests past the tight ring of muscle, we both moan.

"That's it, dirty girl. Let me watch you finger that pussy while I fuck this asshole wide open."

Anna tightens around me, her fingers finding her slick entrance and working their way inside.

Goosebumps pebble my skin at the sight of her, dressed in sexy-as fuck lace where her tits spill out of the top.

And then my cock disappears between her cheeks.

*She said yes. She's gonna meet my pops.*

The thought hits me like a freight train and the rooms spins.

"*Fuck*, Anna ..."

"*Toby*," Anna whines, my cock bottoming out and my balls drawing up so tight I know I won't be able to stop the orgasm this time.

Pulling her legs up, I rest her ankles on my shoulders and lift her ass, my body pinning her to the mattress. The change in angle makes us moan, and Anna's back arches.

"Right there," she whimpers and clenches. "Right there ... I'm gonna—"

The scream that rips from her throat would be enough to set me off all on its own.

But when she clamps down on my cock so hard I can barely move, I roar my pleasure and cum inside her.

"I love you, Anna," I breathe out with a swollen heart, my shaking arms barely holding me up. "It's the only thing that ever made sense."

Her shining eyes stare up at me, seeing right through me, and then a corner of her lips quirk up. "That's Mrs. Prune to you, Jeffers."

The laugh that escapes me has me collapsing against the strength of her legs, only to wriggle between them so that I can prop my weight up on my elbows on either side of her head. "Actually," I start and hold her gaze. "That's …" I pump my hips, and she gasps. "*My girl* to me."

Anna bites her lip.

"I like that."

"Good. Then c'mon. We gotta celebrate."

"Actually … I've got a better idea."

I N LESS THAN SIX hours, my woman managed to not only find a plane that's available, purchased a mouth-watering dress with just enough lace to make my dick painfully hard, and a gorgeous bouquet to hold as she walks the path with me …

But this amazing fucking woman of mine got the two of us back home and directed me to go to the perfect spot to make her mine.

Because while most are all about putting a ring on her finger, I've got something better.

*My ocean of a thousand black X's.*

And while I probably should have told at least one of the guys had we taken the time, this is …

This is so much fucking better.

Anna tucks in at my side, her free hand grasped in mine while she juggles the bouquet she picked just for this.

A tear tracks down my cheek to get lost in my beard.

"Pops …" I say softly to the tombstone. "I want you to meet my girl."

Anna's eyes shine like a polished gem, her glossy pink lips stretched in a smile I can't help but return. "I'm so damn proud of you, Jeffers. Now kiss me so I know it's not a dream."

And I do without abandon because while I know that tomorrow isn't promised, today is everything I didn't know I needed.

Anna is everything I didn't know I needed.

This life I've built with her is everything I was waiting for.

"Tell me that your ass doesn't hurt too bad, Mama," I say, then chuckle when she smacks my pec.

"Not in front of your dad!"

*What a fix.*

# Afterword

As a pantser, I feel like I'm constantly saying that each story I write takes me by surprise. And when you go into something with only a vibe and a pipedream, it's bound to happen. I mean, how can *one* spark of inspiration equal all the things needed to get to the HEA? It seems like an unfathomable feat at best.

But *this*?

The emotions and angst mixed with the banter that still makes me chuckle? The love. The hurt. The *healing*.

I'm still in tears as I'm writing this, having just finished reading it again, even though it's like the twelve hundredth time I've gone through it. Even with the mistakes that are made and the trusts that are broken along the way.

Toby's story, his recovery, is one that will live with me for a long fucking time and I don't know that I'm mad about it.

Just as I'm not mad—*anymore*—that he fucked up my book order when he popped up and demanded his story be written.

Honestly, when I wrote more in this series, I wasn't even positive Toby was going to get a book. He was just a side character, a man with a problem, the quintessential fucked up rock star hanging out in the background. I was dead set on writing Leo's book next when he knocked and didn't stop knocking until I opened that brand new blank document and started typing.

Everything fell to the wayside, including the fmc that I thought Leo was going to get. She just … disappeared. His entire plotline fell through my fingers. The road they were on just *gone*.

*Not the one.*

So I kept it moving, let Toby fuck up my whole process by feeding me tidbits of info out of order. Gave me scenes that didn't make sense. Shit I deleted, scrapped, typed all over again.

He was drunk on the couch in chapter seven when he dropped his love confession on me.

And I was left dumbfounded with how the hell we'd get there. How Anna, another character that was only mentioned and never meant to be a main voice, was going to get through her contempt for the rock star that acted just like the one she envisioned her sister disappearing with. But when we finally did six months later?

*So. Fucking. Sweet.*

Since I mentioned it, I want to touch on the topic of Anna's sister and say that I don't know much more than what was already mentioned. I didn't even know she had one until that news was dropped when I originally wrote the scene where Toby coaxes it out of her. Where he realizes he's not the first addict in Anna's life. And I hope she's out there somewhere. Maybe she'll pop up along the way, or maybe she really is as dead as her parents think she is and Anna can find the closure she needs to finally let the photos display. But until then, I think there's only a dwindling hope that she's still alive. Only time will tell.

Another thing I want to mention is the is the symbolism used to identify the abstinence from alcohol in the final concert scene. The black X on the palms. This is loosely—and I mean *loosely*—inspired by the straight edge movement that occurred in the early 2000-2010's punk culture. *Another stint of research.* And while I recall some things about this from when I was younger, I could not find the origin of the mark itself and there were too many conflicting narratives about the true meaning behind the movement to use it in this book. The entirety of it just didn't fit. Maybe I was just too tired to understand it or looking in the wrong places. I don't know. But to give the guys some way to show their support, they presented the moment where Rex slashes the marker on his own palm during the set and the rest spawned from there. And now, we have our own thing. A thick black X on the palm to ward off the temptation.

If you read my author's note at the beginning, then you know this book took me a lot longer to write than I expected. With all the feels and research that went into making this happen, it just needed the extra time to marinade.

This is not the longest it's taken me to write a book. The Moment took me nine months to get to the end as a brand new writer, typing away in what little spare time I could muster. But having written two other books in the same timeframe and hopes of publishing faster all fell through the cracks when I started this one.

Now I know.

After hours, *weeks,* of research and second-guessing every move I made. Scrapping more than I wrote. Terrified of the journey they were taking me on. Worried that it wouldn't be taken well and the voice of the story wouldn't hold. Angst? Could I really do that? Is that really my thing?

I see now that this is how it was supposed to go. There is no other way for this story to be told, their stories to be told. This is the order they were always meant to be in and these are the loves they were always supposed to find.

We had to have the sweet with Rex and Aria.

The fire from Fin and Cedar.

And now the depth of Toby and Anna.

I believe that these guys are ramping me—*us*—up to what comes next and have been since this all began as a dream and a keyboard.

That they will always give me the story I didn't know I needed, but I'm so fucking glad I got.

As if there was any other way.

$$XXXX$$

If you enjoyed this book, then please consider leaving a review.

# Resources

If you or anyone you know is struggling with substance abuse, there are ways to get help.

You do not have suffer alone. Recovery is possible.

Here are a list of resources, should they be needed.

Substance Abuse and Mental Health Services Administration

Alcoholics Anonymous

Suicide and Crisis Lifeline

Many states in the US have their own resources that are only a google search away. But if you are in immediate need of help, call 988 (the suicide and crisis lifeline for the US) or 911 in most places, even outside of the US.

Your life matters.

# Acknowledgements

Since I did an afterword and I don't normally, I'll try to keep this one short.

My number one will always go to Mr. Stone. The one that keeps the house together while I hide away in my hole and type until my eyes can no longer stay open. The one that makes sure I have tea in the morning to keep me awake, and water for my day job. My foundation when the rest of me crumbles.

Next, to my editor, Zee—*queue the eye roll*—for being an amazingly awesome cheerleader even while she slashes the shit out of my word count.

To Brooklyn for helping me keep these wild assholes in line when they stray too far.

Lori, my cover designer, for always taking the words I spew and turning out a fucking masterpiece.

And to you, the readers. For picking up a little known author's book and loving it just as fiercely as I do.

XXXX

# Content Warnings

Xx

CONTENT WARNINGS INCLUDE ON page abuse of alcohol, addiction, withdraw symptoms including vomiting, enabling of damaging coping mechanisms, grief, therapy sessions, rehab. There are also mentions of obsessive compulsive tendencies, deceit, negative body image, and references to drug use.

References made for **off page** content include over-dosing, pregnancy (only mentioned, not between main characters)and loss of a parent.

Not everyone deals with trauma, loss, and mental health in the same ways. This book is a representation of how these characters dealt with their situations, and is no way any sort of reference for real life use.

The Fix is meant for audiences of eighteen years or older.

# Sneak Peek

WANNA KNOW WHAT COMES next in the As Above series? Keep reading for a snippet from book four. (unedited, subject to change)

Copyright Rae Stone, 2024

---

"CAN YOU JUST FORGET I ever said that?" I stare expectantly at the shrink across from me, only to receive an arch to her manicured brow in response.

"That's not how this works. You know that."

My nostrils flare with my inhale, and a muscle works in my jaw just as my thumb raps a baseline on my thigh.

"But how is that night relevant to anything?"

Doc taps the cap of her pen against her chin and crosses her ankles. "It has to do with the issues you're having with your brother."

"I feel like this is a conflict of interest," I mutter with a roll to my eyes and I pick up the beat in my head with my other hand along my knee.

"It's absolutely within your right to choose someone else to discuss these things with."

Not only does the idea of rehashing all my life's problems to yet another stranger have my stomach twisting up, so does the ease of Doc's statement.

"*That.* Right there." She points that pen in my direction. "What just happened in your mind?"

I sigh again.

It seems to be my favorite pastime every time I find myself seated across from this woman who clearly has all of her shit together.

Which is exactly why I'm seated here, across from all four of her degrees.

And she's there, with her notepad and her head-shrinking notes.

"I don't wanna burden another stranger." Her other brow wings and I roll my eyes. "Right. Watch what I say about myself." I blow out a breath and rub my palms along my jeans. "I don't want to start over."

She nods, jots something, then sets the pad aside. "Back to that night. On the bus with your brother. What happened?"

"I cried like a little bitch."

"About?"

Rae Stone is native to the Midwest, from a town called Springfield, OH. While she no longer resides in the City of Roses, Rae is definitely a misfit of Suburbia that would rather paint her nails black and annoy the neighbors with her loud rock music.

When she's not elbows deep in writing, Rae can be found attending concerts with Mr. Stone, consuming romance novels like water, and letting her fur kids run wild.

Wanna connect? Find Rae on socials below!

Facebook | Instagram | Tiktok | GoodReads | Amazon | BookBub | Newsletter | Website

Need a place to discuss all things As Above?

Check out Rae's reader group here → Rae's Misfits of Romance

www.ingramcontent.com/pod-product-compliance
Lightning Source LLC
Chambersburg PA
CBHW031514010826
48973CB00013B/1285